Captain John Ford's Texas Rangers find themselves facing a band of Comanches while in pursuit of a murderer in "Day of Vengeance" by **James Reasoner**.

Lenore Carroll relates Libbie Custer's affection for her infamous husband—and her own inner strength—in "Sojourn in Kansas."

Bat Masterson must determine how a drunkard got his "Likker Money" and whether or not he murdered one of Dodge City's most prominent citizens in a story by **Jerry Guin**.

and thirteen more tales of . . .

White Hats

WHITE HATS

★

Edited by
ROBERT J. RANDISI

BERKLEY BOOKS, NEW YORK

WHITE HATS

A Berkley Book / published by arrangement with
the editor

PRINTING HISTORY
Berkley edition / April 2002

All rights reserved.
Copyright © 2002 by Robert J. Randisi.
A continuation of copyright credits appears on page 259.
Cover art by Mort Engle.
Interior text designed by Julie Rogers.

This book, or parts thereof, may not be reproduced
in any form without permission.
For information address: The Berkley Publishing Group,
a division of Penguin Putnam Inc.,
375 Hudson Street, New York, New York 10014.

Visit our website at
www.penguinputnam.com

ISBN: 0-425-18426-9

BERKLEY®
Berkley Books are published by The Berkley Publishing Group,
a division of Penguin Putnam Inc.,
375 Hudson Street, New York, New York 10014.
BERKLEY and the "B" design
are trademarks belonging to Penguin Putnam Inc.

PRINTED IN THE UNITED STATES OF AMERICA

10 9 8 7 6 5 4 3 2

CONTENTS

★

WHITE
HATS

INTRODUCTION

Hi-Yo, White Hats

★

Close your eyes. Who's that cowboy you see riding toward you on the large or small screen with the white hat on? How many of you see the Lone Ranger? Hopalong Cassidy? Roy Rogers? Gene Autry? Matt Dillon? Or the biggest White Hat of them all, John Wayne? These are probably the characters and actors who had the most to do with making the white hat a symbol of the good guy. (Okay, maybe Pa Cartwright of TV's *Bonanza,* as well. I mean, who was ever a bigger good guy than good ol' Ben?)

White Hats is the first of a two-volume set, the second being—of course—*Black Hats.* The authors in this book were asked to write stories about real characters from the Old West, people who, while not necessarily lawmen, definitely fell into the White Hat category. It's interesting to see who they came up with, and who they see as the Old West's good guys.

The nice thing about this volume is that it features both famous (Louis L'Amour, John Jakes, Richard Wheeler) and not-so-famous (Sandy Whiting, Lori Van Pelt, Stef Donev) authors as well as famous (Bat Masterson, Buffalo Bill, Ben Thompson) and not so famous (Larry Lapsley, Sally Skull, Libbie Custer) historical White Hat figures from the Old West.

The "mix" is what always makes for an interesting and

successful anthology, in my opinion, and I think we've got a winning mix here. I hope you agree.

Now I've got to go back to my drawing board and come up with the names of some famous Black Hat characters and actors. If you can think of any I should mention, or any historical Black Hat figures you'd like to see written about, e-mail me at Rrandisi@aol.com and let me know.

Robert J. Randisi

St. Louis, Mo.
April 2001

Let the Cards Decide

LOUIS L'AMOUR

You can't know what an honor it is to have a L'Amour story in one of my anthologies. When I conceived the idea for these two collections I remembered this story, and it fit perfectly. You don't know exactly who the White Hat is in this until near the end and it's a wonderful revelation.

I never got a chance to meet Louis L'Amour. The last Western Writers Convention he attended was in 1981, the year before my first. Missed him by a year. This certainly doesn't make up for it, but it's the closest I'm going to get, so I'll take it.

★

Where the big drops fell, we had placed a wooden bucket retrieved from a corner of the ancient log shack. The long, earth-floored one-room cabin smelled of wet clothing, wood smoke, and the dampness brought on by unceasing rain. Yet there was fuel enough, and the fire blazed bright on the hearth, slowly dispelling the dampness and bringing an air of warmth and comfort to the cheerless room.

Seven of us were there. Haven, who had driven the stage; Rock Wilson, a mine boss from Hangtown; Henry, the Cherokee Strip outlaw; a slender man with light brown hair, a sallow face, and cold eyes whom I did not at first know; the couple across the room; and myself.

Six men and one woman—a girl.

She might have been eighteen or a year older, and she was one of those girls born to rare beauty. She was slim, yet perfectly shaped, and when she moved it was to unheard music, and when she smiled, it was for you alone, and with each smile she seemed to give you something intimate, something personal. How she had come to be here with this man we all knew. We knew, for he was a man who talked much and talked loud. From the first, I'd felt sorry for her, and admired her for her quiet dignity and poise.

She was to become his wife. She was one of a number of girls and women who had come west to find husbands, although why this girl should have been among them I could not guess. She was a girl born for wealth and comfort, and her every word and movement spoke of breeding and culture. Yet here she was, and somehow she had gotten into the hands of Sam Tallman.

He was a big fellow, wide of shoulder and girth, with big hands and an aggressive manner. Not unhandsome in a bold way, he could appear gentle and thoughtful when it suited him, but it was no part of the man and strictly a pose. He was all the girl was not: rough, unclean, and too frank in his way of talking to strangers of his personal affairs.

That Carol Houston was becoming disillusioned was obvious. That is, if there had been any illusions to start. From time to time she gave him sharp, inquiring glances, the sort one might direct at an obnoxious stranger. And she was increasingly uneasy.

The stage was headed north and was to have dropped several of us here to meet another stage heading west. We were going to be a day late, however, for our coach had overturned three miles back on the muddy trail.

Bruised and shaken, we had righted the stage in the driving rain and had managed to get on as far as the shack. As we could not continue through the night, and this place was at least warm and dry, we made the best of it.

There seemed no end to the rain, and in the few, momentary lulls we could hear the measured fall of drops into the bucket, which would soon be full.

Now in any such place there comes a time when conversation slowly dies. The usual things have been said, the storm discussed and compared to other storms, the accident bewailed, and the duration of our stay surmised. We had exchanged destinations and told of our past lives, and all with no more than the usual amount of lying.

Dutch Henry produced some coffee, and I, ransacking the dismal depths of the farther cabin corners, a pot and cups. So the good, rich smell of coffee permeated the room with its friendly sense of well-being and comfort.

My name, it might be added, is Henry Duval. Born on Martinique, that distant and so lovely island noted for explosive mountains and women. My family had been old, respected, and until it came to me, of some wealth. By profession I had been a gambler.

This was, for a period of nearly a century, the usual profession of a young man of family but no means. Yet from gambling I had turned to the profession of arms, or rather, I had divided my time between them. The riverboats started me on the first, and the revolutions and wars of freedom in Latin America on the second. Now, at thirty-five, I was no longer occupied with either of these, but had succeeded in building a small fortune of my own in handling mining properties.

But let us be honest. During my gambling days I had, on occasion, shall we say, encouraged the odds? An intelligent man with a knowledge of and memory for cards, and some knowledge of people, can usually win, and honestly—when the cards run with him—but of course, one must have the cards. So when they failed to come of themselves, sometimes I did, as I have said, encourage them a bit.

Haven, the stage driver, I knew slightly. He was a solid, dependable man, both honest and fearless. Rock Wilson was of the same order, and both were of the best class of those strong, brave, and often uneducated men who built the West. Both had followed the boom towns—as I once had.

Dutch Henry? You may have heard of him. They hanged him finally, I believe. He was, as I have said, an outlaw. He stole horses, and cattle, and at times robbed banks or stages, but all without malice and without unnecessary shooting. And he was a man of rugged good nature who might steal a hundred today and give it away tomorrow.

The sallow-faced man introduced himself. His accent was that of the deep South. "My given name is John. I once followed the practice of medicine." He coughed into a soiled handkerchief, a deep rattling tubercular cough. "But my ahh . . . condition made that an irony I could no longer endure." He brushed a speck of lint from the frayed cuff of his faded frock coat. "I am now a gentleman of fortune, whatever that may mean."

Henry made the coffee. It had the strong, healthy flavor of cowpuncher coffee, the best for a rainy night. He filled our cups, saving the best for the lady. She smiled quickly, and that rugged gentleman of the dark trails flushed like a schoolboy.

Tallman was talking loudly. "Sure hit the jackpot! All them women, an' me getting' the best o' the lot! Twenty o' them there was, an' all spoke for! Out in the cold, they said I was, but all right, I told 'em, if there's an entry, I get her! An' this one was extry!"

The future Mrs. Tallman flushed and looked down at her hands.

"How did it happen, Miss Houston?" I asked her. "Why didn't they expect you?"

She looked up, grateful for the chance to explain and to make her position clearer. She was entitled to that respect. "I wasn't one of them—not at first. I was coming west with my father, in the same wagon train, but he died of cholera and something happened to the little money he had. We owed money and I had nothing . . . well, what could I do?"

"Perfectly right," I agreed. "I've known some fine women to come west and make good marriages that way."

Good marriage was an expression I should not have used. Her face changed when I said that, and she looked down at her hands.

"Should o' heard the others howl when they seen what I drawed!" Tallman crowed. "Course, she ain't used to our rough western ways, an' she ain't much on the work, I hear, but she'll learn! You leave that to me!"

Haven shifted angrily on his bench and Rock Wilson's face darkened and his eyes flashed angrily. "You're not married to her yet, you say? I'd be careful if I were you. The lady might change her mind."

Tallman's face grew ugly. His small eyes narrowed and hardness came into his jowls. "Change her mind? Not likely! You reckon I'd stand for that? I paid off her debts. One o' them young fellers back yonder had some such idea, but I knocked that out of him mighty quick! An' if he'd gone for a gun, I'd o' killed him!" Tallman slapped his six-shooter. "I'm no gunman," he declared, "but I get along!"

This last was said with a truculent stare around the room.

More to get the conversation away from the girl than for any other reason, I suggested poker.

John, the ex-doctor with the sallow cheeks, looked up sharply, and a faint, wry smile hovered about his lips. The others moved in around the table, and the girl moved back.

Somehow, over their heads, our eyes met. In hers there was a faint pleading, an almost spoken request to do something . . . anything . . . but to get her out of this. Had we talked an hour she could not have made her wish more clear.

In that instant my resolution was made. As John picked up the cards I placed my palm flat down on the table in the old, international signal that I was a cardsharp. With a slight inclination of my head, I indicated Tallman as the object of my intentions, and saw his agreement.

Tallman played with the same aggressive manner of his talk, and kept a good eye on the cards that were played. We shifted from draw to stud and back again from time to time, and at first Tallman won.

When he had something good you had to pay to stay in the game, and he rode his luck hard. At the same time, he was suspicious and wary. He watched every move closely at first, but as the game progressed he became more and more interested and his vigilance waned. Yet he studied his cards carefully and took a long time in playing.

For me, there were no others in the game but Tallman and John. Once, when I had discarded, I walked to the fire and added a few sticks, then prepared more coffee and put the pot on the fire. Turning my head I saw Carol Houston watching me. From my chair I got my heavy coat and brought it to her. "If you're cold," I whispered.

She smiled gratefully, then looked into the flames.

"I do not wish to intrude on something that is none of my business." I spoke as if to the fire. "It seems that you might be more comfortable if you were free of that man."

She smiled sadly. "Can you doubt it? But he paid bills for me. I owe him money, and I signed an agreement to marry him."

"No one would hold you to such an agreement."

"He would. And I must pay my debts, one way or another. At the moment I can see no other way out."

"We'll see. Wait, and don't be afraid." Adding another stick to the fire, I returned to the table. Tallman glanced up suspiciously, for he could have heard a murmur, although probably none of the words spoken between us.

It was my deal, and as I gathered the discards my eyes made note of their rank, and swiftly I built a bottom stock, then shuffled the cards while maintaining this stock. I placed the cards in front of Henry for the cut, then I shifted the cut smoothly back and dealt. John gathered his cards, glanced at them, and returned them to the table before him. Tallman studied his own, then fidgeted with his money. I tossed in my ante and we started to build Tallman. We knew he liked to ride hard on a good hand and we gave him his chance. Finally, I dropped out and left it to the doctor. Tallman had a straight, and Doc spread his cards—a full house, queens and tens.

From then on we slowly but carefully took Tallman apart. Haven and Wilson soon became aware of what was happening. Neither John nor I stayed when either of them showed with anything good, but both of us rode Tallman. Haven dropped out of the game first, then Wilson. Henry stayed with us and we occasionally fed him a small pot. From time to time Tallman won, but his winnings were just enough to keep him on edge.

Once I looked up to find Carol's eyes on mine. I smiled a little and she watched me gravely, seriously. Did she guess what was happening here?

"Your bet, Mistah Duval." It was John's soft Georgia voice. I gathered my cards, glanced at them, and raised. Tallman saw me and kicked it up. Henry studied his cards, shrugged, and threw them in.

"Too rich for my blood," he said, smiling.

John kicked it up again, then Tallman raised. He was sweating now. I could see his tongue touch his lips, and the panic in the glance he threw at John when he heard the raise was not simulated. He waited after his raise, watching to see what I would do, and I deliberately let him sweat it out. I was holding three aces and a pair of sixes, and I was sure it wasn't good enough. John had dealt this hand.

My signal to John brought instant response. His hand dropped to the table, and the signal told me he was holding an ace.

Tallman stirred impatiently. Puttering a bit, as if uncertain, I raised twenty dollars. The Southerner threw in his hand and Tallman saw my raise, then felt in his pockets for more money and found none. There was an instant of blank consternation, and then he called. He was holding four queens and a trey when he spread his hand.

Hesitating only momentarily, I put my cards down, bunched together.

"Spread 'em!" John demanded impatiently, and reaching across the table he spread my cards—secretly passing his ace to give me four aces and a six.

Tallman's eyes bulged. He swallowed and his face grew red. He glared at the cards as if staring would change their spots. Then he swore viciously.

Coolly, I gathered in the pot, palming and discarding my extra six as my hand passed the discards. Carefully, I began stacking my coins while John gathered the cards together.

"I'm clean!" Tallman flattened his bag hands on the table. He looked around the room. "Who wants to stake me? I'll pay, I'm good for it!"

Nobody replied. Haven was apparently dozing. Rock Wilson was smoking and staring into the fire. Henry yawned and looked at the one window through which we could see. It was faintly gray. It would soon be morning.

From the ceiling a drop gathered and fell with a fat *plop* into the bucket. Nobody spoke, and in the silence we realized for the first time that the rain had almost ceased.

"What's got into you?" Tallman demanded. "You were

plenty willin' to take my money! Gimme a chance to get even!"

"No man wants to play agin his own money," Wilson commented mildly.

My winnings were stacked, part of it put away, yet of what remained the entire six hundred dollars had been won from Tallman. "Seems early to end a game," I remarked carelessly. "Have you got any collateral?"

He hesitated. "I've got a—!" He had started to put up his pistol, but changed his mind suddenly. Something inside me tightened when I realized what that might mean.

Tallman stared around, scowling. "I guess I ain't got—" It was time now, if it was ever to be time. Yet as the moment came, I felt curiously on edge myself. "Doesn't she owe you money?" I indicated Carol Houston. "And that agreement to marry should be worth something."

Even as I said it, I felt like a cad, and yet this was what I had been building toward. Tallman stared at me and his face darkened with angry blood. He started to speak, so I let a string of gold eagles trail through my fingers and their metallic clink arrested him, stopped his voice in his throat. His eyes fell to the gold. His tongue touched his lips.

"Only for collateral," I suggested.

"No!" He sank back in his seat. "I'll be damned if I do!"

"Suit yourself." My shrug was indifference itself. Slowly, I got out my buckskin money bag and began gathering the coins. "You asked for a chance. I gave it to you." I'd played all night for this moment but I was now afraid I'd lost my chance.

Yet the sound of the dropping coins fascinated him. He started to speak, but before he could open his mouth Carol Houston got suddenly to her feet and walked around the table.

"If he won't play for it with you, maybe he will play with me." She looked at Tallman and her smile was lovely to look upon. "Will you, Sam?"

He glared at her. "Sit down! This here's man's business!" His voice was rough. "Anyway, you got no money! No tellin' what you'd be doin' if I hadn't paid off for you!"

Dutch Henry's face tightened and he started to get to his feet. John was suddenly on the edge of his chair, his breath whistling hollowly in his throat, his eyes blazing at the implied insult. "Sir! You are a miserable scoundrel—!"

"Wait!" Carol Houston's voice stopped us.

She turned to John. "Will you lend me six hundred dollars?"

Both Dutch Henry and I reached for our pockets but she ignored us and accepted the money from the smaller man.

"Now, Sam. One cut of the cards. One hundred dollars against the agreement and my IOU's . . . Have you got the guts to do it?"

He started to growl a threat, but John spoke up. "You could play Duval again if you win." His soft voice drawled, "He gave you quite a thrashing."

Yet as John spoke, his attention, as was mine, was directed at the face of Carol Houston. What happened to our little lady? This behavior did not, somehow, seem to fit.

Tallman hesitated, then shrugged. "Yeah? All right, but I'm warning you." He shook his finger at John. "I'm paying no more of my wife's debts. If she loses, you lose too. Now give me the damn cards."

She handed him the deck and he cut—a queen.

Tallman chuckled. "Reckon I've made myself a hundred," he said. "You ain't got much chance to beat that."

Carol Houston accepted the cards. They spilled through her fingers to the table and we helped her gather them up. She shuffled clumsily, placed the deck on the table, then cut—an ace!

Tallman swore and started to rise.

"Sam, wait!" She put her hand on his arm. He frowned, but he dropped back into his seat and glared at me.

Carol Houston turned to me, her eyes quietly calculating. The room was very still. A drop of rain gathered on the ceiling and fell into the bucket—again that fat *plop*. The window was almost white now . . . it was day again.

"How much did you win from Sam, Mr. Duval?"

Her face was without expression. "Six hundred dollars," I replied. "Not more than that."

She picked up the cards, trying a clumsy shuffle. "Would you gamble with me for that money?"

John leaned back in his chair, holding a handkerchief to his mouth. Yet even as he coughed his eyes never left the girl. Dutch Henry was leaning forward, frankly puzzled. Neither Wilson nor Haven said anything. This seemed a different girl, not at all the sort of person we had—

"If you wish." My voice strained hard not to betray my surprise. I was beginning to understand that we had all been taken in.

She pushed the entire six hundred dollars she had borrowed from John into the middle of the table. "Cut the cards once for the lot, Mr. Duval?"

I cut and turned the card faceup—the nine of clubs

She drew the deck together, straightened it, tapped it lightly with her thumb as she picked it up, and turned— *a king*!

Stunned, and more by the professional manner of the cut than its result, I watched Carol Houston draw the money to her. With careful hands she counted out six hundred dollars and returned it to John. "Thank you," she said, and smiled at him.

His expression a study, John pocketed the money.

Haven, who had left the cabin, now thrust his head back into the door. "All hitched up! We're goin' on! Mount up, folks!"

"Mr. Haven," Carol asked quickly, "isn't there a stage going west soon?"

"'Bout an hour, if she's on time."

The six hundred she had won from me she pushed over

to Sam Tallman. Astonished, he looked at the money, and then at her. "I—Is this for me?"

"For you. It is over between us. But I want those IOUs and the marriage contract."

"Now wait a minute!" Tallman roared, lunging up from his chair.

He reached across for her but I stopped him. "That money is more than you deserve, Tallman. I'd take it and get out."

His hand dropped and rested on his pistol butt and his eyes narrowed. "She's goin' with me! I'll be *damned* if I let any of you stop me!"

"No, suh." It was John's soft voice. "You'll just be damned. Unless you go and get on that stage."

Tallman turned truculently toward the slighter man, all his rage suddenly ready to vent itself on this apparently easier target.

Before he could speak, Dutch Henry spoke from the doorway. "You'll leave him alone, Tallman, if you want to live. That's Doc Holliday!"

Tallman brought up short, looking foolish. Doc had not moved, his right hand grasping the lapel of his coat, his gray eyes cold and level. Shocked, Tallman turned and stumbled toward the door.

"Henry Duval, you quit gambling once, did you not?"

She held my eyes. Hers were clear, lovely, grave. "Why . . . yes. It has been years . . . until tonight."

"And you gambled for me. Wasn't that it?"

My ears grew red. "All right, so I'm a fool."

Until that moment I had never known how a woman's face could light up, nor what could be seen in it. "Not a fool," she said gently. "I meant what I said by the fire—up to a point."

We heard the stage rattle away, and then I looked at Carol.

A smile flickered on her lips, and then she picked up the

cards from the table. Deliberately, she spread them in a beautiful fan, closed the deck, did a one-hand cut, riffled the deck, then handed them to me. "Cut them," she said.

I cut an ace, then cut the same ace again and again. She picked up the deck, riffled them again, and placing them upon the table, cut a red king.

Picking up the deck I glanced at the ace and king she had cut. "Slick king and a shaved ace," I said. "Tap the deck lightly as you cut and you cut the king every time. But where did you have them?"

"In my purse." She took my hands. "Henry, do you re-member Natchez Tom Tennison?"

"Of course. We worked the riverboats together a half dozen times. A good man."

"He was my father, and he taught me what I did tonight. Both things."

"Both things?"

"How to use cards, and always to pay my debts. I didn't want to owe anything to Sam Tallman, not even the money you took from him, and I didn't want to be the girl you won in a poker game."

Dutch Henry, the Cherokee Strip outlaw, slapped his thigh. "Women!" he said. "If they don't beat all!"

It was almost two hours before the westbound stage ar-rived . . . but somehow it did not seem that long.

Sojourn in Kansas

LENORE CARROLL

Lenore is the author of *One Hundred Girls' Mother* (Tor, 2001), a true story of Scots Presbyterian minister Thomasina McIntyre. In this story she relates a true tale of George Armstrong Custer's wife, Libbie, and her trip west to Fort Hays to join her husband. Fodder for a future novel, I think.

★

"Libbie, you really oughtn't to tease Lieutenant Weir like that. He's in love with you and you take advantage of it." Anna Darrah poked her needle into the cross-stitch pattern. She and Libbie Custer sat on the deep veranda of the house across from the parade ground at Fort Riley. The porch and trim were green and white, in contrast to the pale stone of the house. They sat on plain straight chairs with their handiwork on a scarred deal table. Libbie moved so much, thought Anna, she never had things as nice as she ought, with Armstrong a colonel.

"I've known him forever. He was in Texas with us. Besides, he expects it." Libbie sharpened her red drawing pencil with a tiny knife and scratched again at the image on the heavy paper.

The day was soft, with a faint blue haze on the grass. A

fresh breeze gusted and was gone. Warm weather had come quickly that spring of 1867. Libbie had warned Anna about the harsh summers and she had brought a supply of cream and glycerin lotion with her to Kansas. She intended to enjoy her stay with the Custers, to find out about army life and perhaps army officers, and never, never be a burden.

"You drop your fan for him to pick up," Anna recounted. "You expect him to bring your tea. He does everything short of carrying your mending basket in his mouth." Anna giggled at the thought, but Libbie scarcely smiled. She continued working on her sketch. "You are merciless," Anna concluded.

"Anna, you are too hard on me. You've only been in the army, so to speak, since you left Monroe last winter. You don't know all the traditions," Libbie said. She picked up her drawing pad and held it at arm's length, tilted it to catch the light.

"I know you pretend you are knights and ladies and chivalry and all that," Anna replied. She tied off one piece of floss and cut another, which she threaded through the big-eyed needle.

"It's harmless. The men delight in doing us favors. When they are in garrison, we make their lives pleasant. There are rules as strict as those of chivalry. If there weren't, it would never do. Tom Weir is my beau ideal, a knight *sans peur et sans reproche.*"

"Tom brings you gifts. In Monroe, a married woman does not accept gifts from men not related to her."

"It is Tom's opportunity to expand his life to include someone besides himself. Bachelor officers have little diversion. We have few chances to exercise our social graces. It keeps Tom Weir's spirits up."

"He has plenty of spirits. From a bottle," said Anna.

"I hope to persuade him to take the pledge," said Libbie. "Autie never touches a drop and he's the better for it.

But poor Tom! He is such a splendid person, except for this one failing." Libbie resumed sketching.

True, Anna didn't know all the ins and outs of army customs. Still, there was something calculating about Libbie. Anna wondered if it was because she had lost her mother so young. Or because she had no brothers or sisters to temper her ideas. Libbie toyed with the young officers, and broke their hearts.

Except for Will Cooke.

Lt. William W. Cooke, who had fought in Virginia with Armstrong, had been very attentive to Anna, even when the scintillating Libbie held forth. He was so tall, so handsome. And his whiskers! The most impressive dundrearies in the regiment—brown, full and uncut, they hung to his chest. Anna stitched her crosses, scarcely noticing what she did, her mind filled with Will's handsome face and his deep, melodious voice. He was so amusing, so *comme il faut*. Sometimes she thought Libbie was a little jealous of Will's attentions to her. But Libbie was the "old lady" and married-married-married.

Sometimes Anna wondered if Libbie and Tom Weir were closer than friends. Certainly he was in love with her. Certainly Libbie encouraged him. But Anna was always present whenever the young officers came calling. Tom escorted Libbie on public strolls. They rode with other officers and officers' wives. There was nothing underhanded.

Anna didn't think there was anything more.

Besides, they were leaving tomorrow for Fort Hays since General Sherman had given Libbie permission to join Armstrong. Libbie's bags were always packed. Anna had spent half the afternoon packing her small trunk. Will and Armstrong had been in the field all spring. If they could all be together at Hays, they would have a merry time.

★

WILL COOKE LOUNGED in his folding chair. Dinner was over and the four of them lingered over coffee after Eliza, the Custers' black cook, cleared the table. The quartermaster had generously allowed them three tents, plus a fly to shelter their outdoor meals. Fort Hays was a white canvas city on the banks of Big Creek.

"You were frightened, too, Libbie," Armstrong teased. The men wore blue flannel shirts and Will wore Indian-cured buckskin trousers with fringe, a far cry from full dress uniforms.

"I never said a word," Libbie answered.

"We couldn't have heard you with your head under the covers," he said.

"I think it was just wonderful that you tried to tie down the corners of the tent," said Anna. She had never been so frightened in her life, but she wasn't going to let them know it. "I don't know how Will slept through it."

"After sleeping without even a piece of canvas for protection, you learn to sleep through anything," Will said. He stroked his extravagant facial hair, a cat grooming its whiskers.

"You've been so brave and intrepid," gushed Anna. She hoped the steady wind hadn't turned her coiffure to frizz. "Even the fright was exhilarating," Anna lied. "I wouldn't for a moment have wished I was home. How can I repay you, Armstrong, for bringing me out here to a life I like so much?" She wanted Will to think her stalwart and unflinching so he would propose. Many young women arrived single at an army post and went home with an engaged. Why not her? "Are you never frightened?"

"When you have gallant comrades, you can manage," Will answered. He and Armstrong exchanged knowing glances. He plucked a blade of grass and chewed the root end. Anna poured coffee into his cup. Libbie's household things had arrived, so they dined off proper china. Armstrong had shooed away Theodore Davis, the *Harper's* artist, and now he and Libbie held hands. Anna was jealous.

"It is so desolate, with no trees, except around the creeks, and very irregular water," said Libbie. "In your letters, Autie, the sun is always shining and the breeze always blows and you always find a camping spot near a creek."

"We manage," said Armstrong. He stroked Libbie's hand.

"Some men like to be on the scout," said Will, implying he was one of those men. "I am never happier than when I'm in the company of men who have shared adversity."

"This company of men had a rowdy party," said Libbie. "After the buffalo hunt."

"Our team won!" boasted Will.

"You girls missed a great feed. The other team kept the total killed a secret," Armstrong complained. "If we had known we needed another buffalo to win . . ."

"You still wouldn't have been able to catch one," Will said. "Never did champagne taste sweeter."

Anna looked at Will. She was losing heart. When he talked about being in the field or hunting, he came alive. When he was with her, he seemed—bored? He said all the proper things, and made love to her with the most charming phrases and small endearing presents. But she never felt she had captured his heart. He never looked at her the way Armstrong—or Lieutenant Weir—looked at Libbie. Perhaps she should set her cap for another young officer and give up on this tall, comely man.

JUST BEFORE HIS companies left to stop Indian depredations, Armstrong directed the soldiers to put Libbie's tents on the highest ground possible. It was a rainy spring and Fort Hays was sodden. They had a few boards to put down for floors. Anna guarded her little trunk, making sure it was placed on an improvised rack off the ground. Libbie made fun of her for worrying about clothes when they were living rough, but Anna had gone to considerable trouble to acquire a decent wardrobe and she intended to wear it. Wherever they were.

"I want people to see me at my best," Anna had declared. She studied her curly dark hair in her traveling mirror and pinched her cheeks to bring some color.

Libbie would put up with anything, including grasshoppers up her skirts, for a chance to be with her husband.

ONE EVENING AFTER Armstrong left, Libbie persuaded Tom Weir to escort her and Anna outside the post, even though there had been threats of Indians. Anna wondered if Libbie were playing a role with Tom, like an actress in a play.

The huge orange sun burned hot all the way down to the level horizon that evening, then a breeze sprang up and carried the smell of cooling grass and wildflowers. Dew dampened their hems as they strolled.

Tom's bland good looks were deeply tanned. His soldierly posture and proper manners were lovely, Anna thought.

Libbie kept wheedling to walk a little farther, and by the time they turned back, it was too dark to see the sentinel. A bullet whizzed past her ears! Tom rushed them to a nearby depression. He shouted, but couldn't make himself heard over the shots. When it was quiet Tom said, "I'll approach the post from the creek and tell the sentinel to let you in." He crept off through the grass.

"Oh, Libbie, I'm too fat. I stick up higher than you," Anna babbled. "I've pulled my skirts as flat as I can."

"Now you want to be slender!" said Libbie.

"Anything to be less . . . prominent." Anna smelled bruised grass and damp earth. "Do you think Tom will find us?" Anna's voice shook.

"He had better." Libbie sounded cool. Wasn't she afraid? "If no one comes soon, I'll crawl in anyway and take my chances that the guard is a poor marksman."

"What's that?" Anna's heart stopped at the sounds nearby. "Oh, Libbie! I hope it's Tom!"

ANNA, NATURALLY, WROTE a lengthy letter back to Monroe about her adventure. Everyone there wanted to hear about Libbie. Anna had been her friend since they were pupils at the seminary, her bridesmaid at the wartime wedding, and a frequent conduit of news about the Custers. She had little to say about herself. Will Cooke returned to the field with a simple farewell, and no promises.

But curiously, Libbie wrote in detail to Armstrong about being caught after dark. Anna thought it strange that Libbie would admit she had disobeyed him and put herself in danger, that she would emphasize Tom's courtesy and resourcefulness, that she would beg to be trusted again, that she promised no more walks beyond the sentinel's line. Anna would have kept her mouth shut, lest she anger a husband less understanding than Armstrong.

On the other hand, Armstrong had written at length of women fawning on him in New York last winter. Maybe Libbie was only getting her own back. Or maybe Libbie thought Armstrong might value her more if he knew other men wanted her. Libbie was too deep for her.

Anna wondered why Libbie had not gotten pregnant yet. It was obvious to anyone that Mr. and Mrs. Custer doted on each other. At the Fort Riley house, Anna and Armstrong's brother joined in the wild romps in the evenings. Shrieks and bellows, hide-and-seek, barricades of furniture, dogs barking and joining the chase, followed by a parade of Libbie and Anna being "toted" about and deposited on a table while the dogs barked and men scrambled like wild Indians shouting and whooping.

Then quiet descended and all trooped to bed and in the dark Anna could hear voices but not words, rustling and shifting in the beds, and she would muffle her ears with her pillows because it was too painful to hear those intimate and physical exchanges.

Libbie told Anna she was afraid to ask for anything, or complain, lest they be sent back to Fort Riley, so for a week she and Anna occupied themselves in their canvas mansion. Anna would just as soon go back to the comforts of the garrison, but she knew that Libbie would strain her utmost to be with her Autie and the farther west she could stay, the better her chances that he could join her.

Then one night after all had gone to bed, a storm began rolling in with vicious lightning and continuous peals of thunder. Anna lay frightened in her cot. The tents had been well spaced for privacy and they were too far from the adjacent ones to cry for help to a neighbor. Rain poured in the dark, drumming on the canvas. The wind tried to rip the ropes loose and the tents luffed like sails.

Then Anna heard Tom, along with some other officers, asking if she and Libbie were afraid. "This is turning into a tornado," Tom shouted. Libbie undid the straps that held the tent closed and the men and Eliza came inside. They struggled to refasten the straps. Anna calmed down when she saw Tom. The great expanses of fabric were tearing loose from their ropes and the tarpaulin which served as a porch flapped wildly. One tallow candle was surrounded by boxes to keep its flame alive.

Libbie called it a hurricane, but whatever it was, it was a frightful storm. The men piled the furniture up and put a zinc-covered board across the wooden hardtack boxes for them to sleep on. The storm passed and the men promised to return if need should arise. Eliza left for her own tent and the two women returned to damp and cold beds.

They had scarcely fallen asleep when a guard shouted, "The flood is here!" Anna and Libbie crept out of the tent and saw, by the flashes of lightning, that the creek, an in-significant trickle when they went to bed, was bank-high. Only treetops were visible along the banks. The creek rose thirty feet in a few hours. As it crept into the kitchen tent, Eliza took command and directed soldiers to remove all the household goods.

Tom and the other officers returned, but the roaring water had created an island where the women were trapped. Anna could hear the despairing cries of men swept into the tempest. She was so frightened she couldn't think. Eliza spotted a man clinging to a tree. The only rope not holding up a tent was her clothesline. Eliza took it, made a loop, and hollered to him to put it over his head. She tossed it and he caught it. He couldn't hear over the rush of the water and the roar of thunder. He looked dazed and the tree he clung to tipped and fell under the bank. Libbie and Eliza and Anna heard him bellowing. Libbie shouted, "Grab the rope!" and at last he understood, grasping the rope. They pulled and dragged the man to firm ground.

He was shaken and wild, with his teeth chattering. He could scarcely walk. Libbie gave directions and Anna fetched one of Armstrong's shirts. Eliza heated coffee to pour down him and Libbie splashed through the water to the Gibbses' tent, where she got whiskey enough to revive him.

But the storm didn't stop and the creek continued to grow, spreading out like a lake. With Libbie in command, they saved two other men that night. Anna and Libbie rubbed them with red pepper and kept the fire red-hot and talked to them until they warmed up. Anna was too busy to be scared. Eliza grabbed another as he washed past their tent. Anna expected to be swept away any minute. Seven men drowned that night.

The laundresses' adobes flooded and the women and children were evacuated in a wheel-less wagon bed, pressed into service as a ferryboat. Eliza broke up her bunk to build a fire to make breakfast the next morning.

Anna had had enough of storms, but the next night Big Creek began to rise again. They had to evacuate.

Tom told Anna she couldn't bring her little trunk with her best clothes.

"I can't leave my things behind!"

"Put on all the outer clothes you can," Libbie ordered.

"They're still wet from last night." Anna held a dark green bodice up and carefully pushed her arm into the damp, resisting sleeve. "Oh, Libbie, what shall we wear tomorrow? Everything we have is wet!"

"We'll wear wet clothes."

"But we'll catch our deaths."

"Anna, don't be a goose. Everybody's clothes are wet. We have no choice."

"I must take my small trunk."

"Forget your trunk. We'll take what we have on," Libbie said.

"Libbie! All my dresses!" Anna began to weep. "What if we should reach a fort? And I'm still wearing the same gown?"

"Anna!" Libbie was out of patience.

But Anna couldn't stop. It was as though this topic was the only one she could grasp.

"The next fort is eighty miles distant and there is only water between here and there," Libbie reminded her.

"Libbie, you don't understand!"

Libbie took a deep breath through pinched nostrils. "Anna, listen closely. Put three dresses on, one on top of the other."

While Anna stood immobile, Tom arrived, picked up Libbie, and carried her through the water to the ambulance. Libbie rested her head on his chest. Mrs. Gibbs and her sons were already inside. When Tom returned for

Anna, he found her at the door of the tent with her little trunk.

"Surely you aren't going to bother with clothes at a time like this," he said. "We need room in the wagon for people."

"I'm not leaving without it."

"It's unnecessary weight," he said.

Anna refused to budge without the trunk.

Tom stalked off out of earshot. What he said was lost in the rumble of thunder. Her trunk went with her.

Days ran together as their ambulance rolled over endless grass. The summer was a continuous ride over wet prairie with Mrs. Gibbs and her sons, and usually with Tom Weir in the escort, until they reached the railhead at Fort Harker. There Libbie learned from General Hancock that she wouldn't see Armstrong again that summer.

Eventually, the women returned to Fort Riley, where Libbie said each day had forty-eight hours and where she prayed for letters from Armstrong.

TOM WEIR TOLD them later that Indians had been all around their train on the way back from Fort Hays. If their wagons had been attacked, he would have kept a promise to Armstrong to kill them before they were captured. Anna felt her blood run cold.

She didn't understand. Libbie was soft and sweet, clinging and silly around Armstrong. Hadn't she proved she truly loved him by traveling across Kansas in blistering heat and living in mud just to be near him? But then she was cool and authoritative as any general when the floods came. She managed Tom, gave orders to Eliza, and kept people amused in camp. Which was the real Libbie and which were roles she played?

Anna always wondered afterward who sent the letter—anonymously, of course—warning Armstrong to "look after his wife a little closer." Libbie accused her of writing it, but Anna didn't know what she was talking about. Some murmured it was Eliza who got Lieutenant Brewster to write. Eliza was always protective of "the Ginnel's" interests. It could have been any of the anti-Custer faction bent on mischief.

When Armstrong got the letter, he raced 155 miles to Fort Harker, arriving at two in the morning. He exhausted his escort and ruined three good horses. He told his sleep-fogged commanding officer he was leaving immediately on the train. He sent an orderly to waken Weir. Armstrong's face was dust-and-sweat filthy, and mud stained his boots and coat. His pale blue eyes showed no fatigue.

He glared at Weir when he shambled into the shelter near the tracks. The train would leave in a few minutes.

"Hello, Armstrong," said Weir. His smile was loose and ingratiating. He was half asleep and half drunk. He had buttoned his tunic wrong and stuffed his nightshirt inside his trousers.

Armstrong pulled a letter from his shirt. "Stay away from my wife!" His voice rang high and crazed.

Weir started, realized this was serious. "But old man, we've been friends—"

"This letter says you're no friend!" Armstrong threw down the paper and lunged at Weir, who backed away, struggling to comprehend.

"What—?"

"It says you and Libbie are becoming 'too attached.' What does that mean?"

"I haven't any idea. What are you doing with your saber?" Weir stumbled, then fell to his knees. "Please, you must believe me. No shadow of scandal has fallen on Libbie on my account."

"How about the time you were riding and got separated from the group at Riley?"

"We got lost and it took us a while to find our way back. Mrs. Dalrymple was with us, she'll tell you. Don't—"

The saber whirred, slashing the air over Weir's head.

"You know how people gossip," said Weir. "I love Libbie. No! not that way. Put that thing down!" He started to rise, but the point of the saber found the hollow of his throat. "My god, man," Weir pleaded. "I have never overstepped my place. I am innocent. Libbie is innocent. Anna Darrah has been with her every moment since you left. Please, you won't gain anything by this. Put that away! Libbie is the most honest, straightforward wife a man could hope for. You are wrong, *evil* to think this of her."

The tip of the saber broke the skin below his beard and a warm trickle of blood ran inside his shirt.

"You can't be serious!" Weir tried to think. "We've known each other since the war. Where is the trust of all these years? I beg you!"

Weir threw himself at Armstrong's feet, utterly abased. Then he had one thought: "If you harm me, you'll prove the rumors are true. If you love Libbie, believe *me,* not that trouble-making letter." Tom felt snot and saliva drip on the splintering floor of the shelter. The sour whiskey on his breath mixed with the smell of coal and the oil from the steaming engine outside.

After an endless time, Weir heard Armstrong sheathe his saber. He looked up and the revolver was back in Armstrong's waistband. Tom started to rise.

"Leave my wife alone!" Armstrong's voice rang thin and high. "Never speak to her again."

"Of course, of course," promised Weir.

The engineer blew the whistle. Armstrong strode out of the shelter and entered a passenger car. The train began its slow rhythm and Weir remained on his knees, waiting until the sound faded into the prairie night.

★

ANNA SAT IN her room, embroidering, at Fort Riley that July morning. She heard the clank of the saber, the quick familiar step on the porch. When Libbie opened the door, there was her Autie. Anna wondered if he came out of love or because he suspected Libbie was unfaithful. They had a blissful reunion, then that same day a wire from his commanding officer called him back to Harker immediately to face court-martial charges for his actions. He had risked his career to be with Libbie.

After that, the joy went out of things for Anna. Will Cooke stayed in the field and she never saw him again. She could scarcely claim to be jilted, but she wept nonetheless. The court-martial was horrid, with Armstrong accused of dreadful things. Libbie put a brave face on and pretended it didn't bother her, but Anna knew she wrote pages and pages in her journal in Armstrong's defense. Anna moved to Fort Leavenworth with the Custers while Armstrong served his sentence, then she returned to her home in Monroe.

ANNA SAW THE Custers on their occasional visits to Monroe. Then came the dreadful news in July 1876 of the tragic events at the Little Big Horn. The town was stunned. Besides Armstrong, his brothers Tom and Boston were killed, along with cousin Harry Armstrong Reed, James Calhoun, and George Yates. Libbie helped plan the memorial service, and later, even though her stepmother worried about her depression, Libbie helped Frederick Whittaker, a dime novelist, with a biography of Armstrong. It was rumored that Libbie was destitute, with no income and burdened with Armstrong's debts.

"Read this letter from Tom Weir to me, please, Anna," Libbie asked. The two women sat sewing in Libbie's morning room. Libbie handed Anna a letter written weeks earlier, on November 28, in a large, legible hand, such as

officers develop to make their reports clear. "I can't read it
for weeping."

Libbie looked beautiful in black. Anna thought it
brought out the pallor of her complexion, which was recovering from years of dry wind at prairie garrisons. It became her black eyes and graying hair. She had lost weight
since she returned, but looked the better for it.

Anna began the letter from Tom Weir and Libbie took
out her handkerchief halfway through. Anna, who thought
she had shed all the tears she had in her already, could
hardly finish. Tom Weir, always *comme il faut,* never overstepped himself, but his letter overflowed with affection
for Libbie.

> *"I will visit soon, my beloved widow, when I regain
> my health. If you and Maggie Calhoun and Annie
> Yates and I were together in your parlor at night,
> with the curtains all down and everybody else
> asleep, one or the other of you would make me tell
> you everything I know. When I come, I will be able
> to say something to you all that would make you feel
> glad for a little while at least. What I could tell you
> would vindicate forever our dear friends."*

Anna dried her tears on the corner of her embroidery.
Not an hour later, in one of those coincidences so natural
you must accept them, the cook brought in the day's mail.
Libbie opened a bill, then a letter and gasped and handed
it to Anna. Lieutenant Weir had died on December 9.

"Oh, Libbie, now we'll never know!" wailed Anna. She
read the letter from Weir's physician through again.

"I cannot bear to know any more," Libbie said.

"What are you going to do, now that the book about
Armstrong is published?" Anna asked. "Are you going to
stay here in Monroe?"

"I must begin my life again," said Libbie. "I must de-

fend Armstrong's memory against those awful things people are saying."

"What will you do?"

"I will go to New York where I can respond effectively
to comments Whittaker made about the General."

Anna was puzzled. Hadn't Armstrong been a lieutenant
colonel when he died? Hadn't Libbie helped Whittaker
with his biography?

"Surely there is some occupation there, in charities, or
perhaps writing, that a respectable woman could do. Besides, if I don't protect the General's reputation, the carp-
ing of lesser men will tarnish it."

Anna remembered the charges at that court-martial.
Some of them had been true. Armstrong was not perfec-
tion.

Libbie was too deep for her. She knew Libbie loved
Armstrong, but there was always some other motive at
work under the surface. Anna wondered if Libbie were
playing another role. She thought about it as her needle
outlined flowers and leaves in bright floss. The playacting
of ladies and chevaliers was over. Monroe was dull. Libbie
would write a new role: the widow of the glorious hero.
Then Anna banished the thought. It was petty of her to
think Libbie had motives like that.

"You must do what you think is right," said Anna.

"I shall," said Libbie. "I shall."

On Peg Leg's Trail

JON CHANDLER

Jon won the prestigious Western Writers of America Medicine Pipe Bearer Award for Best First Novel of 1998 with his impressive book, *The Spanish Peaks*. He is also an accomplished poet and songwriter. In this story he recounts a story of his great-great-grandfather, F. M. Ownbey, and his relationship with the infamous Tom Horn.

Of this story, Jon writes:

> The story of the Cotopaxi Robbery is a vivid part of frontier Colorado's history. It's also the first time the notorious Tom Horn became recognized as being on the proper side of the law. Horn and Doc Shores, a legendary Colorado lawman, teamed up to catch several hard cases responsible for the robbery of the Denver and Rio Grande Railroad near the town of Cotopaxi, Colorado. The robbery and its aftermath are chronicled in the Autumn 2000 edition of Colorado Heritage, *the publication of the Colorado Historical Society. Author Larry D. Ball, of Arkansas State University, does a masterful job in bringing the incident to life.*
>
> One of my ancestors, Francis Marion (Frank) Ownbey was peripherally involved, most likely as a deputy sheriff of Huerfano County, Colorado. A letter from Ownbey to Horn, sent when Horn was imprisoned and soon to be hanged in Cheyenne, is included in Horn's autobiography

(Tom Horn, Written by Himself. "On Peg Leg's Trail" is a whimsical, and very fictional, attempt to re-create the closing of the Colorado frontier through my ancestor's eyes.

★

The whole thing was one big damn mistake.

First of all, I never even knew a train went through Cotopaxi. Hell, the only man I ever met from Cotopaxi was Nestor McNabb, a scrawny weasel who shoveled coal on the Denver and Rio Grande and swore, between spittin' cud, wiping black snot on his sleeve, and tossing another shovel full of that dusty, soft Colorado bituminous into the inferno, he'd never go back. Hated the place, he said, after his ma hooked up with a Kentucky miner and left seven kids alone in an abandoned cabin south of town, one of 'em a pretty gal who promptly shacked up with a railroad man who got her younger brother Nestor a job shoveling coal so as to stop her whining. Kentucky, McNabb told me, must be the true location of hell, 'cause it sure spawned the devil what stole his ma. Hated every southerner who breathed God's clean air, he said, until I pulled back my coat to show him both my pistol and my badge and conveyed to him in my Dixie drawl how much I missed my native Georgia.

McNabb never mentioned, as I led him off the train and locked him up pending extradition on a petty theft charge from Raton, that the Denver and Rio Grande actually passed through Cotopaxi. So I was surprised when Ed Farr came bursting into the sheriff's office in Walsenburg, slammed the door behind him, tossed a wire from the U.S. Marshal in Denver on the desk, and earnestly said, "Frank, it looks like they robbed the train at Cotopaxi."

There I was, writing out a report about a drunk and disorderly disturbance the night before, listening to the lout I'd busted on the noggin whimpering in the cell in the rear, and trying not to scream from a foot that was swollen to twice its size from the gout. Now, Ed was a fine deputy, but lacked some in the communication department.

"*Who* robbed *what* train at Cotopaxi?" I said.

"Dunno. But it says in that wire they got away with about thirty-five hundred dollars," he answered.

"There's a train goes through Cotopaxi?" I asked.

"Well, sure," Ed said, a little haltingly, as he picked up the sheet of paper and began reading.

"McNabb never told me that," I said under my breath.

Ed's mouth moved along with the words, and he had a puzzled look on his handsome, black-bearded mug. He was working up to asking a question.

"Frank," he finally said, "it doesn't say here where Cotopaxi is. You know?"

"Well, sure, Ed," I answered. "Up north there around Canon City, there at the Sangre de Cristos. Didn't know the Denver and Rio Grande ran through there, though."

"Yep, they do," responded Ed confidently, "and now the train's been robbed."

Like I said, that was the first thing.

Second, I wasn't smart enough to figure out how a train robbery at Cotopaxi had anything to do with the Huerfano County Sheriff's Office, it being a hundred fifty or so miles southeast of Cotopaxi. There I was, an ex–Pinkerton agent with the gout so bad I considered shooting my good foot just to get my mind off the pain in the other. I hadn't set a proper horse for five years since I began riding trains for the Pinkertons and later for the Denver and Rio Grande, which made me feel stupid as a Missouri carp since I didn't even know the damn line went through Cotopaxi.

"Hand me that wire, Ed," I said. "Who they got involved in this wild to-do?"

I read the wire and saw Ed had missed a few particulars. U.S. Marshal Albert Jones sent word that some of the Wet Mountain Gang, whoever they were, had kin in the Cucha-

ras Valley down our way, and they may be taking flight to
that area. I was trying to figure who in the hell lived on the
Cucharas River that might have blood with a proclivity for
train robbery when Ed broke my train of thought.

"Frank," he said, "why's they name it Cotopaxi?"

I sighed and answered, "Ed, there are some mysteries
even I don't know the answer to. Maybe there was somebody named Cotopaxi, some Aztec god or a Messican from
Sonora."

"Oh," Ed responded. "Does sound Messican, doesn't it?"

It took a couple of days and a half dozen wires to understand this Wet Mountain Gang business. It took Deputy
Sheriff Ed Kelly to toss the whole mess in my lap.

Here's what I remember. Marshal Jones kept sending
wires care of the sheriff's office in Walsenburg, answering
questions I'd been sending back his direction. He was dealing with me, the lowest deputy sheriff on the totem pole, instead of Sheriff John Mertz because we'd worked together
a couple years earlier when I was a Pinkerton agent, trying
to find out who set fire to an old creosote-soaked trestle and
bridge near Pueblo that damn near caused a mile-long coal
train to take a dip in the Arkansas River. Never did find the
culprit, although we managed to get the train stopped before an unplanned baptism occurred.

I left the Pinkertons a short time later, or maybe they
left me, and went back to farming and mining at La Veta,
a little west of Walsenburg. Planting corn and spuds is
rough business after a few years of finer living. Digging
coal is damn near impossible. So I went back to the law,
first as a railroad detective and then signing on with Sheriff John Mertz, all the while keeping my sights set on the
office of justice of the peace, or perhaps even that of sheriff itself. I figured I was as electable as the next fella.
Maybe even more.

Marshal Jones let on that the railroad detectives and the
marshal's office really knew who the genius criminals be-

hind the Wet Mountain Gang were: some family named
McCoy, along with a few gunmen named Watson, Curtis,
Parry, and Boyd. Some rancher near Cotopaxi said Watson
or Curtis had either kin or close friends down my way, although he didn't know any names. Naturally, Jones wired
me, asking me to keep on the lookout for some fellas who
might be robbers and who *might* be headed my direction
because they *might* be connected up with someone in that
pretty Cucharas Valley. I almost wired him that I *might*
have time to look into it.

Watson only had one leg since his other had been shot off
in some fracas, so he was called—hold on, you'll never
guess—Peg Leg. Criminals in general, and outlaws in particular, aren't the most inspired people in the world. If
they're big old boys, they're always called "Tiny." If they're
up out of Austin, they're named "Tex." If they're young,
they're called "the Kid." There must be some confederation
of villains that bestows these silly names, 'cause they all
seem to have them. Frankly, if my leg had been shot off in a
gun battle, which, believe me, would have hurt substantially
less than the gout, I would have put a bullet through the first
man to call me "Peg Leg." I'd have adopted a less pre-
dictable moniker. "Ahab," probably. "Captain Ahab Ownbey" suits the ear, I think. Or "Long John Silver Ownbey"
after that pirate in Stevenson's book, or better yet, just "Silver." "Silver" Frank Ownbey, I'd be, and anyone who asked
why that peg-legged fella was called "Silver" would be told
it was because Silver Frank Ownbey had culture.

My own brother did the same thing. Adopted a more
dignified name, that is. He took to referring to himself as
"Colonel," although the closest he'd been to military service was selling whiskey to the quartermaster at Fort Lupton.
He wound up calling himself Colonel John Ownbey, even
though his name was James, and somehow managed to
convince our second or third cousin, that old windbag J. P.
Morgan, that he should invest in land and mines in Col-

orado. James, or John by then, ran such holdings, of course, and being called Colonel went a long way in making both miners and greenhorns show appropriate respect. I have to give him credit, 'cause it worked for a while.

Anyway, Peg Leg and his accomplices were stretching their run throughout the Sangre de Cristos, and Jones wired me he needed help in tracking those boys down. We had five deputies in Huerfano County, each working for Sheriff Mertz. There was Ed Farr, of course, and me, of course. Then we had Roberto Sanchez and Ernest Duran, both good men who'd watch your back.

My gout being what it was, I got Sheriff Mertz to send Ed on up toward Salida to hook up with my old pal Doc Shores, probably the best lawman Colorado ever knew. Cy Shores was a little feisty, all right, but he had reason to be. He'd been shot at, bushwhacked, blackjacked and left for dead, shot at again, forced to guard and actually feed that ungodly man-eating cannibal Al Packer, and called a liar by a Gunnison rancher whose son was caught with most of his neighbor's cattle. Why Doc stayed in the law business always perplexed me. When I'd ask him, he'd say he had a reputation to uphold.

Ed joined Doc somewhere in South Park while the rest of us supposedly followed Marshal Jones's admonition to keep an eye on the Cucharas country. If I'd done exactly that, I would have saved myself a pile of trouble.

I mentioned we had five deputies. Well, the fifth was another Ed, the aforementioned Ed Kelly, who somehow or another got to be called "Black Bill" Kelly in documents of record on down the road. I never heard one living soul call him Black Bill, or Wild Bill, or Buffalo Bill for that matter. His name was Ed, and that's what we called him. I don't know exactly why Sheriff Mertz hired him, but he'd been with the sheriff's office a year or so longer than me, and I put up with him—him and his stories. Why, if you ever climbed a mountain, he climbed one higher. And steeper. If you ran a race, he ran faster. If you shot a ten-point buck, he shot a twelve. If you caught thirty or forty of those pretty spotted trout, he caught a hundred, and bigger ones, to boot. It was like that. It got to the point where we started calling common, everyday exaggerations, "Ed Saids." Even Ed Farr caught on to the fun, not taking any offense in light of the fact that he shared his first name with the object of our levity.

Oh, we had some fine "Ed Saids." Like Roberto hauling in that fella who was riding Stan Fink's gelding off up North Veta Creek. The man said the horse found him, and it was probably smart enough to open the corral gate itself. He forgot to mention he aided the gelding by saddling it, and helping it don its rigging, as well. Roberto looked at the scoundrel and told him he better come up with a few better "Ed Saids," just before he slapped the guy in the ear with his sap. A confession was forthcoming.

So why was *I* stupid enough to believe what Ed said? How come I listened to him tell me he knew what Peg Leg and those other boys were up to? Why did I almost let him get killed out there on the prairie between Walsenburg and Trinidad? My only excuse is the gout.

The gout has no peer when it comes to the aches and pains of everyday living. It's insidious, evil, and, well, just plain *bad*. I stepped on a pitchfork when I was a kid in Georgia, back before my pa got killed at Chancellorsville. I don't recollect it hurt near as bad as the gout. When I was twenty-three and first put on a badge, I took buckshot in the rear part of my anatomy from a bank robber's scattergun at Las Animas. The gout's worse. I got knocked from my horse Dixie by lightning on Mount Blanca in eighty-one. Killed the horse and left me smoldering in the rain, not able to hear a thing and with a broken leg where Dixie fell on me. Didn't compare to the gout.

I hate the gout.

If you ever drop an anvil on your foot, then crush it in

a vice before you run it over with an ore cart, you'll get the idea. The only thing that's worse than putting weight on your foot is taking weight off. And vice versa. I heard of some men who got the gout in both feet at the same time. I believe I'd just end it all right there and then. Suicide is preferable to the gout in both feet, and it is all that consumes your thoughts about a week into the suffering when it's only in one foot.

My wife, Sarah, as strong willed a daughter of the South as ever breathed, learned to live with me during my spells with the gout, but her sympathy over the years waned considerably. "You'll live," she'd say, and I would. But I wouldn't want to.

I figure my judgment must have been clouded by the gout miseries when Ed Kelly strolled into the office after a couple of days of being out and about, and began telling me how he knew just about everything there was to know about the Cotopaxi robbers. My foot actually felt a little better, but I was still taking powders every two or three hours and a stiff shot of Ritter's rotgut twice during the day trying to control the pain. I had an old pair of boots in the tack shed, so I slit the right one from toe to instep so I could jam my foot down in and hobble to and fro. When Kelly sat down on the edge of the desk, I was just putting the foot up to rest on the other side.

"Why's your boot all cut up like that, Frank?" he asked.

"The gout," I answered. "Hurts like a son of a—"

"The gout," he interrupted with a shout. "You ain't never seen the gout 'til you seen me with it. My foot swells up like a melon, I tell ya. I was up on Texas Creek once where I actually took a knife and nicked my ankle to try to let the gout bleed on out. Keep my foot in the creek for a half day, but it still didn't work. Heck, I even had the gout in my knee and elbow. Tried soaking my elbow in mescal once, but it didn't—"

"Ed," I broke in.

"Yeah, Frank," he said.

"You got something to tell me?" I asked in my most exasperated tone. The gout was hurting and Ed wasn't helping.

"Yeah, uh, yeah, Frank," he answered slowly. Ed had a doleful look about him, with his little line of a sandy-haired mustache and his eyebrows pointing down at the same angle.

"I was down there north of Trinidad night before last," he continued, "and came up on a camp there by the crossing. You know, one'a them places where drifters camp."

"What in the hell were you doing in Trinidad, Ed?" I broke in. "I thought you were taking a couple of days up at your place on the Cucharas."

"Well, I was looking for clues, Frank," he stated with a quick nod of his forlorn little head. "Looking for clues."

"But you told me you were headed over to the river to dig up those spuds you been growing," I challenged.

"Well, for a bit, I did," he sputtered, "but then I got to thinking about that church robbery down to Trinidad, and how nobody from town would actually do such a thing, and that it must be a drifter. I couldn't just stay there digging spuds with that on my mind, so I took off to see if I could find them blasphemers."

Something wasn't right, but my gout-clouded mind couldn't comprehend it at the time. Looking back, it seems like it was all laid out there for me. But then, looking back always makes you think of a hundred ways you could have avoided misery.

Ed began talking, and I began listening, and for some reason the whole thing seemed to make sense. According to Ed, he came on a campfire with a couple of drifters and thought he'd feel them out about the cash missing from the poor box at Immaculate Heart of Mary. He hailed the camp and joined them, pulling out a little coffee from his pack and tossing it to his new campfire pards before making himself a place to bed down by the fire's edge. Ed said it was one of those quiet summer nights you get out on the prairie and, except for the crackling of the fire, you could hear the coyotes yipping all the way up to the Spanish Peaks.

Before he got to asking about stolen tithes and such, he said a bottle of strong spirits suddenly appeared, so he and the boys started drinking and talking, talking and drinking. Pretty soon, his campmates were whooping it up and laughing themselves sick about robbing a train up around Cotopaxi. Four of them pulled it off, they said. Funny thing was, nobody got rich, they said, 'cause the proceeds from their dirty deed went to pay off lawyers from the chief crook's murder trial.

Pretty soon, one of the presumed robbers staggered up to go relieve himself, and it was then Ed noticed he had a wooden leg. It was a pretty involved contraption, according to Ed, and when the fella returned, he unlatched it and set it to the side before crawling into his bedroll.

The other potential criminal had already nodded off, which left Ed with a dilemma. Should he draw down on them now, or wait until morning to get help? Full of strong spirits, he fell asleep while pondering the problem and woke up just in time to see the newly confessed robbers saddling their ponies. They waved good day and took off across the prairie.

Ed scuffled around as fast as he could, he said, and packed everything up. Near the fire, he found a set of false whiskers and threw them in his pack.

It was the whiskers that convinced me. The whiskers and the gout, I guess. Marshal Jones's wire said one of the Wet Mountain Gang was wearing fake whiskers, so I figured Ed was on to something.

When he finished his story, I slowly lowered my foot to the floor, grimaced, and stood, knowing I had three wires to send, gout or no gout. I began steeling myself for the walk to the telegrapher's office.

I only had one question for my fellow deputy.

"Why do you think they talked about this heinous crime in front of you, a total stranger?"

"I don't know, Frank," Ed said deliberately while tugging on that skinny lip hair. "I believe it must be because I have an honest face."

I stared at Ed for a moment, shook my head, and hobbled for the door.

"Frank?" Ed asked. "What's heinous?"

My first wire was an advisory to Marshal Jones in Denver. My second was to Doc Shores in Salida, asking him to join me in Walsenburg. I was jotting down the third when I started smiling at the thought. I handed the text to the clerk and watched him go to work.

On the receiving end, to the best of my recollection, the note read: Mr. Tom Horn *stop* Pinkerton Agency *stop* Denver, Colorado *stop* Needed at Walsenburg immediately *stop* On the trail of Peg Leg *stop* Doc Shores notified at Salida *stop* Yours, F. M. Ownbey.

Tom Horn. That name means something these days. It brings up images, most of them not within a week's ride of the truth. There's a fine line between being foolhardy and brave, between fact and brag, between legend and lie. Tom walked that line better than any man I ever knew. Cowman, hard case, gunman, stock detective—whatever he called himself, he always had an eye on creating something bigger than life. Not that he bragged. He didn't. He just left enough out of a story to let you fill in the missing parts. And because he had a, well, *certainty* about him, I guess, the omissions were always filled in in his favor.

Back then, before infamy and myth set in, Tom was just the name of a man I'd met over a year earlier on a train platform in Pueblo. I remember four events in my life with perfect clarity—my first glimpse of the Spanish Peaks as a boy on a wagon train two thousand miles from my home in Georgia; the day Sarah and I were hitched in La Veta;

the birth of my daughter, Louise; and the day I met Tom Horn.

If you're lucky, you'll meet three or four people in your life who you just take to, and who take to you in return. It was like that with me and Tom.

I'd been sent to Pueblo by the railroad to investigate a missing lockbox that was full of pay vouchers. The Pinkertons were involved, so an agent was dispatched from Denver. We were to meet at the station in Pueblo. I'd heard a thing or two about this Horn from a detective in Denver, as well as from Doc Shores, but wasn't quite sure what to expect.

I was talking to the stationmaster and puffing on a nickel stogie when the train pulled in from Denver. We were just talking about the county elections coming up in a couple of months when someone grabbed my shoulder from behind, spinning me almost 180 degrees.

"You Ownbey?" the man asked. He was tall and fair haired, about thirty or so, with a tan, broad-brimmed hat jammed down on his head.

"Could be," I answered.

"Well, they said Ownbey'd be here and that he was a portly fella with a big black mustache and a black hat. That'd seem to be you."

I looked him up and down and sensed more bluster than danger.

"They got the mustache part right, now, didn't they?" I said. "And the hat. That portly business is open to interpretation, though. I prefer substantial."

He snorted softly, then said, "Well, portly or not, you're a railroad dick, and I got no use for railroad dicks."

I excused us quickly from the stationmaster and hobbled a couple of steps on down the platform. The irritable man followed.

I picked up the conversation with about as much menace as I could muster.

"That's all right, I guess, 'cause I got no use for two-bit

casino robbers, even if they're wearing Pinkerton clothes. I'm supposed to meet one here named Tom Horn."

The man looked taken aback, and stammered, "Well, you . . . you met him."

We locked eyes for a few seconds before I broke into a chuckle and said, "Don't look surprised, Horn, Doc Shores wired me all about you. Said you'd come on like a Wild West outlaw and that I should take you down a peg by mentioning a misunderstanding at some casino in Nevada."

Horn's eyes narrowed, then widened as he shook his head and said, "Ol' Doc. Doc set me up, he did. Gave you the goods on me. I hate when he does that."

"Well, if it's any consolation," I said, "Doc says you're innocent."

"That I am," he mused. "I sure am."

I started walking from the station's platform toward Main Street and the sheriff's office. Tom grabbed his pack and followed.

"Why are you limping like that?" he asked. "Get shot or something?"

"Um, something like that, all right," I confirmed.

Tom reached into an outside pocket on the pack and pulled out a little bottle of mash. "Hey, hold up," he said.

We stopped at the side of the station and he held the bottle out to me.

"This oughta help."

I hesitated for a moment, said, "What the hell," grabbed the bottle, and took a lengthy pull before handing it back to Tom, who did the same.

I then reached into my inside coat pocket, pulled out my bottle of Ritter's, and offered it to Tom. He smiled, said, "What the hell," and took a snort before passing it back to me so I could follow suit.

You could say we had mutual interests.

Once Tom was registered at the hotel, we sat down in

the lobby with a bottle of Ritter's finest to discuss the problems presented by the missing vouchers. We never got the chance. I started talking about coming to Colorado as a boy of fifteen in 1865, and how the place had changed so much. He started talking about growing up in Missouri, winding up in Santa Fe and then Arizona, scouting for Crook and Miles. I started speaking a little Ute I'd picked up at the mines, and he countered with a sentence or two in Apache, learned when he was an interpreter. I told him about Tom Tobin and he told me about Al Seiber. I talked about meeting Red Cloud's Cheyenne off to the east, and he talked about meeting Geronimo off to the south. I talked about leaving the Pinkertons and he talked about joining them. Before I knew it, the time was late, the bottle was empty, and morning was on its way.

I had a new friend.

We never did catch the culprit who made off with the vouchers. Another railroad detective in Denver did that for us. Turned out the thief was a man named Bates who had a wife and five kids and a mistress and two kids. They all lived north of town in a two-room shack. It seemed the detective busted in with pistol drawn after finding one of the vouchers had been cashed by the desperado in question and hearing from the cashier that Bates was a mighty bad man. He managed to shoot one of the kids and the mistress before he realized he was firing at helpless people. Bates had deserted them and taken off for California with a Larimer Street working gal. Even the railroad couldn't fight the power of the press when the *Rocky Mountain News* picked up the story. The Denver and Rio Grande settled with Bates's families for $3,000 and payment of medical bills.

In the meantime, Tom and I spent a couple of days together in Pueblo, investigating and chumming, chumming and investigating, before hearing from Denver that a railroad dick was busy shooting at women and children and the case was solved. We managed to become pretty good pards.

Now it was a year and a half later, and Tom and I were hooked up again. He walked into the sheriff's office in Walsenburg grinning like the cat that ate the bird, reached into his duster, and pulled out his little bottle of mash.

"This oughta help," he said.

And it did.

I'd arranged to stay in town that night rather than taking the wagon back out to the spread. Earlier that morning, Sarah had given me one of her "Francis Marion Ownbey, you are genuinely teched" looks when I told her I'd be out on the prairie for a few days searching for ruffians and criminals. She reminded me that my prowess with livestock had waned considerably over the past few years of devotion to the law, even if my skill with a rifle had not. Plus, there was the gout involved, and a gout-ridden foot did not mix well with a hard stirrup. I told her if she needed me she should send in our son, Les, or one of our daughters' husbands, and a deputy would likely find me somewhere out toward Kansas.

Doc Shores came in on the morning train, all crotchety and charming at the same time, glad to see both Horn and me. Doc was a fair-sized man, a little older than me with a sad little mustache and eyes that challenged. I knew he was a hard man, but I'll swear he was never hard to me.

My foot was feeling better, perhaps from Tom's mash or perhaps from the sixth batch of medicinal powders I'd swallowed over the previous twenty-four hours. I was even riding pretty well, having borrowed my friend Nathan Patterson's mare, Dixie, named after my late, lamented lightning-struck mount. Nate's boy Morgan would a couple of years later become my son-in-law, and was always my superior in handling that horse.

By noon, we'd rounded up more horses, supplies, and

Deputy Sheriff Ed Kelly. We were off on what Doc termed a "manhunt."

The prairie out east of Walsenburg and Trinidad is a mighty brown place in early September. Now, that's not necessarily bad. Brown feels like the color of home on the high desert of south Colorado. It's a vast space, that great prairie, and the horizon is impossibly far away. Looking east, it seems you can actually feel yourself being drawn down the creeks and arroyos toward another place, a place that was left long ago. But, even though there's a yearning to go back and see that place again, you're disturbed at having to leave the high peaks and valleys. Old John Francisco always said the prairie calls, but the mountains command— words of wisdom. One look back at the Spanish Peaks from out on the prairie is enough to make your soul sing. There's nothing like those two hills in the world, I suspect, twin peaks of vivid blues and deep greens—massive granite mountains that dominate the landscape for a hundred fifty miles. Rumors of hidden gold mines, lost treasures, ghosts and haunts, and graves of Spanish conquistadors abound. The Utes even believed there was a place to find eternal life on the Wa-Toy-Uh, their word for the Spanish Peaks. Mexican settlers called them Huajatolla, their version of the Indian term, and legends of great haciendas that once flourished at the base of the east peak are still passed on.

Riding east from the peaks is like entering another world. Brown, as I said, but just as alive as any place on earth. Deer and pronghorn populate the prairie where buffalo grazed just a few years back. Coyotes and prairie dogs are common. Every kind of bird in the world flies about and rattlers seem to take pleasure in spooking skittish horses. It was on the brown prairie between Walsenburg and Trinidad that we began our search for the outlaw known as Peg Leg.

We decided to head almost due south, while bearing a bit to the east. Ed had let it be known that even in his sleep he could find the drifters' camp where the famous Cotopaxi robbers had confessed their evil deed. Why, according to Ed, there was really no reason for four of us to be out riding the prairie, as he could probably just follow the trail himself. He was still talking when Doc, Tom, and I spurred our horses, drowning him out.

Doc Shores and Tom Horn presented fair imitations of centaurs, riding like they were attached to their horses. Ed rode all right, but kept one hand firmly attached to the saddle horn. After a few years of riding trains and gaining an extra twenty pounds, my rear end saw considerable daylight, and between the gout, the pounding my nether regions were taking, the numbness in my knees, and the fact I had never before ridden this particular Dixie horse, I knew I was in for a rough ride. I would be damned rather than let anyone know it, however.

I mentioned two reasons why this whole "manhunt" was a mistake. Well, there was a third. Anytime you put more than two lawmen together on a case, it's like planting a boot in the middle of a red anthill. Did you ever throw an old dried ear of corn into a fire? Well, it's like that when you let lawman from four or five jurisdictions chase after the same ne'er-do-wells. Things start to scatter—things like facts, and truth, and good sense. While making progress down toward Trinidad, Doc filled us in on the chase, and how it seemed we were not dealing with mental Titans, on either side of the law. I got to laughing so hard when Doc said they figured Peg Leg was involved, because of the holes his wooden leg made in the soft ground at the robbery site, Dixie seemed to settle down, probably thinking I'd lost my mind. Tom wasn't quite guffawing, but I saw him blow a bubble of snot when he snorted at one of Doc's descriptions of a county deputy who carried only one bullet—said he'd used his quota for the month shooting rats at the dump, trying to work on his aim, of course, and the sheriff wouldn't give him any more. Ed looked kind of perplexed at the story, like a man who laughs too loud at a joke he doesn't understand. Anyway, Doc's recitation of the mistakes and mishaps associated with the "Peg Leg" case reminded me of one of Bill Shakespeare's comedies, only funnier.

In a nutshell, here's what happened. Old Dick McCoy, a rancher up near Cotopaxi, was a southerner, just like me. Unlike me, however, he rode with that butcher Quantrill when he was a kid, and he seemed to have retained the habits of his youth. It took the U.S. Marshal and the railroad powers-that-be about a half minute to figure out who was behind the train heist. Old Dick was up for murder in Canon City, and his lawyers had refused to continue representing him until they were paid. Dick had a few of his boys, including Peg Leg Watson and Bert Curtis, abscond with the railroad's cash in order to pay said lawyers. (Now, lawyering used to be a fairly noble profession. But, more and more, it seems lawyers are the kind of folks who don't mind being paid with stolen money for defending murderous scoundrels. Something must be done!) Not being the most discerning robbers, Peg Leg, Curtis, and two others first broke into the mail car, automatically attaching a $500 federal reward to their scalps. They then shot open the door to the express messenger's car, where they reaped both $3,600 and the ire of the Denver and Rio Grande Railroad. The reward was upped by another $500.

When asked for a description of the bandits, the messenger said, "Well, now, one of 'em seemed to be wearin' fake whiskers, but it was ol' Bert Curtis under there. Then there was that old boy with one leg, what do they call him—that one-legged fella? I forget. He had a scarf over his face, but I still seen that wood leg."

Now $1,000 is a lot of money, and messing with the federal government tends to bring out a lot of lawmen. Doc estimated over one hundred were on the case within twenty-four hours. People were being arrested right and left, peg legs or no peg legs. I read later Tom claimed he

was arrested—erroneously, of course—at least twice by
deputies during the chase, which was impossible since he
was with me for most of it, and I sure didn't arrest him.
Like I said, Tom did manage to stretch a tale now and again.

So now there were federal marshals, railroad detectives
and special agents, Pinkerton agents, state police, county
sheriff's deputies, deputies from at least five cities, a few
bounty hunters, and maybe even the Pope's own Vatican
Guard itself out scouring the Rocky Mountains looking for
bank robbers and rewards. In the meantime, Old Dick was
sitting on his porch telling the authorities he had no idea
what happened and, like me, didn't even know a train went
through Cotopaxi. He had more on his mind than robbing
trains, he said, like his daughter's husband trying to shoot
her new man friend.

By Doc's count, at least twenty-three lawmen had so far
been arrested by other lawmen. Civilians, hearing about
the reward, began arresting each other in record numbers,
bringing in anyone who didn't share blood to the local authorities. One old gal even marched her son-in-law into the
Salida sheriff's office, all the while pointing a scattergun
directly at his head and demanding the reward. While the
deputy on duty disarmed her, her prisoner calmly picked
up the deputy's nightstick and struck her senseless. The
two shared a familial cell that evening.

Then Doc got a wire from me saying Ed Kelly had become inebriated on the high desert northeast of Trinidad
with wooden-legged, fake-whiskered fellas. It seemed like
as good a lead as any, and since Tom was along as well, it
seemed like a good opportunity to catch up on old times
and at the same time get away from the posses of the Sangre de Cristo Mountains.

So there we were, traipsing off across the prairie, following the lead of "Ed Said" Kelly. Tom commented that
he'd heard there was Spanish gold hidden on the Huajatolla. Ed said he'd found it, and someday was going to go

back and dig it up, just as soon as the time was right. Doc noticed mule deer sign heading down into a little dry creek. Ed said he shot three elk and a moose the previous winter within a mile of where we were then riding. I kidded Doc about his days as sheriff in Gunnison when they brought Al Packer into his jail. Ed said Al Packer ate his uncle.

Tom finally told Ed the ride would be smoother if Ed just didn't talk until someone spoke to him. Ed opened his mouth to answer, but then caught a glimpse of Tom's eyes. "Steely eyes" is the term, I believe. He swallowed the thought and rode off to the side for the rest of the afternoon.

We camped in a little wash with plenty of dry wood and protection from the wind. Of course, there was no wind. It was a beautiful September, even for a place with the most beautiful Septembers in the world. The weather was perfect, and we had a fine little fire going in no time. There was sign the campsite had been used for generations, and our talk was of the Colorado both Doc and I used to know. Cold beef, warm beans, and strong coffee were on the menu, and nothing ever tasted better. The sunset behind the mountains was lovely.

I threw my bedroll on some soft ground beneath a pinon pine about twenty-five yards from the fire. Ed unrolled his blankets within a few feet of the flames, causing me to worry about his well-being. He was snoring before I could ask him to move, though.

Tom and Doc chatted a bit, then took off into the darkness to their respective prairie beds. I carried my copy of the Colorado Justice Manual with me, particularly in light of my aspiration to the office of justice of the peace. I positioned myself so the fire would illuminate the pages and began reading the chapter dealing with jurisdiction in criminal matters. I didn't read long, as the stars in heaven kept vying for my attention. A coyote yipped in the distance, and all was right with the world.

I opened my eyes before dawn, interrupting a pleasant

dream having to do with quail hunting with an old boy-
hood pal from Union County, Georgia. I cleared my head
and started to sit up to face the new day. Now, it had been
a few years since I camped out after a hard ride, but I
surely couldn't remember my body responding in such a
manner. *Sore* was not the proper term. *Excruciating* was
more like it. The spot I'd picked for my bedroll was actually little more than an inch of dirt covering thick sandstone. How in the world that pinon grew there, I'll never
know. When I went to roll over, every single muscle in my
body protested. It was all I could do not to scream for help.
Between pulled muscles, bumps and bruises, numbness
from the hard ground, and the gout, I was a candidate for
the boneyard. If I could have reached my pistol, I may
have used it to end my misery. Instead, I reached out to
steady myself and put my hand directly over one of those
little barrel cactuses, or cacti, as Sarah would correct me.
This time, I did let out a yelp, and sat directly up, causing
every nerve in my body to protest and, at the same time,
rolling into a yucca a few inches from my bedroll.

I sat for ten minutes in the near darkness pulling cactus
needles out of my left hand and making sure no yucca
spines had taken up residence in my backside. Then, de-
ciding I had to get up sometime, I stifled screams of agony
and stood, willing myself toward the fire, where I stoked it
and got it to give up a few tiny flames. Ed Kelly lay there
snoring, like he had all night, and I would have booted his
rear end if the gout would have permitted it. Instead, I
threw a couple of branches on the fire and began hobbling
out toward the darkness to loosen up.

The morning air was invigorating without being cold.
The sky was getting lighter and I could see the outlines of
the mountains to the west. I limped to a big old cottonwood
at the bottom of a soft slope leading down to a shadowy
ravine, and stretched up against it, moving up and down,
scratching my back and limbering my tortured muscles at

the same time. I was about to let out a sigh of contentment when I saw movement to my right. I instinctively reached down for my pistol, which was, of course, back at camp. I was on the prairie in the predawn darkness, searching for outlaws, hobbled by gout, bruised muscles, and cactus wounds, and without a weapon. A fine lawman, I was. The sky lightened almost imperceptibly as I willed myself to stay still as a post. I spied the movement again, about thirty yards to the east. I was sure anyone listening could hear my heart trying to escape my rib cage. Then, in a flash, I witnessed a profound sight that will always stay with me, as the first light of dawn spread over the prairie and the biggest mountain cat I ever saw walked to the edge of the ravine, looked back at me, and disappeared over the rim.

I told Doc, Tom, and Ed about the cat later as we were packing up to hit the trail. My gout was passable, my aches and pains were responding to movement, and the wonder of the encounter with the cougar was still as new and mysterious as a first love.

"Lion coulda et ya, stumblin' around in the dark like a fool," Tom said with a grin.

"I believe you were sleeping somewhere out that direction, Tom," I countered. "I'm surprised he didn't drag you off to his den for a little snack."

"Cats don't like man meat," Doc chimed in. "Scares the heck out of 'em. Tastes like pure danger, I 'spect."

"My uncle got ate by a mountain cat," Ed chimed in. "He was brother to the one got ate by Al Packer."

Tom's steely eyes reappeared as he slowly looked Ed up and down and said, "That's enough out of you, Kelly. Now, let's ride to that camp you were telling us about. I want to find those bandits' trail before it gets any colder."

And ride we did. We rode long and we rode hard. We rode dang near to Trinidad, then out on the eastern prairie. We doubled back toward Walsenburg, then actually headed west for a while. We rode and rode and rode.

I asked Ed late in the morning how far we were from the camp.

"Hold on, it's coming right up," he said.

A couple of hours later, Doc said, "Kelly, where's that camp?"

"Hold on, it's right up yonder," he answered.

An hour after that, Tom said, "The camp, Kelly, where in the hell's the camp?"

"Hold on," he said, and spurred his horse.

By late afternoon, we knew something was wrong. Ed was on up ahead, just over a little ridge, when Tom rode up next to me and said, "Frank, you know this fella. Do you think he's just a fool and can't find the camp, or is something else going on here?"

Doc was off to the side, and pulled his horse in closer to hear the conversation.

"I don't know if Ed's that conniving, Tom," I answered, pulling Dixie from a trot back to a walk. "Lord knows he's just a potato farmer who does deputy work to make ends meet."

And then it struck me. Struck me as hard as the slap in the face I received when I was eighteen from Mrs. Stimmel when she mistook me for my brother, James, whom she heard had made untoward advances to her daughter, Emoline. All at once, I knew exactly what had happened. Ed had met the outlaws at a drifters' camp, he told me, when he was really supposed to be at his little place on the Cucharas digging spuds. Marshal Jones had wired me that some of the Wet Mountain Gang, which turned out to be Peg Leg and his cohorts, of course, had friends or even family on the Cucharas. Ed was either their kith or their kin, and a lying son of a bitch, to boot.

I never felt as foolish in my life. I should have suspected Ed's story from the beginning, in light of my familiarity with "Ed Saids." Instead, I had let my little miseries cloud my judgment, not exactly a superior trait for a peace officer.

I brought Dixie to a complete halt. Tom and Doc pulled their horses up and I began at the beginning.

"Well, boys," I fumed, "I believe that damn Ed's led us down a very wrong road. You see, he was supposed to be up digging spuds on the Cucharas . . ."

I finished the story, and thought Tom's head might explode, he was so red. I didn't blame him. I hadn't taken the Lord's name in vain so frequently since I learned of my pa's death. I think Tom and I would have just run Kelly down and shot him on the spot, but before we could take off after him, Doc said, "Hey, settle down, boys. Here's what needs to be done. Let's catch up with Ed, there, and get to the bottom of this. Let me question him, all right? It's something I do as a matter of course, and I'm pretty good at it."

He stopped and gave both Tom and me a stern look.

"You understand, Tom? Frank? I'm gonna get it out of him. You boys just settle down."

I mumbled my assent and Tom actually managed to say, "Yep," before we all three took off over the ridge like a Comanche war party.

Ed was standing a few feet from his horse relieving himself when he saw us come over the ridge. He did his best to get buttoned up, mounted, and off toward New Mexico before we got there, but managed to trip on the rein he'd left trailing on the ground. His horse started spinning around and managed to kick him a couple of times before I raced over and grabbed the other rein.

Ed stayed on the ground for a few seconds, then began untangling himself.

"Thought I mighta cracked a rib, there, but I 'spect it's all right," he said with a grimace. "You boys come over that ridge pretty fast. Made me a little jumpy."

"Aw, there's no reason to be jumpy, Ed," Doc said. "We

were just stretching our horses out a bit, you know—letting 'em run off a little energy."

Ed smiled and stood up, then reached for the reins, both of which I now held. I didn't hand them to him.

"Um, Frank, I need to . . ." He mimicked mounting the horse.

"No, Ed," Doc said, "we're all gonna get down and have us a little chat."

Ed's face went white as a lace kerchief as we dismounted and faced him.

"We been all over God's prairie the past couple of days, looking for some criminal types you came upon at a night camp somewhere near here—that right, Ed?" Doc said.

"Yeah, yeah, Doc," Ed answered. "That camp's right up ahead. I'm sure it is. I just know it."

Doc nodded his head with great sympathy, then said, "Ed, Ed, Ed. We all know there's no camp, now, don't we."

Ed swallowed hard. Doc began to speak again. I stood there with my arms crossed over my waistcoat, my gun belt plainly visible.

Tom—well, Tom did exactly what Doc told him not to. He broke in over Doc and yelled, "Kelly, you know those uncles that got ate by mountain cats and cannibals? You're gonna wish you was one of 'em when I'm through with you."

Tom started to rush Ed, when Doc pushed him from behind, knocking him off to the side and keeping him from grabbing Kelly. Tom was furious, but Doc took the distraction in stride, latching on to Kelly's waistcoat lapels with both hands and shaking him.

"I'll let Tom loose on you, Kelly," he screamed. "God knows I will unless you tell us what's behind this runaround."

"All right, all right," Kelly whimpered. "Just—just—just listen to me for a minute and don't go hurtin' on me."

Doc pushed him back and told him to start talking. Talk

he did. He damn near talked our ears right off our heads. We learned about him and Bert Curtis being second cousins, only Bert Curtis wasn't really Bert Curtis's name. It was Frank Elliot, although he also called himself Dan Breckenridge. We learned about him and Frank growing up together, their mothers being first cousins from Missouri. We heard about them stealing apples from orchards, and bullying younger boys for their pennies. We found out about young Ed and Frank-Bert-Dan robbing a store in Oklahoma and making it out of town on stolen horses with bullets whizzing by. We learned the experience cured Ed of his wayward proclivities, and of his split-up with his larcenous cousin, only Frank-Bert-Dan visited Ed's place on the Cucharas pretty regularly. Ed told us about Frank-Bert Dan's hookup with Old Dick McCoy and his subsequent friendship with Peg Leg Watson. We found out about Ed going to his place on the Cucharas to harvest potatoes, only to find Peg Leg and Frank-Bert-Dan waiting for him with news of the Cotopaxi robbery. We learned the bandits' haul truly had been handed off to another of McCoy's confederates to be used to pay his lawyers, and that the robbers planned on lying low in Oklahoma for a few months before heading back to the Sangre de Cristos, whereupon McCoy would reward them handsomely.

Then, an hour or so into his tale, Ed let us in on their brilliant plan. The bandits had learned Doc Shores was on their trail after meeting up with a posse ten miles from Cotopaxi and acting like lawmen themselves. Although the posse was looking for a wooden-legged man, they apparently noticed nothing suspicious about Peg Leg. The bandits hightailed it to Ed's place on the Cucharas, where they decided that Ed, being a deputy and all, would serve as a dandy decoy. Ed let on that I knew Doc Shores. They figured once I was convinced the bandits were in the area, I would wire Shores to show up, and Ed would then lead us in circles out on the prairie, giving Peg Leg and Frank-

Bert-Dan at least a couple of extra days to make their way
to Oklahoma. Ed hadn't counted on me wiring Tom and
inviting him along, him with his bad attitude and all.

My gout-addled mind had fallen for it. Silly Ed Kelly
had played me like an evil genius. God, I was mad.

But not as mad as Tom.

When Ed was through, Tom was even more red than before. "So," he began, "your bandit cousin actually was
down here, only not at some drifters' camp."

Ed nodded his assent.

"And," Tom continued, "we spent two days riding
around this cactus-infested prairie dog town so you could
let your cousin and his partner escape."

Once again, Ed nodded.

Tom thought about it for a moment, then walked over to
his horse and pulled his rifle from its scabbard. From a distance of less than fifteen yards, he said, "That's aiding and
abetting," leveled the rifle, and shot point blank at Ed Kelly.

Both Doc and I ran for Tom as he raised the rifle, and
Doc quickly knocked it back down after the shot. I turned
and ran toward Kelly, who was breathing in short gasps
with eyes wide as saucers, his hands holding his chest.

"I . . . I . . . I," he stammered, and that's when I noticed.
He was standing there shivering with fear, more scared
than a rabbit at a coyote gathering, without a scratch. No
blood. No hole with daylight shining through. Nothing.

To this day, it's still hard to believe Tom missed.

Well, Doc settled Tom down, and I tied Ed up. We spent
a sleepless night out on the plains, Doc sitting right next to
Ed with a keen eye on Tom.

In the morning Tom and Doc took off for Oklahoma
where, in due course, they caught up with Peg Leg and
Curtis and brought those bad men to justice. I was given
the task of taking Ed back to the Walsenburg jail, and listening to him whine all the way. At one point I stopped the

horses, looked him in the eye, and said, "Ed, I truly wish Tom Horn had better aim."

When we got back to Walsenburg, Ed managed to convince Sheriff Mertz he could actually help find the bandits since he knew their real trail, being in on their plans and all. Mertz bought into Ed's new "Ed Said" and they took off toward Oklahoma with a posse, leaving Roberto and me in charge. Roberto laughed so hard he like to cried as the posse rode out of town.

I resigned from the force and took up coal mining.

Over the years, I kept up with Tom and Doc, and we saw each other as much as common. Tom got harder over the years, and his stories got wilder, but I still recognized the friend I'd met on a station platform in Pueblo, especially when we'd pull out our little bottles and toast the tracking of Peg Leg.

They hanged Tom quite a few years ago up in Cheyenne. He got caught up with some of those big cattle ranchers and wound up killing a few men, it's said. It's also said he murdered a young boy, mistaking the kid for his father. It was a shot of over three hundred yards in the fog. I never believed for one second that Tom could have done such a thing, although, like I said, he did have a contrary attitude.

I wrote to Tom in the Cheyenne jail, altering the facts of the Peg Leg affair just enough to hopefully cause doubt among his captors.

Denver, Colo. January 24, 1902

Mr. Tom Horn,
County Jail
Cheyenne, Wyo.

Dear Tom:
I see by the papers that you are in serious trouble. After reading an account of the charge preferred against you, I can not for the life of me believe it is

true. Knowing you for so long and knowing you so intimately, I can not comprehend how a man of your sense and ability could be guilty of so great a charge as is preferred against you.

Now, Tom, you will remember the Cotopaxi robbery, which was committed several years ago by "Peg-leg" and Curtis, and the long, hard chase we had after them, endeavoring to catch them. You will remember Ed Kelly, of Walsenburg, who first put me on the trail of Curtis and "Peg-leg," and you will again remember me wiring you and Doc Shores to meet me at Walsenburg—that I was on the trail of the robbers. Doc Shores, as you know, is with the Rio Grande Western as their special agent; he formerly was sheriff of Gunnison County, and his reputation is beyond reproach. We went down on the prairie between Trinidad and Walsenburg, and Kelly went back on all his first statements and endeavored to throw us off the trail. You will remember we would have been killed down there on the prairie and left for the coyotes to devour had it not been for your interference.

Now, Tom, I am at a loss to believe, after your protecting such a character as Kelly from being shot out on the plains, where mortal man would have never known anything about it, that you would be guilty of murdering a fourteen-year-old boy in cold blood. You know that scoundrel Kelly would have been shot for lying to the officers had it not been for your interference.

Tom, I do not believe you are guilty of the crime. I am writing this in all justice to you and the community at large; knowing you as I do, and knowing your ability and sense, I can not believe you would stoop so low as to murder a fourteen-year-old boy for the small sum of five hundred dollars, when you could in all probability have made that amount in a week, legitimately.

I live in Loveland, Colorado, and if there is anything I can do for you, or aid you in any manner as far as it is right, I am at your service. You can write me at Loveland, Colorado, box 271, and tell me what you think about it. I will give a copy of this letter to the press this afternoon, to be published in your behalf, as I do not believe you guilty of the crime. Write me and tell me if there is anything I can do to aid you.

As ever your friend,
F. M. Ownbey

P.S.: I will write Doc Shores this afternoon (although I presume he has seen an account of your trouble), and see if there is anything he can do for you. My sympathies are with you, Tom, because I believe you innocent.

Tom was hanged anyway, and I visit his grave over in Boulder now and again, close to where my brother James once had that granite mansion, before everything in his life went bad. Tom was a good friend, and a good man, and I knew he could never have killed some kid with a circus shot. The fact was, as Ed "Black Bill" Kelly, Doc Shores, and I learned out on the prairie between Walsenburg and Trinidad, Tom Horn couldn't hit a barn wall at ten paces.

That's how I remember it.

Who Would Kill a Dead Man?

STEF DONEV

Its author a newcomer to the Western field, this story is
probably best introduced by Stef himself:

> As a reporter for the Chicago Times, John T. Finerty became
> America's leading Indian War correspondent, fighting "the
> savages," as he called them, while he rode along with the
> army. He covered five major Indian campaigns, more than
> any other reporter. He related some of his experiences in War-
> Path and Bivouac: Or the Conquest of the Sioux," written in
> 1890. This story takes place after the Apache Uprising of
> 1881, at Cibecue Creek, Arizona, an uprising that Finerty
> covered. Finerty eventually gave up reporting and was elected
> to Congress from Illinois.

This is one of several stories in this collection that tell a
mystery in a Western setting, illustrating the versatility of
the author.

★

"Now one of the things that good, honest, law-abiding and
God-fearing people like yourselves usually want to know
is why there are always thirteen loops on the nooses I use
when I hang people," intoned the tall, cadaverous, bearded

hangman standing on his fresh-built gallows, explaining the intricacies of his craft to the several hundred people looking up at him. "Always thirteen," the low, rumbling voice continued. "Always thirteen.

"It's the same reason there are thirteen steps leading up to this here gallows, the last thirteen steps your Mr. Geoffrey 'Hot Stove' Stover—or any other condemned brigand—will ever climb before he takes that long drop through man's final justice on his way to meet God's. That step, by the way, will be long, but quick. I am very scientific about my trade. His neck will snap. He will go fast. You can count on that, just as you can count the thirteen steps leading to my gallows. Exactly thirteen. No more. No less. And there are thirteen for a good reason. A holy and sacred reason."

The hangman paused. With all the aplomb of a great actor, he waited for his audience to demand that he continue. His audience complied. In less than a minute, every man, woman, and child gathered around the gallows in the middle of the dusty Arizona street was screaming for his answer.

People who had witnessed other hangings were already telling their friends that this would be the best one ever, and Hot Stove hadn't even swung yet. He hadn't even been pulled out of his cell.

"The reason it's thirteen," the hangman continued after a long pause, "is because of our Lord and Savior, Jesus the Christ. And let us bow our heads in his memory." He paused, but any solemnity was destroyed by the sight and sound of a pair of dogs loudly making puppies in the nearby alley.

"It is because Jesus died on Good Friday, and as all good Christians know, it was a Friday the thirteenth. So those thirteen steps and thirteen loops are a hangman's prayers for forgiveness for having to carry out man's harsh law. Harsh but just. The law of the Bible that calls for an eye for an eye. A tooth for a tooth. A life for a life."

John T. Finerty shook his head in quiet admiration. He didn't know if he believed a word of the hangman's spiel, but it would make good copy. This would definitely be the finest hanging he had ever seen, let alone written about. He was already preparing the story he would telegraph back to the *Chicago Times*. In it, the hangman, William Marwood, Jr., would feature as prominently as the condemned Stover.

Everything about Marwood was black—hair, beard, hat, shirt, neckerchief, vest, pants, boots, even the handle of the six-gun in its black leather holster just visible underneath his long black duster. The buttons and buckles on his clothing and gun belt were also black. Even his eyes seemed black, staring out from the dark, deep shadows of his gaunt and angular face.

Finerty planned on having another talk with him. The telegram he had received from his newspaper that morning had confirmed his suspicion. William Marwood was the name of the chief executioner of London, England. *I know hangmen routinely use aliases,* the reporter thought to himself, *but why Marwood? It's either an alias, an amazing coincidence, or the Arizona Territory's William Marwood, Jr., is son and heir to England's own Chief High Executioner. In any event, it just makes the story even better.*

Finerty was glad that he had accepted Amos Colby's invitation to stick around. The town marshal had promised the reporter that he would get a good story out of it, and his old friend was right. It was a good enough story to keep Finerty in the middle of the desert and away from his beloved Chicago for a few extra days.

Thinking about his friend reminded him that he had to pick up the condemned man's last meal, as well as lunch for the marshal and Deputy Pete. Luckily it was only a half a block to the diner. The tall and lanky reporter made the trip quickly, his long legs using few strides to travel the dirt street, a street baked rock hard by the Arizona sun.

"THERE'S THEM WHAT says his last meal should be wormy beans and moldy bread. And after what he did, especially to folks right here in Frying Pan, I almost agree. He left a lot of women crying, and even some men, too. But I'll not let any man meet Peter at the Pearly Gates and have a saint thinking that Adelaide Gertrude McMullen don't know how to feed a body right."

"So you think he might actually be going to heaven?" John Finerty asked the gray-haired, matronly woman.

"When pigs sing! No, you can tell your newspaper readers that as far as Adelaide Gertrude McMullen is concerned, St. Peter will have his good, stout Irish bog walkers on, and he'll boot Geoffrey 'Hot Stove' Stover, an English name if ever I heard one, all the way down to the bottom-most pit of hell itself. He'll burn in that pit in hell for eternity, knowing he'll never again have anything anyway near as good as my peach cobbler."

"Not even in heaven, Adelaide. Even if St. Peter were to let him into heaven itself, he'd still never taste anything as good as your peach cobbler."

"Awww," she cooed. "So it would be a piece for yourself you'll be wanting too, then, John T.," she said with a smile and a wink, adding extra pieces to the wicker picnic basket that the reporter was carrying. "And what part of the old sod do you harken from? I meself high from Skibbereen, in County Cork, down around Fishnet Harbor. Now there are extra pieces of cobbler for the marshal and young Pete, too. Heaven knows he deserves it. But the big one, that's yours."

"From County Galway, Adelaide, but I know Skibbereen well. And I'm looking forward to your pastry as much as I am a chance to be back to the Emerald Isle my-self. But while the cobbler is in my future, home is not."

"So," she replied, giving him a knowing and sympa-thetic look, "the Brits have you on the run?"

"That's the truth of it, the sad but whole truth of it. You speak out for freedom for Ireland while in Ireland, and they put a price on your head."

"What do you expect from the Brits, a race that pro-duces back-shooting cowards and bandits like Stover? Back home he probably would have been an English gen-tleman, an officer in the British Army."

"Assigned to Ireland, no doubt," Finerty said. "I've met many like him."

It was Mrs. McMullen's month to feed whatever pris-oners were locked up in the small town jail in the center of Frying Pan, Arizona. She and Mrs. Woodly, who owned the other diner in the small desert town, alternated months. Normally a deputy would pick up the meals, but with the hanging approaching, and every deputy and part-time deputy busy, Finerty had volunteered to do it.

As Finerty carried the large wicker picnic basket back to the jail, he saw that the crowd had grown. The hanging wouldn't be until noon, still several hours away, and the gallows was already surrounded. It seemed as if everyone in the territory wanted to see "Hot" Stover, leader of the Hot Stove gang, swing for his sins, and hear the hangman describe exactly how he would swing him.

Finerty was confident that his article would get good play in the paper. His editor, Wilbur F. Storey, believed in keeping his readers interested. His motto was that the job of a newspaper was "to print the news and raise hell." Storey did just that. And he loved a good hanging. In fact, the *Chicago Times* had once headlined a hanging story: JERKED TO JESUS. Reporters and editors would regularly sit around and try to dream up a better headline for a hanging story, with no success. The longer Finerty thought about it, the more he thought that the focus of the article should be on the hangman. Then he could suggest that the headline be: JERKING THEM TO JESUS! Storey just might like that. And if anyone ever stood in need of jerking, Finerty thought, it was Stover.

Frying Pan had one main street, five blocks long, going east and west, parallel to the train tracks connecting the small village to the rest of the country. The jail was right in the middle of the street, on the north side. At the moment, much of the jail was in the shadow of the gallows that had been built in front of it, blocking off the entire street. What little horse and wagon traffic there was ran along the back of the stores and buildings lining the main drag. People were gathered on three sides of the gallows, but sawhorses kept a clear space between the front of the jail and the back of the gallows.

It was thirteen paces from the front door of the jail to the back side of the gallows. That was where the steps were, the thirteen "prayers," leading up to the noose.

There were two windows in Stover's cell. One faced the side street that was little more than an alley that ran alongside the jail. The other faced the main drag, giving him the best view of the gallows. There was a guard outside the jail watching those windows, and anyone who came close to them. Whenever Finerty walked past, he looked at the window. Sometimes Stover was staring at the gallows with the fixed look of a cobra facing a mongoose. But not this time.

Marwood wound up his presentation by "hanging" a sand-filled scarecrow as part of his demonstration of the science of execution. A piece of wood served as a surrogate spine in the sand-filled scarecrow, and it snapped loudly when the trap was sprung and the "body" dropped down below the trapdoor of the high gallows, down and into a pit sunk six feet below ground level. Digging that pit in the rock-hard street had been a major undertaking, but

Marwood had convinced the town council that it was necessary.

"The secret to a good, clean hanging," Marwood had told the town council, "is the long drop. A man of your Mr. Stover's weight and height has to drop at least fifteen feet from the end of the rope. Don't dig a pit that's at least five feet deep, my gallows will have to be five feet higher, and that will make it that much harder for the people to see."

Digging the pit and hiring extra guards had been only two of the problems the town council faced once Stover had been arrested, tried, convicted, and sentenced.

Two locals, Adam Clayton and Stan Dumbrowski, had demanded the right to perform the hanging. They'd even got into a fistfight at the council meeting over which one had more of a right to personally hang the outlaw. The town council had finally sent to the territorial governor for an official hangman. Finerty agreed with their decision. The two men had just cause, but the Irish reporter was glad it was being done by a professional. There is nothing more unsettling than an amateurish hanging with the condemned man slowly choking to death at the end of a swinging rope. It tended to upset the audience, especially the women and children.

Choosing the executioner had been easy compared with the final decision—entertainment. After hours of debate at an open meeting, a meeting at which almost everyone had their say, even Mexicans, women, and other people ineligible to vote, the town council had agreed to maintain the dignity of the event, but only by a five-to-four vote.

The owners of the Golden Saddle, Pearl, and Easy Money saloons, and their supporters, had wanted to put a piano on top of the gallows and let the dance hall girls perform. Instead, the town council had ruled that the entertainment would be more subdued and in keeping with the solemnity of the occasion.

Once that decision had been made, the council had

spent another two hours determining just who would perform. Emma Mae Patterson, the Baptist pastor's wife, would play her fiddle, the choirs from both the Baptist and Catholic churches would sing some hymns, the Jorgenson brothers would play their guitars, and Galliano would sing.

Galliano was a popular choice. All of the locals had heard the stable owner sing in the Catholic chorus, at the town Christmas party, at weddings—even at some of the Baptist ones—and at other events, as well as to his horses. Even though only a few dozen people in town understood Italian, everyone appreciated his voice.

The golden moment had come. Now that the hangman had finished his demonstration, it was Galliano's moment to shine. Finerty stopped on his way back to the jail to listen to the Italian stable owner sing. *There is something about singing on a gallows,* he thought, *that makes a sad song even sadder.*

Even Marwood, who'd come all the way from Tucson to supervise the building of the gallows and perform the actual execution, seemed to be enjoying Galliano. Finerty noticed the executioner underneath the gallows, humming to himself as he prepared the actual rope he would use to hang Stover. It was a new rope, and it had been well stretched to make sure that there was no give to it. Marwood silently tipped his hat to the reporter, who returned the compliment.

"Morning, Mr. Finerty," the overnight deputy said when the reporter entered the jail. "Coffee's on."

"Morning, Pete. Where's Amos? I brought you both—"

"In here!" they heard the marshal shout. "Now!"

Finerty dropped the basket on the marshal's desk and joined Pete in running to the door leading to the back section of the jail, where the cells were. Between hearing the shout and reaching the door to the cellblock, Pete had his gun drawn, and Finerty wished he had not left his in his hotel room.

★

"POISON. IT WAS definitely poison," the doctor pronounced. "Probably cyanide."

"Poison?" Colby asked. "Couldn't it have been a heart attack?"

"No," replied Doc Armstrong. "It was cyanide. Look inside his mouth at his gums. Cyanide turns the tissue cherry red."

The men each looked. It sure was red.

"I was at a gold mining camp a few years ago. They use cyanide in gold mining. Silver, too. So I've seen more than a few cases of cyanide poisoning. Cut him open and you'll see his blood's the same color," Armstrong continued. "Then there's the smell."

"Smell?"

"Isn't it supposed to be something like bitter almonds?" Finerty asked. "That's what I've read, at least."

"I've read that, too," Armstrong agreed. "Problem is, I don't know what bitter almonds smell like. But I do know what dirty socks smell like. That's what cyanide smells like to me, and that's what I'm smelling now." He stopped as everyone inhaled deeply through their noses, and then quickly started breathing through their mouths after a few coughs to clear their lungs. "Since all of us, including the deceased, are wearing boots, but he still smells like dirty socks, his gums are cherry red, and he looks like he died while fighting to take a deep breath, I'm calling it cyanide poisoning. That's what goes on the death certificate."

"Well, damn," Colby muttered. "Double damn."

Everyone else, aside from the recently deceased, of course, nodded agreement.

"He was right, you know," Pete said, looking down at Stover's face, locked in a hideous grimace.

"Right? Right how?" the newspaperman asked.

"A couple of days ago, when the two preachers came by, Reverend McGee and Father Hastings. They came by to talk to him. Since no one knows what church he was raised in, if any, they both came by together, to offer him a choice. He told them both to go to hell. Told them he didn't need no praying because we'd never hang him."

"Which is what he told me when I interviewed him yesterday," Finerty said.

"The hanging!" Colby exclaimed. "Pete. Get the judge. Don't let him know why. Don't let anyone know. Just get him here." Before Pete could get to the door, the marshal stopped him. "Then go find Adam Clayton, Stan Dumbrowski, and . . ." Colby paused. "And you better bring in Adelaide McMullen, too. All of them. But don't tell them why."

"NOW JUST WHO on earth would want to go and kill a dead man?" asked the Honorable Leland Talbot, chief and only judge of Frying Pan County. He was in the now-open cell, looking down at the blanket-covered corpse of the dead outlaw. The jail cell and corridor were packed, the crowd including three reluctant guests.

The judge's question seemed to just hang in the air.

Finally, after a long pause, the marshal answered.

"I don't rightly know, Judge. But that's why I had Clayton, Dumbrowski, and Mrs. McMullen brought in. I figure they're a good place to start."

The three looked confused until Amos continued.

"Stover was murdered. The investigation starts right here and right now."

As soon as the three realized that they might be murder suspects, each reacted in a different way. Dumbrowski started swearing in his native Polish. Clayton lunged for Colby. Mrs. McMullen fainted.

Two deputies pulled Clayton back from the marshal. Pete sweated and strained to carry the diner owner to the worn leather couch against the wall, underneath the rifle and gun rack in the office. Dumbrowski just stood there, swearing.

Ignoring the commotion, the judge turned to Finerty, who was writing in his notebook. "You must be that reporter I've been hearing about."

"That I am, Your Honor, John T. Finerty of the *Chicago Times*. At your service."

"And you came all this way just for our hanging, Mr. Finerty?"

"No, Your Honor. I was covering the recent Apache uprising at the San Carlos reservation, up north of you a bit. I looked Amos up when it was done. He told me about the hanging, I decided to stick around. Chicago readers are familiar with the Hot Stove Gang and its crimes, even though the gang did seem to stop riding three years ago."

"Three years and one month to the day of his capture. I'll be honest, Mr. Finerty. When he was spotted at the old Hoffman spread, we sent a posse out. But we didn't really think he'd be stupid enough to hide so close to Frying Pan. After three years, if we'd thought of him at all, we'd assumed he'd taken his loot and gone to San Francisco, or Europe. His gang had stolen thousands over the years, but when we brought him in all he had was three American dollars, two dimes, and a handful of Mexican pesos."

"And he's the only one that was ever caught?" Finerty asked.

"True. Only one we even had a name for. Frying Pan could be filled with his old gang, and we wouldn't know it. The only way we learned Stover's name was that he bragged about it in a bank in Prescott eight, nine years ago. Told the people they had had the privilege of being robbed by the legendary Geoffrey Stover and his gang. He'd spent two years in Yuma Prison before that, so we knew what Geoffrey Stover looked like."

"Well, from my experience, brigands like Stover are

better known for braggadocio, meanness, and viciousness than for intelligence."

"True," the judge agreed. "Very true. But tell me, how do you know Amos?"

"It goes back a few years, five to be exact, the Yellowstone and Big Horn expedition against the Sioux, in seventy-six."

"Ah yes," the judge replied. "Amos was an army scout then."

"With General Crook. I was covering the campaign for my paper."

"Saved my bacon while doing so," Colby interjected. "Some reporters played it safe, stayed behind, far behind. But not John T. He rode with us and fought with us. We called him the fighting pencil pusher. When three of us got separated from the main force, and some of Sitting Bull's braves had us cornered, Finerty came in with a squad of troopers and got us out of there alive."

"A fighting reporter?" the judge asked, somewhat incredulously.

"When necessary, Your Honor. When necessary. When it comes to fighting Indians, neither God nor the U.S. Army has any use for a noncombatant."

"But dealing with hostiles is simple compared to what we have here," Colby said.

"What we have here," bellowed Adam Clayton, "is an outrage!"

"No, Adam. What we have here is a murder. And I'm going to ask Doc Armstrong to tell you about it."

"So you think," Clayton eventually asked when the doctor finished, "that one of us killed him?"

"Afraid so," Colby replied.

"Now just wait one minute here, Amos," Dumbrowski interrupted. "I wanted him dead. I wanted to hang him myself."

"You tried to shoot him," Colby reminded him. "You

were part of the posse that went after him. Remember? We
had the drop on him. He had his hands in the air. He'd
dropped his guns and his rifle. Surrendered. But if Pete
hadn't pushed your gun hand down when you fired, we'd
be hanging you today."

"Yes, Deputy Pete," the Polish-born mining engineer
said, contemptuously, looking at the young lawman. "I
never thank you for that. You, of all people." Then, turning
back to the marshal, he continued. "I know why you bring
me here. And Adam. He want Stover dead as much as me.
Maybe more. But why Mrs. McMullen?"

"Yes, Marshal," the matronly woman asked. "Why am
I here?"

Colby looked a bit uncomfortable.

"Aside from me, and my deputies, of course, only three
people have had any contact with Stover in the last few
days. Stan, you were here last night. Adam, you were here
just before him."

"But I've never even met the man," Mrs. McMullen
wailed.

"Now, I cannot imagine you killing him. Or anyone.
But you have been feeding him, and he did die of poisoning."

Mrs. McMullen lunged at Colby before he could even
finish speaking.

Finerty would later say that while he had never actually
heard the legendary Irish banshee's screech, he figured
Mrs. McMullen's caterwauling probably came close.
While it had taken two deputies to stop Clayton from lunging at Colby, it took all three of them, plus Finerty and the
judge, to pull the Irish woman back.

"I would guess," the winded judge said to no one in particular after Mrs. McMullen had stopped screeching,
scratching, and screaming, and was finally sitting down,
"that before her hair turned gray, it was a dangerous shade
of red."

★

"I WANTED TO see him hang. Watch him die. Hear his neck snap," Clayton said to the group gathered in the front office. "Paid a Mexican kid a silver dollar to hold me a good spot in front of the gallows. He's been there since last night, keeping my place. Why would I poison him and then miss actually being able to watch him die?"

Dumbrowski interrupted before Colby could ask Clayton anything else.

"I have spot right next to him. Another Mexican kid hold it for me," Dumbrowski said, his Polish accent giving his words a harsh sound. "Yes. I do want to shoot him when I was with posse. Yes. I want to hang him. I can prove I not kill him."

"You can?" Colby asked. "How?"

"Your deputy searched me last night. Take my gun and my knife before he let me see Stover. He watch me while I talk to Stover. Stover was alive when I leave him. If I kill him I stay to watch him die. Watch him die like he made me watch my boy die. Now I am cheated of his death. I should have shot him when I had chance."

"Pete," the marshal asked, "what exactly happened last night?"

"It was the same procedure for each," the nervous deputy replied. "Mr. Clayton came by first, around six. Handed over his sidearm. He was unarmed. Honest to God."

"And then?"

"I went in with him. I didn't unlock the cell. Mr. Clayton just stood there and stared at Stover. First Stover ignored him. Then asked what he was doing there."

"I told him," Clayton said. "I wanted to see if he could face death as easily as he handed it out. And the son of a bitch laughed at me. Laughed. Told me he wouldn't hang. Told me he'd live long enough to piss on my grave, like he pissed on Samantha's. Told me Samantha had liked it. That it wasn't rape. That she'd asked him to do it again."

Clayton was a big man who looked more like a blacksmith than the town's apothecary. But he didn't look big as he recounted his last meeting with Stover. The pain of the memories—his talk with Stover, Stover's laugh, of the rape and murder of his wife—drained all life from him.

"Come here now, Adam," Mrs. McMullen said with gentle warmth. "Let me get you a cup of coffee." She led him over to the couch she had so recently vacated and helped him get seated, and then poured him a cup of coffee from the pot on the jailhouse wood stove. Neither Colby nor the judge bothered asking Adam Clayton any more questions. It would have been a waste of time. Only his body was present.

Instead, Colby turned to his deputy.

"I don't suppose Adam handed Stover anything."

"No, sir. Honest to God."

"What about Stan?"

"Him neither. And before you ask, I did the same with him. He didn't go in until I was sure he was unarmed. And I didn't open the cell."

"And what did you tell Stover, Stan?" Colby asked.

"Tell him? I don't say words. He come over and start talking about getting out of jail and coming after me. He threaten me. Tell me I'll be as dead as my son."

"What did you do?" Colby asked. "What did you say to him?"

"I say nothing. I spit in his face. Right in his face. Then I leave."

"Pete?" Colby asked.

"Just that, Marshal. He spat right in Stover's face. Honest to God. I thought Stover was going to have a heart attack. He was that mad. He started screaming at Mr. Dumbrowski, saying he was going to kill him, going to cut his guts open and watch him die. But Mr. Dumbrowski just walked out of there. He ignored him. Honest to God."

"ARE YOU ASHAMED of yourself, Amos? Or haven't you caused enough pain yet?"

"I'm just doing my job, Adelaide. Just doing my job."

They were back in the jail's front office, and everyone was working real hard at avoiding eye contact with everyone else, except for Mrs. McMullen and Colby. She was glaring and he was taking it.

"Then why aren't you asking me if I gave him the poison? I fed him."

Realizing that both an explanation and an apology were in order, and being unused to either, the middle-aged marshal broke off eye contact and scratched his head.

"Now hold on a minute there, Adelaide," he said, finally. "I jumped the gun having you brought in. Soon as I saw you, I knew it was a mistake. I doubt if a meal ever gets to a prisoner without one of us stealing a taste, and I know you—"

"Me?" she said, cutting him off. "I'm not talking about what you're doing to me. But we will have that conversation one of these days, Amos Malachi Colby. You can count on that. No! I am talking about you accusing either Stan or Adam."

"I am not accusing. I am questioning."

"And a fat lot of good it did you. Pete himself told you that neither one of them handed Stover anything. So how did Stover get the poison?"

"In this!" Finerty announced as he and Pete came into the front office from the cell area, holding up an empty whiskey bottle. "I found it tucked in his blanket at the foot of his bunk," Finerty explained, handing it to Armstrong.

"That's just where it was," Pete said.

"Whew!" Armstrong exclaimed after taking a whiff of

the empty bottle. "This is it," he said, handing the bottle to Colby. "The smell of the whiskey would have overpowered the smell of the cyanide. But with the bottle empty you can tell that there was something extra in it. This is your murder weapon."

Colby was just opening his mouth when Pete started talking.

"Honest to God, Marshal. Ain't no one handed him nothing anytime I was in there with him. Honest to God. And no one went in to see him without me or one of the other boys being there. We followed the rule book, just like you taught us. And you put deputies outside, by the windows, to make sure no one got at him."

"HE'S AS MUCH a problem dead as he was alive," Colby told Finerty as the two sipped on their coffees and looked down on Stover's covered body lying on his bunk. The rest of the group was in the front office. "He was a problem even before I got here."

"So Clayton and Dumbrowski aren't the only two in town with a score to settle."

"Not by a long shot. In fact, during the trial . . ." Colby stopped and looked up at the cell's ceiling, thinking.

"Pete!" he shouted after his moment of silence. "Pete! Get in here!"

The deputy ran in to find Colby looking at him intently.

"Why didn't you ever mention that Stover had killed kin of yours?"

"Why?" the stunned deputy asked. "I thought you knew. Everyone else does."

"I didn't know, until just now," Colby admitted. "The way Stan talked to you made me wonder. Then John T. made me think even more. Until I remembered that during the trial someone asked if you'd be testifying and you said no, your brother could tell the story without your help. I was still new in the job, and up to my neck in paperwork, so I never got around to asking just who of yours he had killed. Who was it?"

"My pa," Pete replied calmly. "My brother testified because he was there when it happened. I wasn't."

"Is that why you volunteered to pull the duty inside the jail?"

"Right. Thaddeus and Hal both have seniority, but they knew this was important to me, so they let me have it."

"And you just watched him?" Colby asked. "That's all you did? Watch?"

By this time everyone in the jail had moved into the back room.

"That's right, Marshal. I watched him. I would have paid for the privilege. I was looking forward to walking him to the gallows. Helping the hangman adjust the noose. Adam and Clayton had to pay to have their places held for them in front of the gallows. I was going to be up top of the gallows myself. I was going to climb all thirteen steps with him to his death. Having him die like this . . . It just ain't fair! Honest to God! It just ain't fair!"

Colby looked at everyone crowded into the cell area of the jail.

"Blast it!" he shouted. "Somebody killed him. And I have to find out who."

"Why bother?" Mrs. McMullen asked. "He was sentenced to die and he's dead."

"But I sentenced him to hang," the judge said. "Not to death by poison."

"The hangman!" Colby said. "Somebody better go and get him and . . ."

And the hangman walked in.

It's as if Death himself has entered the room, Finerty thought to himself. *This man truly is an executioner.* While no one said anything aloud, it was obvious that the tall, black-draped man had a similar effect on everyone else

there, including Colby. Finerty had spoken to the hangman
once, in the Silver Slipper Saloon, and the man had seemed
somewhat dour, but approachable. When he'd seen him
lecturing on the gallows, the executioner had appeared im-
posing, much like a hellfire-and-brimstone preacher
threatening sinners with damnation. Now, in prison, at the
hanging hour, draped in and radiating death, he was an in-
timidating force.

"It is time," the hangman intoned. "In fact, it is past
time. Both the crowd and justice are waiting."

"I'm afraid they will both have to wait a little while
longer," Colby said after taking a long breath to regain his
composure. "We have a problem."

Finerty watched the hangman as Colby explained what
had happened. The hangman didn't seem disappointed or
upset, or even surprised by the news. He just stood there,
taking it all in.

"Since my work is done, been done for me, I should say,
you have no further need of me," the hangman said. "So I
shall take my leave of you and of Frying Pan." Then, after
a pause, he added: "By the way, I do think someone is
going to have to address the crowd. I do not think they will
be happy to hear the news."

The hangman was just starting to turn to leave when
Colby stopped him.

"I think you better stick around for a while, Mr. Marwood," Colby said. When the hangman opened his mouth
to protest, the marshal continued. "The town council will
want to talk to you. After all, you were paid to perform a
hanging."

Finerty watched as the hangman started to say something, thought better of it, and decided to look around for
a seat. Once seated he seemed ready to speak, but changed
his mind. Finally he said, "I was paid to come to Frying
Pan, build a gallows, and conduct a hanging. I have completed my part of the contract. It's not my fault he died

early." He then stood up. "This is foolishness. The town council can write me about their concerns, care of the territorial governor's office."

"Sit!" Colby ordered. "Things around here are crazy enough. You will wait here until the town council is finished."

"Marshal!" the hangman countered, still standing. "You are talking to an officer of the court, the chief executioner of the Arizona Territory."

"And you are talking to me, and this is my town. I've got a hanging to cancel, a murder to solve, and a town council to keep happy. And you will help me take care of that last item by sitting out here peacefully and quietly, or you'll sit back in one of the cells. But you will stay here until I say you can go. Now sit!"

The hangman sat.

Finerty hoped the hangman realized just how much tension there was in the room. Everyone, even Mrs. Mc-Mullen, was looking for a fight, for an excuse to blow up. If the hangman didn't shut up, he'd be providing it for them.

FINERTY HAD SEEN numerous hangings being performed. Now he watched a hanging being canceled. Canceling a hanging, he and everyone else in town discovered, takes longer than actually holding one. Eventually the last spectators were cajoled—in some cases, threatened with arrest—to get them to leave. Finally, the town was back to normal; except, of course, for the large and still-unused gallows in the middle of the main street.

Since he was directing the un-hanging of "Hot Stove" Stover, which was how it would enter local legend, Colby was fairly busy. But Finerty did have a chance to have a private chat with his old friend before they all returned to the jail.

★

"WHY MARWOOD?" FINERTY asked. "Why William Marwood, Jr?"

"He's . . ." The hangman stared into his cup of coffee before starting again. "He's my hero."

"Your hero?" Colby asked.

They were all in the jail's office. It was crowded. The judge was there, Dr. Armstrong, Pete, Mrs. McMullen, Clayton and Dumbrowski, and several other deputies. They were waiting for the town council to show up so they could settle the financial arrangements about the cancelled hanging, and then continue the murder investigation.

"I've seen my share of bad hangings," the hangman said. "A bad hanging is a crime. A hanging should be an execution; a quick, clean death, without the torture of spinning at the end of a rope waiting for the last breath to be squeezed out of you. So when I took up my craft, I insisted on doing it proper. I have been corresponding with Mr. Marwood in England for several years now, learning from him. He is a true genius, a master, and he has given me his kind permission to use his name in my work."

"What is your real name?" Finerty asked. "What were you before . . ."

"That is no concern of yours or your readers," the hangman interrupted, tartly. "The territorial governor knows me. No one else needs to."

"I'm sure he knows the name you gave him, and maybe it is your real one," Finerty replied. "But I doubt that he knows what you did before you became a hangman. I doubt, for example, that he knows," Finerty stood up and spoke slowly and clearly, "you rode with the Hot Stove Gang. You murdered Stover. You . . ."

Finerty stopped talking and dropped to the floor because guns had taken over the conversation. The hangman was fast. As soon as he went for his gun, both Colby and Pete shouted "Freeze!" But the hangman ignored them.

Since Colby and Pete knew what was coming, they were ready. Pete had his pistol drawn, and was holding it by his side, out of sight. Colby's hand was on the handle of his .45. Even so, when the hangman jumped up he almost managed to get a shot off before Pete and the town marshal each put a bullet into him. Although late to the draw, Colby and Dumbrowski were also shooting before the hangman's body hit the ground.

"THE REAL MIRACLE is that no one else was hit," Doc Armstrong said that evening as he joined Colby for his regular after-dinner nightcap at the jail. Tonight the jail was crowded. Colby, Dumbrowski, Mrs. McMullen, and the judge were all there, along with Finerty, Pete, and several other deputies.

"Well, we figured our angles and knew we could get the drop on him. But he sure was fast," Colby said, "a lot faster than I expected."

"Or me," Pete said. "If I hadn't already had my gun out, he probably would have gotten the drop on us. Honest to God! That man was fast!"

"Speaking of that man," Armstrong said. "Do we know his real name?"

"We know the name he gave the governor. The telegram from Tucson came through about fifteen minutes ago. It's William Calcraft," Colby said. "Now it's up to the governor's office to track down the truth."

"And now, the big question," Colby continued. "John T.?"

"It was a lot of little things," Finerty replied, taking another sip of the large glass of whiskey the marshal had poured him.

"I found it odd that he came into the jail to get Stover. In every hanging I've ever seen, or read about, the hangman always waits on the scaffold for the condemned to be brought to him. It's tradition, and Calcraft kept the traditions. Remember his lecture on the significance of the number thirteen?

"Then there's the simple fact that he was the only one who needed him dead before the hanging, and the only one who could have given him the bottle of whiskey."

"But he couldn't," Pete said. "I was there when he met with Stover, and nothing changed hands. Nothing. He measured him, asked him his weight, and he left. Aside from Stover answering a few questions, they didn't talk."

"That was then," Finerty said. "But I'm sure they had a number of conversations through the jail window."

"But they were guarded," Colby said.

"I'm sure they were, and the only people who could get near the windows were the guards and the hangman. Now I'll wager that if you talk to the guards they'll admit to taking an occasional break to go to the privy, and you'll find that Calcraft was more than willing to cover for them."

Several of the deputies looked a bit sheepish.

"Well, hell," Colby said after an uncomfortable silence. "If you can't trust the hangman to watch a condemned man while you take care of nature's business, who can you trust? I'm sure I would've done the same thing if I'd pulled window-watching duty."

Finerty continued, ignoring the signs of relief from the deputies. "This is all an assumption, seeing as he's dead. We needed him to draw, to show that he was guilty. The plan was to stop him, and then question him later, but as we all know . . .

"Anyhow, here's the way I figure it. Marwood, or Calcraft, or whoever he was, became a hangman, a fairly natural job for a killer. But when he was told he had to hang Stover he had a problem. He knew that Stover would identify him.

"I figure he talked to Stover through the window while he was building the gallows, and told him that he had arranged a jail break. All Stover had to do was sit there and wait. He wouldn't hang, he'd be set free."

"Which explains why he got so sure, all of a sudden, that we'd never hang him," Pete said. "He was waiting for the jail break."

"Which was never going to happen," Finerty continued. "Calcraft poisoned the whiskey and slipped it to him through the bars in the window sometime last night so Stover could start celebrating breaking out of jail a bit early."

"When, exactly, did you know?" the judge asked.

"I didn't know anything for certain until he drew his gun once I accused him. But I first started to think there was something odd when he showed up to collect the prisoner himself. I'm sure he was just too nervous to wait any longer to find out if Stover was dead. He had to come in and find out.

"After that, it was just a matter of looking at everything else; at all the elements in a confusing story, arranging and rearranging them until they all finally made sense."

Later that night, when only Colby, Finerty, and Armstrong were left in the jail office, Armstrong asked if he planned to write the story about how he had solved the murder. Finerty just laughed, poured himself another drink, and motioned for Colby to answer for him.

"No," the marshal said, "I figure we'll get the credit, all of us. John T. doesn't believe that a reporter has any business getting too involved in his stories. Of course, he keeps doing just that, but to hide it he always gives the credit to someone else."

"It's very simple," Finerty explained. "Reporters are boring people. All we do is watch what goes on around us. No one really wants to read about us. That's why we have to find interesting people to write about.

"Wilbur Storey, lord and master of the *Chicago Times,* just loves stories about hangings, and now neither Stover nor Calcraft will hang. And knowing my editor, who is a bit of a wild man even by Chicago's journalistic standards, and not always completely rational, he'd probably decide that somehow it was all my fault, and he'd fire me."

Likker Money

JERRY GUIN

Also a mystery in a Western setting, this story features a rather famous White Hat of the West, Bat Masterson. A good choice for a submission, as I am a great fan of Bat's— and now of Jerry's, as well.

★

In the fall of 1877, former buffalo hunter, scout, and gunfighter Bat Masterson, age twenty-four, was appointed sheriff of Ford County, Kansas. His older brother Ed, age twenty-five, was already marshal of the busy railhead cattle town of Dodge City. The brothers were seated around a lone desk, having their morning coffee, when the front door to the sheriff's office was jerked open.

"Sheriff! Sheriff! Come quick, T.C. Shaw's been stabbed dead!" Aaron Grubbs, the store clerk, stood wide-eyed and breathless in the doorway of the sheriff's office.

Bat and Ed Masterson both grated their chairs then stood at Aaron's declaration.

"Where?" Bat Masterson asked.

"In the alley, next to the City Hotel," Aaron sputtered, then pointed out the door in the direction of the City Hotel, across the street and a hundred yards away on Front Street.

The lawmen grabbed their hats and headed for the door.

Aaron turned and the threesome began quick-stepping toward the alley between the hotel and the general store where Aaron spent his days working the counter.

"How'd you find him?" Sheriff Masterson asked in midstride.

"I was emptying the trash buckets," Aaron offered. "I seen him laying there stabbed in the back!" he exclaimed.

"Did you see anyone?" Sheriff Masterson implored.

"No. No one," Aaron stammered as they reached the alley entrance from the street.

"There, over there!" Aaron pointed into the alley.

Scarcely twenty feet from where they stood lay the body of T.C. Shaw. He lay facedown, arms stretched over his head. The pockets to his pants and jacket were turned inside out. T.C. Shaw was the apparent victim of a robbery.

The white handle of a large knife was sticking from his back.

T.C. Shaw was a wealthy and respected man. One of Dodge City's pioneers. It was mainly due to his influence and money that the railroad chose to run their tracks through this section of the country, making Dodge City a prosperous town. T.C. had enemies for sure, as he owned and ranched most of the good land to the west of Dodge City where his sprawling Top Side Ranch was located. The Top Side's notable brand of a *T* imposed over an *S* made it almost impossible for thieves to rebrand any of the herd with a running iron.

Smaller neighboring ranches, if not envious of T.C. and his holdings, were dependent on him for water for their meager spreads, as the only stream flowed from Top Side property and could easily be diverted.

Before Bat Masterson was appointed as sheriff of Ford County, it was the Top Side Ranch with T.C. Shaw and his many riders that kept the law in the area even though Larry Degen was the sheriff. Marshal Ed Masterson had told his brother Bat, just after he took the sheriff's job, that Larry Degen acted only on T.C.'s orders.

T.C. Shaw could have been a politician but declined mayorship of Dodge City, allowing James "Dog" Kelly the honor instead. T.C. opted to spend his time ranching and running other business enterprises. In Dodge City he owned various businesses—a livery, the bank, a freight company, and the general store that Aaron clerked at.

Bat Masterson checked the time on his silver open-faced Elgin then knelt beside the still body and felt for a pulse on the side of the man's neck. Finding none, he stood, studying the body and obvious drag marks that the toes of T.C.'s boots had made in the soft dirt of the alley from the street to where he lay next to the hotel wall. The body was hidden from view by some wooden crates. The crates had been placed over the drag marks. Someone took a chance to go to extra lengths to hide the body.

"Sheriff!" Aaron called out.

"Look!" He pointed down the alley. A few feet away, a wooden crate rocked back and forth, then stopped as first a hand, then a head, emerged from the back side of the crate.

A slight, grubby figure stood, steadying himself while holding to the side of the crate.

It was Hector Jones, the saloon swamper and well-known town drunk. It was obvious that Hector had spent the night behind the crate. He still clutched an empty whiskey bottle to his breast with his left hand while holding on to the crate with his right.

"What are you doing here, Hector?" Bat Masterson asked as he and Ed, followed by Aaron Grubbs, approached.

Hector looked through red-rimmed, bleary eyes, teetered a little, steadied himself, then answered, "I don't know, Sheriff. I guess I musta fell asleep here."

Before anyone could say anything else, Aaron quickly

stepped forward and reached into Hector's tattered suit jacket pocket and pulled out a wad of bills, then declared, "Arrest him, Sheriff. He done killed T.C. Shaw."

Aaron held the money out, shaking it, as if the sheriff and marshal could not see it.

Marshal Ed Masterson grabbed hold of Hector's bottle hand, causing him to drop the bottle. He produced a set of handcuffs and began putting them on the passive Hector's wrists. By this time some townsmen, hearing the commotion, began gathering on the street at the entrance to the alley.

Bat Masterson spoke up, "How about it, Hector? Did you kill T.C. Shaw?" He pointed to the body a few feet away.

Hector looked, his eyes widening when they focused on the still form. Hector's lips moved, but nothing came out. Then he expelled, almost in a sob, "I didn't kill nobody, Sheriff!"

"He's lying. He killed T.C." Aaron fumed. "Look at this money!" he exclaimed while holding the money aloft for the growing crowd to see.

"Everybody knows Hector ain't even got likker money most of the time. He drinks it up before he even earns it. Begs it off Ernie, the saloon keeper, long before closing time!" Aaron explained.

"That's right," a man from the crowd called out.

"Let's string him up!" Aaron yelled at the crowd, to a chorus of agreement as the townsmen began to surge forward.

Sheriff Bat Masterson stepped in front of Hector and Ed Masterson. He drew his silver-plated, white-handled six-gun with his right hand while holding his left out as a sign for the moving crowd to stop. When they kept coming, Bat Masterson pointed his six-gun straight up and fired one round. The crowd stopped immediately.

"Hold it right there!" Bat Masterson barked out. "This

man is in my custody. There will be no hanging unless Judge Parker so decrees!" Bat Masterson stood stiff legged and pointed the gun again at the menacing crowd. He motioned to Bill Campbell, the blacksmith. "Bill, you and some others take T.C. over to the undertaker. Aaron, give that money to Ed. I want somebody to ride out to the Top Side and fetch that foreman, Miles Jenkins. I need to talk to him."

"I'll go," Lester Holmes, a neighboring ranch hand, offered as he stepped forward.

Bat Masterson nodded then motioned his brother Ed and Hector forward while holding the six-gun erect. They slipped through the disbursing crowd and headed for jail. Aaron caught up to the three and said, "I know he did it, Sheriff."

Before he could say any more, Bat Masterson cut him off. "Aaron, I don't want to hear any more out of you." He stopped and forced Aaron to stop and face him. "Unless you seen Hector do it?" Bat Masterson gave Aaron a stern look. "Well, did you?" he asked.

"No, no, I didn't," Aaron murmured while avoiding Bat Masterson's piercing gaze.

"Then make use of yourself," Bat commanded, "and go fetch Ernie from the saloon." With that, Bat Masterson holstered his six-gun and continued to escort Hector and the marshal to the jail, slamming the door behind him after the three had entered.

By midday things had come into focus for Sheriff Masterson a little better. Or rather, the process of elimination had come into play. Ernie Banks, the saloon keeper, confirmed that Hector, as usual, had panhandled drinks throughout last night's business hours, but was sober enough to do the cleaning of the saloon.

Hector had not stolen any money, or a bottle either, as far as Ernie knew, for Ernie always put the day's take in a very good safe and took a daily inventory of stocks.

T.C. Shaw had been in the Lady Gay Saloon a good part of the night, playing poker and drinking. He had bought a bottle to take with him when he left at closing time.

T.C. had won a considerable sum, and was the last to leave the saloon. The losers had left promptly after the game was over. Ernie named all the players, which included two Top Side cowboys.

There had been one cowboy, from the neighboring Diamond B Ranch, who had left the game in a huff, apparently after losing his pay. No harsh words had been said. No one in his right mind, at least no one from Dodge City, would have accused T.C. Shaw of cheating. He was known for his hard work and honesty.

Ernie produced a bulging, sealed envelope with the initials *TCS* on the front. "That was his winnings last night, Sheriff. T.C. didn't want to pack it around. Said he'd pick it up in the morning. I locked it in the safe, so the killer did not get much," Ernie concluded.

"Just about the amount that was in Hector's pocket," Ed Masterson stated under the watchful glare of Bat Masterson.

Miles Jenkins, the Top Side Ranch foreman, knew T.C. Shaw better than anyone. He had been with him for over twenty years. When he arrived in town, he went directly to the sheriff's office.

"T.C. Shaw wasn't afraid of any man, Sheriff, but he wasn't a fool either," Miles Jenkins began. "He was always cautious about not flaunting what he had. Sounds just like T.C. to lock the winnings into the safe and to go to his favorite room in the hotel for a few drinks before bedding down. He spent a lot of nights at the hotel if he had business in town the next day, which he had today," Miles advised.

"Somebody that didn't know him well killed him. That's if it was for money, 'cause T.C. never carried much.

He said it was inviting trouble," Miles explained, then stood.

"They say that old drunk, Hector, stabbed him to death, Sheriff. That right?"

"I don't know yet, Miles. It may take a jury to figure that out," Bat Masterson replied.

"You owe that badge you're wearing to T.C. Shaw," Miles Jenkins said. "Before you was made sheriff, in place of Larry Degen, we at the Top Side took care of things like this. They ain't going to take this easy out at the ranch," he concluded, then turned and stomped out the door. Perhaps Miles Jenkins did not press further for he knew of Bat Masterson's reputation as a man of nerve and coolness despite his youth and overall appearance. He usually wore a tailor-made black suit and a bowler hat with a high curled brim. A crack shot with a handgun, Bat Masterson spent hours daily target practicing, "sweetening his gun," as Masterson put it.

Bat Masterson knew that Miles Jenkins would not let this go easily and that he and others from the Top Side would be back, possibly to cause a ruckus. Bat Masterson figured he would deal with that when it happened. He spent some time grilling Hector, trying to get him to recall, as best he could, all about last evening. He learned that Hector had spent the evening bumming drinks until it was time to go to work at midnight, when he swept and mopped the floor, cleaned the spittoons, and took care of various other routine chores he performed nightly after closing time. His pay was not much, and he usually did squeeze enough drinks out of Ernie each night to more than wipe out what he had coming.

Ernie was a kind man, however, and felt sorry for Hector, allowing him to sleep in the storeroom on bad weather nights and then always leaving one drink in a glass for Hector as a nightcap. Hector was dependable enough that if he left the building, he would lock the door, for he preferred sleeping in a stall at the livery to the damp store-room of the saloon.

Hector could not explain the money found in his pock-ets, but he remembered finding the full bottle of whiskey lying in the alley entrance between the general store and the hotel. He went into the alley because he was afraid that whoever had lost the bottle would come a-looking for it. He hid behind the crate and opened it. That was all he could remember.

IT WAS NEAR dark when a large group of riders rode slowly into town, pulling their mounts to a stop in front of the jail.

Bat Masterson heard them, knowing that it was the Top Side riders.

"Bat, you might as well bring that old sot out here," Miles Jenkins's voice reverberated.

Bat Masterson opened the jailhouse door and walked out unarmed. He stood on the walkway and faced Miles Jenkins and the group. "You could take that old Hector out and hang him, Miles. That's the way it was done ten or twenty years ago. I'd even guess that T.C. Shaw would be leading you if he wasn't the victim in this case. But things have changed. I was appointed the sheriff. That brought an end to the need for vigilante justice. Now there's Judge Parker in Fort Smith," Bat Masterson advised.

"Enough talk, Masterson, we want him," Miles stated. He motioned and a dozen cowboys dismounted and began walking forward while a dozen more looked on.

Bat Masterson held up his hand as a signal to halt. "You'll be hanging the wrong man," he stated.

"How's that?" Miles demanded.

Bat Masterson folded his arms then began talking. "Hector isn't the one. He had no motive, and besides, he isn't even strong enough to have lifted T.C. and dragged a man of his size down the alley. Hector found the bottle after T.C. had been killed. He slipped down the alley right past the body, but didn't see anything. Then he sat and drank the whiskey.

"The killer had not found what he was after on T.C.'s body at the time of the stabbing, so he returned near daylight to search further. That's when he moved the crates to hide what he was up to and in so doing discovered Hector passed out nearby. It was too perfect an opportunity to pass up, so he planted the money on Hector and let things unfold, pointing the finger at Hector."

"So who is the killer?" a solemn cowboy from the group asked. Bat Masterson looked at the group, then the ground, then to Miles Jenkins again and said, "The man you're after is still free. A man with a grudge, perhaps, fiery enough to make him kill. Or a man that figured T.C. had a lot of cash on him, cash that he and others had just lost to T.C. in the poker game."

Bat Masterson reached into his back pocket and produced a bulging envelope. He said, "T.C. left this with Ernie to put into the safe. There's money in there. There's also an I.O.U. made out to T.C. by the killer."

"What's the name on that paper?" Miles demanded.

"Why, it's the man that made sure Hector was found this morning along with a small wad of money. The name is Aaron Grubbs," Bat Masterson said matter-of-factly.

"Where is he?" Miles asked softly, seeing that Masterson was so confident.

"Right now he's about fifty miles from here, on a train headed east," Bat Masterson replied. "He sneaked onto the noon train to Wichita hoping he'd made sure Hector was safely tucked away. I wasn't really on to him until after Ernie had named him as one of the players, but when we opened the envelope and found the I.O.U., I sent for him. He couldn't be found, but we learned he bought a ticket to Wichita at the last moment.

"He'll be arrested as soon as the train arrives in Wichita. I wired the marshal there. Aaron will face Judge Parker at Fort Smith and will be under the protection of the army provost stationed there," Bat Masterson concluded, then turned and entered the jailhouse.

Miles Jenkins and the riders turned their horses toward the Top Side Ranch.

On the Peck

R. C. HOUSE

Dick House is one of my oldest friends in the Western field. I spent all of the 1980s attending WWA conventions, and always a centerpiece of those gatherings was Dick's recitation of "The Face upon the Floor" ending "campfire" parties in my room. But more than that, Dick has been a centerpiece of WWA itself for many years, even serving at one time as president. His Western novels, including *Ryerson's Manhunt, Stouthearted Men,* and *The Sudden Gun,* among others, have always had a ring of truth, which made him a natural for this collection. Dick chose as his White Hat Liver Eatin' Johnston, and his partner X. Beidler. In his letter to me Dick said this is a story of "a best-laid plan that goes slightly awry."

The only thing better than reading this story would be hearing Dick recite it.

★

Liver Eatin' Johnston and his old friend X. Beidler were mad, fightin' mad. That dried-up miserable wretch of a Ned Storch was headed for his stronghold just south of the line in Square Knot, Wyoming . . . with their money. All they had in this world.

Ned Storch was a bony goat of a man who wouldn't

make a square meal for a coyote. Still, he was some mean
son of a bitch. He kept himself busy knocking over
coaches or holding up solitary travelers for whatever
goods they had worth carting off. Mostly money and gold
dust; often watches and jewelry and other such valuables.
To cross him only got you a ride back to town in a hearse
or over a saddle. Just one word to describe Ned Storch:
ugly; in looks and in disposition.

The two sat stewing about it in Johnston's cramped constable's quarters in Red Lodge, Montana.

"Back from the first damned trip in my freightin' business," X. said, "and that little pimple on the pecker of
progress has to show up and clean me out."

Johnston, a tall, erect, solid man, scowled. "Four hundred dollars! Two hundred of that mine." He wore a full,
gray beard.

X. turned sadly philosophical. As he piled on the years,
X., once lean, added girth. "Yeah, John. I was fixin' to pay
you back the minute I got to town. The team and freight
wagon your money bought for me is out yonder." He
shrugged. "They're rightly yours now, I suppose, seein's I
can't settle my scores." X.'s mouth drew down in an angry
pout. "In my book, a promise made is a debt unpaid. I
won't go back on my word."

"Here, now," Johnston chided, "you'll get back on your
feet in due time, X. I hereby grant you an extension on that
loan. With no increase in interest, which was zero to start.
I insist. We've been friends too long. Well before you and
your vigilantes dangled that traitorous sheriff Henry Plummer on the scaffold in Virginia City, what, twenty years
ago?"

X. brightened. "I'm obliged with respect to the loan.
And for your generosity. Yeah. Those were grand days,
huh? While you was beatin' the brush for the Crows' best
braves and eatin' their livers raw." He slyly watched Johnston for a reaction.

His companion bristled, his scowl deepening. "You and I both know that's nothin' but night-fire and bar-talk bull-shit!"

"So? It earned you a fame nobody else'd have. I seen men go pale at just the mention of your name."

Johnston chuckled. "Yeah, and that fact has saved my hide more'n a little bit. Lawkeepin's best when you can intimidate. Ain't too many come along wantin' to fuss with the Liver Eater." He paused. "So, X., we still got one out."

"How's that?"

"Go after the runt. But it's risky. Risky as hell."

"So what? But damn right. Let's go. I catch hold of that monkey, John, I'll wring his neck like a chicken."

Johnston chuckled again. "Or like a monkey?"

"Huh?"

"Aw, nothin'. Just that we both know Square Knot's chock full of Ned Storches goin' around under other names. Each one orn'rier'n the one before him. You figure to head in there, X., you by God better wear your cast-iron union suit."

"Most of 'em, too, half our age. We're gettin' to be old jaspers, John. Only two of us. That'll be some pack to tie into."

"You afraid? Hell, figure it this way. Nobody on earth yet has braced the Liver Eater and the invincible Vigilante Enforcer ridin' in together. That's like having a troop of Custer's Seventh Cavalry comin' along behind us."

"Some consolation that is! You know how they wound up."

"Okay, pantywaist. So how about Sittin' Bull's Sioux beefed up by a bunch of Comanches?"

"You commence to make sense."

"Like you said about me, I've heard of owlhoots seein' X. Beidler traipsin' along with a coil of rope, and them hightailin' it the other way tippy-toed, eyes big as bowls, disappearin' down an alley. Them Virginia City vigilante

hangin' stories strike fear; and you were right-smart
smack-dab in the middle of it all. You got your name because the writer-guys down at the paper figured your victims were noose-worthy. We got the edge on the Square
Knot gang in spades, pard."

"Reputation is one thing, John, but facing down a
crowd like that, we got three-, maybe four-to-one odds
against us."

"So it depends on a combination of our scare tactics,
heavy weapons and careful strategies. And timing. Think
about that."

"Heavy weapons?"

"In that situation, us having to flat confront a whole
town of hardcases, I got two bobbed double scatterguns in
that rack yonder. They got to be our major ordnance. Win-
chesters and plowhandle Colts ain't but popguns for what
we're goin' up against. But that's how they'll be heeled.
Pilgrims, greenhorns, morning-after drunks and amateurs,
all playin' tough guy. We still got to come in with some
heads-up heavy artillery. 'Cause there's gonna be a right
nasty batch of opposition. Sawed-off shotguns'll be the
only real Old Equalizers at the frolic."

"You sure make it all sound so attractive."

"You thinkin' of duckin' out?"

"Not on your old tintype. I want my money back. I owe
you. Bein' stiffed for a hard-earned four hundred dollars'd
put any man on the peck."

Johnston's mind was elsewhere. "When they come at
you, they'll be bunched up. If it gets down to gunplay, one
charge from one barrel'll right now chew one man in half
and put a couple of those close on either side of him down
in the dirt with hellacious tummy aches. And you still got
another barrel primed and ready for the next relay."

"That right now ought to take the starch out of the rest
of 'em." X. shivered with excitement.

"Not the starch of the Ned Storch cronies of Square

Knot, it won't. To them, men are expendable. That's why we're going to have to have us some tricks."

"Tricks? What tricks?"

"What they taught us in the war. Use your knowledge of the terrain. Always worked before. Catch 'em off balance. Use their disadvantage to your advantage. The way to win."

"So what do you know about Square Knot? And terrain."

"Hell, son, I been there. Figured it was time to scout ahead. Year or so ago. Just to keep myself wise. Be smarter'n my competition. I seen the town layout. So I've got a few ideas."

"How in hell did the Red Lodge constable get in there . . . or, for that matter, get out?"

"Well, sir, first whack, I got me a dignified haircut; got this wild mop all slicked down. Shaved off my beard, and you'll never believe this. I put on a white shirt and tie and a suit of clothes."

"You? In a suit of clothes?" X. was dumbfounded. "I figured they'd have to hog-tie you first. That ain't your way."

Johnston chuckled in recollection. "I went down there posing as a whiskey drummer. Hell, those dumb bastards didn't know me from Adam's off ox. There was a sight of them ruffians had seen me before, I'm sure."

"Glory be!"

"Went in there, b'God, chummy as hell. Spent the whole day. Drank with 'em. Singled 'em out. Coaxed 'em to do the braggin'. Got to know their strengths. Their weaknesses. Their troubles. And their fiendish delights. How the land lay. Hell, wun't a one of 'em including the boss I couldn't't've drunk under the table." Johnston's voice turned gruff and he squinted in wisdom. "That wun't why I went there, X. I got that town and its inhabitants bracketed in my sights."

"What's so special about it?"

"Nothin'! Not a damned thing. To a legendary cannibal and a fearsome vigilante hangman, it's a pushover. 'Cept it ain't square and it ain't in a knot. Main stem runs straight as a string, north to south. Long rows of buildings, both sides of the street, some with common walls, but a lot of alleyways between 'em to run a wagon or a buckboard through to load or unload out back. A few vacant lots. Usual business: bunch of saloons, hurdy-gurdy dance and billiard halls, mercantiles and general stores, liveries, three or four bagnios—whorehouses to you—freight businesses, greasy spoons, newspaper, hock shops and a blacksmith shop, with a few shyster lawyer offices and questionable land speculators throwed in for good measure here and there. Truck such as that. All operatin' mostly off stole money and dust and valuables. Shacks and wickiups scattered out from there where they live, on the plains and in the foothills, random as raindrops."

"Sounds like Bannack and old Virginia City. Likely that town could use a vigilance committee. A little overnight hangin' could bring some sense of law and order."

"Don't seem to me there's too much call for it in Square Knot, X. Not too many there are disturbed about profitin' from the fruits of evil. You got to have that first, an outraged citizenry. They're too happy down there livin' off the fat of the land. They don't rob one another in Square Knot."

"But, John, that ain't even in your jurisdiction."

"Hey, when somebody snatches my roll, son, the ground that man stands on is my jurisdiction. And speakin' of jurisdiction, there's another high-class owlhoot down there I'd delight in pinnin' his ears back."

"Who's that?"

"Every town like that has to come equipped with a strong man. Somebody who calls the tune so everybody else can dance."

"I'm waitin'."

"You're not going to believe this. The head honcho, meanest of the bunch, callin' the shots in Square Knot, Wyoming, is, so help me Hannah, a heavyweight by the name of Honor Bright."

X. guffawed abruptly. "You're jobbin' me!"

"Swear to God."

Beidler waved his arms. "I've heard everything now!"

"Hell, X., that damned place is a mecca, a magnet, for every scalawag and scofflaw in that part of Wyoming, like flies drawn to a smokin' turd. And the maggots that'd like to be. Not all of them lives there but they go up there for a wing-ding after they score a big hit. Birds of a feather and all that. Plenty of dough in town. Honor Bright exacts his tribute from the madams and the merchants."

"Another Sheriff Plummer and them of kindred stamp. Ought to be strung up off the nearest telegraph pole or barn rafter. The way we damn well did it in Virginia City."

"Ah, give old Bright credit. He keeps his hand on the tiller. And, of course, in the till. Town's wide open, but them youngsters get too raspinorious and start tearin' up the place and shooting the local folks, Bright's got *his* enforcers to call a halt. The unruliest are taken out of town and told not to come back. Others that get too carried away get carried away; fresh soil come morning up on Old Boot Hill." He paused. "So there's your Honor among thieves." He chuckled at his own word choice.

"Commences to sound like we may be bitin' off more than we can chew."

"There you go gettin' back to them livers again. I spoke of intimidation. These are the kind, like we was saying, that go pale when they hear of the Liver Eater and his bloody Bowie, or tippy-toe fast the other way when the famous Vigilante Hangman-Enforcer comes by totin' a long hank of hemp. Specially with a thirteen-hitch hondo and a noose."

X. basked for a glorious moment in the warmth of John's words. Then he came awake. "Still don't see how we face down that mob, John. We may get six, eight with your scatterguns, but them left standin'll shoot us to rags in a wink."

"*We* don't face 'em, X."

"Huh?"

"*You* do."

"Me?!"

"Yeah, you. All by yourself."

Now it was X.'s turn to go pale. "All of a sudden that damn four hundred dollars don't sound all that important. Why me? Where the hell do you come in?"

"I told you about tricks. I'm gettin' to that."

"Don't seem like much of a trick to me. Sounds more like sudden death."

"I'll be there. Don't get your underwear gnarled. Listen."

"At this point, I'm by God listenin'. Better'n bein' there."

"Then settle down. I told you about them alleys."

"Yeah."

"We separate—on horseback—north end of town. You ride the main stem. I go 'round back of the buildings, east side, to your left, hidden for the most part."

"I'm listenin'. Thank God I'm still able to."

"A place called the Painted Lady is the saloon, dance hall and whorehouse preferred by most of the locals; Ned Storch, Honor Bright, and such as them hang around there. Our major opposition. It's got a big sign. You can't miss it. That's where our standoff is likely, if my reconnoiter means anything."

"I got that. What about the alleys?"

"Timing's essential. Everything. We ride in at a walk. As you pass those alleyways on your left, and with just a glance out the corner of your eye, you'll see me at the end of each alley. And know our plan's working. You'll keep track of me. Trust me. You'll stop maybe fifty feet ahead of the Painted Lady and call out and challenge Ned Storch. I'm sure he'll be there. He's got four hundred dollars of our money to burn, and that place lights his fire."

"I still don't like the smell of it."

"Son, it's all we got. You got to trust me. I don't want to reach my strategic support spot too soon. When Ned Storch comes out at your call, I'm figuring the saloon crowd'll empty out, all of 'em groggy, wondering who the hell is this upstart old jackanapes who figures to all alone brace a whole roughneck town such as those scoundrels."

"I commence to wonder that pretty strong myself."

"Dammit, X., trust me. We got 'em off balance, and we do the unexpected, first whack."

"All right, John. We're pretty much just talking here. I ain't signed my name to nothing yet."

"Here's the trick. There's an alley just south of the Painted Lady. At the moment everybody's out there, facing you, I step out of the woodwork behind 'em with my docked scattergun cocked. I'm figuring the element of surprise, and them not knowing which way to turn, and two sawed-off shotguns at close range afore and aft will cause them to think twice about false moves." Johnston slid closer to Beidler as he unfurled his plan, his voice again gruff, his eyes tight. "Here's the clincher. We strike at early to midmorning of a Sunday . . . Sunday next, for a fact."

X. looked at Johnston quizzically. "Why on the Sabbath?"

Johnston's tone became a low growl. "The best of times, my friend; the best of times. For us. The worst of times for them. Saturday night's when the squires of Square Knot pulls the plug and goes up for the grand larrup. Cuts the wolf loose. John Barleycorn rules as does the lure of the shady ladies and the faro boards and the monte cards. The tinkling piano and the tinny banjo. Big balls in town, son, big balls in town. Ned Storch likely has happily called—still bein' flush with our money—for all kinds of setups on him the night before. We take advantage of the bleary nature of their soggy Sunday morning-afters. When we hit, they are still staggering with the enormous colly-wobbles, suffering what some aptly term the inside sweats. They're in the Painted Lady gingerly and painfully testing and testing the hair of the dog. And we noisily appear, ag-gravating them like the approach of the mighty apocalypse from out of nowhere. Get it? Shock the livin' bejeebers out of 'em. All we want is Ned Storch and our four hundred bucks."

Johnston got up to walk around and stretch cramped muscles.

"But, X., I got to get there—behind them—at the exact moment they'll be outside facing you and them too off bal-ance to shoot straight. Not too soon, not too late. And hope the mastodon hangovers cripple them with the jitters, their reflexes slow, some with the dry heaves, their eyesight blurred, and yet out there in a crowded bunch. It's risky, but we assure our edge."

"God, how I hope so."

"Hell, son, the way we got it figured, we can't miss."

SATURDAY MORNING DAWNED chilly as they feasted royally on steak, eggs and grits at the Red Lodge Ritz, washed down with coffee stout enough to float a mule shoe. Outside in the cold gray light, at the hitch rack, their horses were saddled, loaded sawed-off shotguns in the boots, and a pack horse burdened with their bedrolls, camp fixings and provisions.

Warm and content with full bellies, feeling good—and eager—they mounted and rode south. Any reservations X. Beidler had about the expedition had vanished; he was confident now they'd pull it off and retrieve their money.

At least some of it; and he was sure old John Johnston would figure a way to milk the rest of it out of the crowd. He'd take no more than was rightfully theirs.

Johnston didn't speak much until they were clear of Red Lodge and headed into open country.

"We got us a spot, X., a garden spot, for camp tonight, north a few miles of Square Knot. Come across it that time I snuck in there. Been back a couple of times for a few days whenever I felt the need to knit up the raveled sleeve of care."

"The what?"

"Aw, nothin'. You probably wouldn't understand anyway. High and a little breezy. A grove of pine and spruce with a centuries-old bed of needles perfect for uncurlin' a bedroll in a flat, uncobbled place. You'll sleep like a sultan. About an acre of rich grass to keep the horses content. A sweetwater spring rises there with waters so crystal clear and cold you won't need any booze for intoxication."

"Sounds grand, John."

"Perfect place to gird for our confrontation in the mornin'. I call it the Land. I don't own it. Wouldn't want to. It's open range and ought to stay that way. A place to rest easy for tonight. And a place to make another camp for us sometime."

AT DARK, AGAIN well fed, in trail coats to fend off the growing chill, they sat across from each other, illuminated by a small night fire, as they perched on logs and made small talk.

"You weren't exaggeratin' about this place, John."

"Speaks for itself, don't it?"

"Downright pleasurable. A comfort just to sit around here doin' nothin'. Don't know as I've seen a place that suits me so."

"Well, son, we'll come back sometime and stay a few days."

"Sounds prime to me."

"Somethin' I been meaning to ask you for years. What's the X. stand for?"

"My middle name. X. is enough."

"Close about it, ain't you?"

"First name was John, but, hell, about every second man I ever met was named John, includin' you. So I dropped that and because I really hate my middle name, I took to going just by X."

"My middle name's Jeremiah."

"Biblical, I suppose."

"Likely. Seldom use it."

"Recollect years ago when you and me had that wood-cutting station for the steamboats on the Missouri?"

"Eh-yah."

"And we had them Sioux come after us. Them takin' exception to us, and the canoe-that-walks, bein' in their jurisdiction."

"Eh-yah." Johnston grunted in a sort of reverie.

"You went at that one brave with your Green River knife, that same toad-stabber you got there right now."

"Yup. One and the same. Some greenhorn saw me comin' back with my bloody knife, and to scare him I had to go and say I'd et my valiant enemy's liver to take strength from his bravery. That's how the word started to spread like a disease. All manner of variations came after that."

"That's how I remember it."

"I'd as leave not said that and got that thing goin'."

"Like them always asking me what the X. stands for. Gets to be a pain in the ass."

"It irritates people when you won't own up about such things. So they go ahead and make up more stories about you."

★

LATER, WHEN THEY had tucked themselves into their
blankets and soogans and waterproof tarps under the ever-
greens, X. called through the deep dark. "John? You
awake?"

"Well, I guess I'd better be," he said with resignation.
"What's on your mind?"

"If I tell you a secret, promise not to repeat it?"

"Depends. But probably."

"My middle name."

"I can handle that."

"It's Xenophon."

Johnston giggled in the dark. "Xenophon?! Sounds like
something you'd take for a head cold."

"That's why I keep it secret. Name of a character from
long ago. Maybe from the Bible."

"Well, I can hardly pronounce it. Your secret's safe with
me. Now go to sleep. We got a big day comin' up in the
mornin'."

"Least now you know why they call me X."

"Hee hee. John Xenophon Beidler! As I live and
breathe. Sounds more like a fire-and-brimstone preacher
than a vigilante hangman. Go to sleep."

Though the night was chilly, they slept snug and toasty.
Filled with a whopping breakfast of fried eggs and sow-
belly, with ample fluffy biscuits Johnson had baked in his
little Dutch oven the night before, slathered in sorghum,
and nearly finishing a hefty pot of camp coffee, they rode
into Square Knot at midmorning. After the previous day's
easy trails and reminiscing, and a fine camp, they rode
confident of—and competent for—properly concluding
their mission.

As they approached the town, Johnston spoke softly.
"Here's where we split, X. See that lane leading off to the
left? Toward the rear—east—of the buildings? That's my
trail."

X. nodded.

"You bear straight in. Watch for me down the alleys. When you get the Painted Lady in your sights and to your call-out spot, give me half a minute to secure my horse and get up the alley close to the building front before you yell."

"Got it."

Johnston turned dead serious. "Now, X. If anything goes wrong and the shootin' starts, save yourself. Get the hell out. Forget about me. Good luck." He reached across to give X. a firm handshake.

X. grinned. "It'll work, John."

Johnston grinned back. He watched as X. took a deep breath and touched his knees to the horse's ribs. Their ominous, suspenseful stalk of the Painted Lady began. X. thought he'd be nervous. Instead he sensed calm and determination, a need to focus on what had to be done. There was a strange power in camaraderie; they were in it together. To the end.

At the first alley, with a surge of thrill, X. saw Johnston and his horse standing strong in place; and the next and the next. They nodded silently each time. His confidence grew; it was working.

The Painted Lady sign was high and jutted from the building. X. halted his horse gently, dismounted to tether him and slid the shotgun out of the boot. He stepped closer to the Painted Lady. Johnston would be tying his horse near the far rear corner.

Movement along the storefronts south of the alley brought him alert that way with a spear of alarm; his heart leaped.

The man, head down, stumbling toward him, was pint-sized and incredibly spare: Ned Storch!

"Oh, hell!" X. muttered under his breath. Johnston's grand plan was suddenly blown to bits; John wouldn't be in place for about thirty seconds. That now seemed like an eternity. Time to think fast. X. looked around. No nearby alleys for him and his shotgun to hide in. Storch was badly hung over: an advantage.

Ned was about to step across the alleyway. X.'s shotgun would be all but ineffective at the range, but any second, Ned might spy him, or John coming up the alley. He'd be sure to go for his Colt and raise a cry.

X. took the bit in his teeth. He drew back his head for a bellow: "Ned Storch!"

Ned came erect; he stiffened and stopped. He instinctively bent slightly in a palsied gunfighter's stance and went for his holstered Colt. His feeble fingers missed his first slap. On the second try, the gun dropped in the dirt. Ned panicked.

Face pale, his bloodshot eyes fixed on X., Ned stooped for the gun. X. jumped with elation as Johnston loped like an avenging angel the few steps out of the alley to ram his shotgun's muzzle against Storch's cheek. His growl was loud. "Leave it, Ned!" Both raised up. Ned meekly obeyed, his terror obvious.

Bat-wing doors clacking, seven or eight men, aroused by the commotion, boiled out in a bunch, eyes on John and Ned a few feet away. They were all considerably under the weather.

X. kept his position; no one had noticed him.

A shaky voice rose from the crowd. "It's the Liver Eater! He's got Ned!"

"Turn him loose, Johnston!" came another voice; this one of authority.

"Well, as I live and breathe! There's Honor among thieves! Why don't you quit hidin' behind your cronies' petticoats, Bright?" Johnston's voice was a bark.

A man big and beefy as Johnston, in a big black hat and black broadcloth suit, emerged. "What's your game, Johnston?"

Johnston kept his gun on Storch. "I'll tell you, and listen well. Ned Storch is going back to face charges of armed robbery. Maybe witnesses to some of his murders'll come forward too. I'll see that my good friend and law-keeping associate, X. Beidler, the dreaded Vigilante Hang-man of Virginia City, skillfully handles the execution."

"If he's so goshalmighty great, why ain't he here?"

"If you're man enough, take a look behind you."

Bright cranked his neck slightly; others in the group gasped. X. stood there resolute, grinning, and spread-legged, ready to cut down four or five with his handy how-itzer firmly shouldered and sighted. Bright's bravado dimmed.

Johnston barked again. "You been euchred, Bright. One false move and they'll bury Ned Storch in two pieces. But you won't be there. My next barrel's for you, and maybe one or two of your hard cases. What I miss, Beidler'll get. It'll take 'em a week to scrape up and scrub off the blood and mincemeat. Order those men back inside and stay back from the door."

Bright was furious. "We'll come after you. Chase you down."

"Dust clouds are seen a long ways in this country, friend. X. and I'll set up our own ambush. Where you least expect us. I'll shoot high on you on purpose, you lily-livered son of a bitch. That pale morsel of yours that I'll have for supper'll be like eatin' a box of candy."

X. heard somebody loudly vomit; maybe, he thought, it was three or four in unison.

Bright blanched. He turned and muscled through the crowd and was followed into the Painted Lady.

Johnston yelled loudly after them. "If there's any more of this monkey business, I'll come back after you, Bright!"

He shoved Storch toward X. "Tie his hands," he or-dered angrily. "Take off his boots so he can't run. We'll blind-swap his horse, wherever it is, for one of them yon-der."

They heard a familiar clacking sound behind me. Somebody'd come to look, then ducked back. Johnston pivoted and unleashed both barrels. The Painted Lady's bat-wing doors dissolved into kindling. The shotgun's roar and the sounds of splintering wood hung in their ears for several seconds.

He turned back to X. "That'll show 'em, b'God. We'll tether his mount to our pack horse for the trail."

Johnston regarded a terrorized Storch. "You got any of our money left, big man?"

Storch's chin and lips trembled as he tried to make words.

"Mebbe m-m-more'n half. R-r-right side p-p-pants pocket." Johnston thrust his hand into the pocket. "Don't worry, Ned. I'll not grab your cheesy nuts!" He fished out a small, wrinkled wad of bills. "Not much left here, X.," he said sadly.

Beidler nodded grimly as he went about getting Storch ready to ride.

"Anyway, X., it's time to go get my horse and take our goodies and head for home. We won, pard. We won!"

The Winning of Poker Alice

JOHN JAKES

I am deeply indebted to John Jakes for allowing me to reprint this story in *White Hats*. Busy as he is, he had no time to write an original, but when I found this story I knew it belonged. John is not only a bestselling author, but he edited one of the highwater Western anthologies in recent years, the wonderful collection *A Century of Great Western Stories* (Forge, 1999). His own collection, *In the Big Country*, will soon be reissued by NAL.

★

W. G. (for George) Tubbs belonged to the tradition of the gentleman gambler. He realized that here, as everywhere else, social levels existed. At the lowest rung came the card sharps, the professional cheats who used every trick in the book to fleece the wary Westerner of his cash. Higher up the ladder were the semi-honest gamblers; they cheated only when absolutely necessary. And at the very top stood the gentlemen of the trade, and such a one was Tubbs.

Not only were professional ethics important to him but also the matter of one's attire. The more ragtag was a man's dress, the less he belonged to the finest tradition; poor clothes stamped him as nothing but a shady tinhorn. Since the gentleman gambler enjoyed a spotless reputation for honesty and straight dealing in all the raw frontier towns, Tubbs felt that it was up to him to look the part.

Tubbs was large and red-faced, with friendly blue eyes and well-manicured fingernails. It was in the 1870's, when he was forty or thereabouts, that he thrived in the roaring Black Hills. He was regarded as one of the cleverest gamblers in Deadwood.

That is, until Poker Alice came along.

No one knew exactly how she arrived in town. One evening she was there, that's all. She walked into the Poker Chip Saloon, a big woman, dressed in an inexpensive but tasteful gown with her slightly grayed blonde hair piled fashionably high on her head. There was a determined, rugged cast to her jaw, and her eyes were shrewd. But they were also clear, straightforward and honest.

Nobody paid much attention to her at first. She strode up to the bar, with only a few of the local honkytonkers giving her haughty glances and being secretly envious of the fine-looking woman who no doubt would be equally at home in a luxurious drawing room. She waited for the bartender, Sherm Clagfield, who also owned the Poker Chip, to come to her.

"What'll it be, ma'am?" Sherm asked, his eyes glinting humorously.

The woman did not smile. "Rye."

Sherm almost hollered his head off with laughter. He wanted to, that is. But something about the woman—her air of determination, perhaps—kept him from it. Trying to keep a serious expression on his face, he set the glass of liquor down before her. She tossed it off with one gulp. Sherm felt a pang of admiration.

The woman seemed to hesitate a moment. "Anything I can do for you, ma'am?"

She surveyed the room. "Yes. I'm a gambler. I want to set up shop here. My name is Alice Duffield."

Sherm couldn't contain himself this time. He let out a

loud *Haw!* He doubled over with mirth, but when his eyes came to rest on Alice Duffield again, he stopped laughing. A pistol muzzle, held in her steady hand, poked at him. A wicked-looking .38 on a .45 frame.

"Are you going to stand there and laugh like a jackass," Alice said softly, "or are you going to shut your mouth and give me a chance?"

Clagfield saw that she meant it. From the way she held the gun, she was no greenhorn. "Sure, ma'am, you go on over to table six and tell Whitey I said for you to take over. What are you good at?"

"Stud or faro," she said briskly. "I prefer faro, however."

"Well, number six is stud."

"That'll do nicely."

She thrust the pistol back into her carpetbag which she had beside her, and walked over to table number six. Whitey didn't believe what she said. He too got a look down the business end of the gun, and saw Sherm's amazed nod. Whitey got up fast and Alice Duffield sat down. A crowd of curious, eager men thronged around the table. Alice faced them coolly. "Gents," she said, "sit down and play some cards. You'll get treated fair."

A few men slid reluctantly into place, pushed by their comrades who haw-hawed at the idea of a woman being a good card player. The game got under way. "The sky," announced Alice, "is the limit."

It was a fair, even game. One of the men lost a hundred and eight dollars, another won a hundred and forty. The crowd grew larger. The other saloons in town drained of their customers. Business boomed at the Poker Chip as the night wore on. Players left their chairs and new players sat down. But always, Alice sat there, watching the faces of the men, her own face unmoving as stone. By dawn they knew that she was square. A real gentleman gambler, if you could call a woman that. And in spite of her expressed preference for faro, they had already coined a name. Poker Alice.

Shortly after sunrise Alice approached Sherm Clagfield again. "Are you satisfied?"

Sherm nodded rapidly. "You want a job here?"

"That's why I came."

"Well, you're hired." So began the career of Poker Alice in Deadwood.

And now W. G. Tubbs re-enters the picture.

For you see, he had been on a trip, all the way down to St. Louis, when Alice arrived in Deadwood and made her sensational entrance. He rode confidently into town on his moderately well-cared-for mare just before noon one day, put on fresh clothes—light trousers, a colorful vest, broadcloth coat, white shirt with flowing black tie and tall beaver hat (for the dress of the true gentleman of the tables was highly conventional)—ate lunch at Mame's Cafe, and wandered over to the Poker Chip to let Sherm know he had returned.

A game was already in progress. Faro this time, with Alice handling the box. As usual, she had a large crowd of spectators around her, for the novelty of a woman gambler had not yet worn off.

Mildly surprised, Tubbs approached Sherm who stood at the bar. There was none of the pleasant foolish conversation about, How was the trip? and It was fine. Instead, Tubbs jerked a thumb at Alice. "Who's that lady?"

"Poker Alice," Sherm said. "Our new dealer."

Immediately a frown creased the broad forehead of Tubbs. He saw a problem. Several of the other dealers—Johnny Red Dog, Louisiana Irwin, The Count, among them—sat idle at a corner table, playing a listless game of twenty-one. Apparently Poker Alice was a threat to his livelihood. As if he had sensed what Tubbs was thinking, Sherm said, "Yep, nobody wants to gamble with anybody but Alice."

"Oh, is that right," Tubbs said, irritated. Well, the fad wouldn't last. The boys would come back to George Tubbs for a fast, honest game when they got tired of this female.

But the boys didn't come back. The weeks dragged on and Alice kept raking in the money. Tubbs played on a salary, but his self-respect grew battered and worn. Beside, the boys didn't care two hoops about him any more. If Tubbs had two men playing with him on a Saturday night (the liveliest time of the week, of course) he was lucky. Whereas Alice could never bee seen, there were so many men crowded around her table.

Tubbs realized that something had to be done. He found out more about Alice, and the more he found out, the greater grew his envy. She had learned to play cards, it was rumored, down in New Mexico. In fact, a bawdy story stated that instead of spending her wedding night with her husband, Frank Duffield, a mining engineer, she spent it in the Silver City, New Mexico, saloon, fascinated by the card playing. The wide-eyed bride had evidently learned fast and well, studying the expressions of men's eyes when they played, the uncontrollable nervous tics that showed when they bluffed, all those mannerisms that might betray them to the wary dealer. Alice herself stated that she took up gambling as a career after Frank Duffield got blown up in a mine accident in Lake City, Colorado.

Tubbs contemplated violence. He sat there at his generally empty table, glaring at the crowd of laughing rowdy men around Poker Alice. But violence, he decided, was out. One night a young punk of a kid got smart with Alice. That lady drilled him neatly in the shoulder with her .38 on the .45 frame before he could bring his own shoulder gun clear of the harness. And besides, Tubbs was not a violent man by nature. He made his way by the code of the gentleman . . .

One afternoon Alice approached him. She had often spoken to him, but he had snubbed her. "Mr. Tubbs," she said, sitting down across from him and pouring herself a drink. "I'd like to know why you don't take to me."

Tubbs stared gloomily at the table. "How do you expect me to? You're wrecking my business."

Alice nodded. "I heard you were a good man. Popular, too."

"I was. Before you came along."

Alice extended her hand. "I'd like to call a truce."

"No thank you," Tubbs said politely, and turned away from her, fuming. She shrugged and left the table. He couldn't help following her with his eyes, though. She had a certain mature, rugged attractiveness. For a moment he almost regretted not having accepted her offer.

Gradually, the novelty wore off and Alice assumed her place as just another of the dealers. Tubbs got business again, though he grudgingly told himself that Alice was just a *little* more popular than any of the men. But as the days passed and he watched her work the faro and stud games, his envy changed slowly. Now that the threat to his job had removed itself, he began seeing her in a more favorable light. As downright attractive, in fact. But he didn't exactly have the courage to approach her, after having rebuffed her once. After all, he was a gentleman, cool and calm, unused to rash impulses and actions.

But she grew more and more attractive in his eyes. None of the men of the town seemed romantically interested in her, for they were always moving on and new ones took their place. At last Tubbs determined something had to be done. He spoke to Alice now, a casual "Hello" and "Fine day" now and again, but nothing more. With the natural guilty feeling of a rather shy man, he followed her home one evening, at a safe distance, to learn that she roomed at Kate Colby's Boarding House.

If anyone had seen him ride out of Deadwood the next day, and had followed him, his reputation would have been ruined for good. He rode out across the countryside, always turning around for signs of pursuers, but there were none. He chose one spot, decided it was too public, and rode back up into the hills a little further until he came upon just the place. Quiet, secluded, and he could hear any horses coming that might happen to ride his way. He climbed down off his mare, clutching the section of newspaper. He still felt highly embarrassed, but something bigger than himself made him go ahead with his plan.

Carefully, he picked a bouquet of wild flowers and wrapped them up in the newspaper.

He rode back into Deadwood soon after that with the bundle clutched tightly under his arm. He was in a state of high nervous tension all afternoon, and did not go near the Poker Chip. Poker Alice had the habit of returning to Kate Colby's Boarding House at around six in the evening, eating dinner and resting in her room for a while, and then going back to the saloon about eight for an all-night session with the cards. So when his expensively-fobbed watch showed just seven-thirty, Tubbs dismounted before the boarding house, still clutching the flowers. He'd had them in a vase of water in his room all afternoon, with the shades pulled down, to keep them fresh.

He stole past the dining room unobserved by the few late eaters. He already knew which room Alice kept. He had, in fact, worked out an elaborate spy system among his town cronies so that he knew her movements almost exactly. He walked determinedly down the hall and stopped at the door of Alice's room. He fumbled self-consciously with his string tie for a moment and then knocked.

"Come in," said a wary voice.

Tubbs opened the door and his jaw dropped.

Alice was crouched down behind the bed as if expecting an attack. Her gun was leveled at Tubbs' ample stomach, and to add to the strange scene, a large black cigar stuck out of one corner of her mouth, curling up smoke that wreathed her blonde-gray head.

"What do you want, Tubbs?" she said sharply.

He held out the flowers awkwardly. "Just . . . just wanted to pay my respects." He felt his face getting hot and, presumably, red.

Poker Alice rose to her feet, seemed to debate with herself for a moment, and then put her gun away. She flicked an inch of cigar ash neatly into a brass spittoon by the bed.

"Well, close the door, it's drafty," she said.

Tubbs fumbled for words. He stared at her cigar with a peculiar expression.

"Well, what's wrong with it?" Alice exclaimed. "Other women smoke cigarettes. I like something stronger." She blew out a large puff of smoke. Tubbs was getting hold of himself now. He extended the flowers again and Alice took them. She unwrapped the package and a smile spread across her face.

"Why, Mr. Tubbs, they're very nice. Thank you." She began putting them into a vase. "I'm sorry I jumped at you like that, but I was looking out the window and I saw you ride up and you looked so odd that I thought maybe you had something bad on your mind. A woman can't be too careful."

"No," Tubbs murmured, sinking down into a chair. He sprang up again immediately. "Well, I guess I'd better get down to the saloon."

"Sit still," Alice said. There was a hint of authority under the friendliness of her voice. Tubs sat. "I'm glad to see we've called off the feud, Mr. Tubbs." She offered him a cigar and he lit up. "A woman gets lonely in a town like this, and you always appeared to be such a gentleman, though I did get angry when you refused to shake my hand."

Tubbs felt a little more at ease now. The cool demeanor of the gentleman that had left him so rapidly a few minutes earlier was returning. "Yes'm," he said, smiling. "I just thought we could be friends and maybe go for a drive now and then . . . I've got a buggy . . . and the front porch of this place seems like it would be mighty pleasant and breezy in hot weather . . ."

And so they talked on, the gentleman gambler and the cigar-smoking woman who handled cards and a gun like a professional. Their relationship made its way forward from that night on a very friendly basis. They took their drives and ate Sunday dinners together (for Alice refused to play cards on the Lord's Day) and sat on the front porch of Kate Colby's Boarding House. But the situation had not yet smoothed itself out completely.

For W. G. Tubbs was by nature a cautious man. The gentleman gambler, he could never forget, did not let himself be guided by rash impulses. Tubbs often considered matrimony, but even then he would put himself off, saying mentally, *I'd best think about it.*

Nearly a year passed that way. Tubbs and Poker Alice had accepted each other, and their rivalry over the gambling tables was now an amicable one, and Tubbs did not mind kind of taking a back seat, for the woman was always just a *little* more popular than any of the men.

Tubbs was relaxing in his room one Sunday morning, thinking of the dinner he and Poker Alice would eat together in an hour or so, when the door opened quickly. Alice stood there in her best gown. A humorous light shone in her eyes but the .38 on the .45 frame pointed at Tubbs' stomach with unmistakable authority.

"Get your shirt on, Tubbs. I've been thinking for a long time that it'd be a good thing if we were married. We'd double our income and we wouldn't have to eat that boarding house food all the time. I know you were too frightened to ask me, so I thought I'd better do the asking." She waved the gun. "Now hurry up."

The Rev. Billy Watters married them in the Poker Chip Saloon, with Sherm Clagfield standing up for them. Sherm had a cabin back in the hills, so they got into Tubbs' buggy and drove off for a little holiday. Tubbs didn't seem at all unhappy about the shotgun, or rather six-gun, aspect of the marriage. And so they rolled out of Deadwood, Poker Alice Duffield Tubbs, queen of the gambling halls from Colorado to the Dakotas, and W. G. (for George) Tubbs. The gentleman gambler and the lady who smoked cigars.

Buffalo Bill's Last Dream

ARTHUR WINFIELD KNIGHT

A heartrending tale of Buffalo Bill's last days from the expert pen of poet and playwright Arthur Winfield Knight. Little more needs to be said. You'll see what I mean when you read it. I step out of my role as editor here to tell you this is one of my favorite stories in this book.

★

"I want a divorce," I say. "I'll give you whatever you want. I don't have a lot left, but it's all yours if you give me my freedom."

"Why should I give you anything?" Louisa asks. "You've made my life hell, humiliated me with your floozies."

"I didn't mean to humiliate you," I say. I tried settling down right after we were married. I managed the Golden Rule Hotel in Salt Creek, Kansas, but it was a small, dingy place, and I had big dreams. I would have died there. I'd already fought Indians for the army and shot buffalo for the railroad. Buntline had already written a book about me.

Louisa and I sit on the porch swing at Scout's Rest Ranch in western Nebraska. It's dusk and we watch the bats fly out of the loft above the barn, and I wonder where they go every night at this time. I wish I could follow them, disappearing into the darkness.

"How do you think I felt when I came to New York and phoned your hotel room and one of your whores answered?" Louisa asks. "Couldn't you at least have kept her in a room down the hall?"

"I'm sorry," I say, touching her shoulder, but she pulls away. She's always pulled away. "I think I'll go in and pour myself a whiskey."

"That's your answer to everything," she says. "Whiskey."

The doctors told me my liver "flopped" when I was in my forties. It was a hot, rainy night in Pittsburgh, and I felt like I was suffocating under the big tent. The doctors said I'd be dead by fifty if I didn't stop drinking, but that was fifteen years ago and they didn't have to live with Louisa. "Why did you marry me?" I ask.

"I've thought about that for thirty years because it's made me so . . . bitter."

"I know."

"All I can decide is that I was young and foolish and impressionable," Louisa says. "I think I fell in love with the legend."

THE "LEGEND" HAS been drinking all day and his prostate is inflamed so he has a difficult time mounting his horse. He has rheumatism and neuritis and he's gotten paunchy from all the booze; he can't see his penis when he stands on the scale, naked, weighing himself, but he tries not to dwell on that.

Sometimes it helps if I think about myself in the third person, distancing myself from my pain, but it doesn't always work. The pain's real.

I don't know if I'll be able to get through my act, riding out into the ring and making my speech, without peeing in my pants. I grit my teeth when I swing my right leg over the saddle.

Someone standing next to me asks, "Are you all right, Colonel?" I was never a colonel, but they call me that because I've survived all these years.

"I'll be fine," I say.

I spur my horse into the ring, circling it, waving my hat to the crowd. I hope my hairpiece doesn't come off. I remember the day it did. I rode out of the ring into the bewilded loneliness of a blazing afternoon, the crowd's laughter ringing in my ears. It was a bad moment for the old scout.

I stare into the lights, blinded by them, and say, "This farewell visit will be my last 'hail and farewell.' I'm about to go home for a well-earned rest. Out in the West I have my horses, my buffaloes, my sturdy, staunch old Indian friends—my home and my green fields." I've given this speech for five years now, but I always mean it, always think it will be my last. But I keep coming back because I need the money.

I say, "I want to see nature in its prime and enjoy a rest from active life. Thirty years ago you gave me my first welcome, and I'm grateful for your loyal devotion to me. During that time many of my friends among you and many of those with me have long since gone to the great, unknown arena of another life—there are only a few of us left.

"To my little friends in the gallery and the grownups who used to sit there, I thank you once again. God bless you all. Goodbye."

Then I spur my horse out of the spotlight into the darkness and wait for someone to help me dismount.

THEY GAVE ME the Medal of Honor for my bravery and skill in fighting Indians forty-five years ago. I led the troopers to within fifty yards of the Sioux camp before they discovered me, then I killed one of the warriors in hand-to-hand combat and shot two others.

Now Congress has ruled the Medal of Honor can't go to civilians so they've taken mine away.

I've had the medal more than half my life so the shelf where I kept it seems empty now; I've been running on empty for a long time.

The Wild West show bearing my name is owned by someone else and I can't control my kidneys.

When I heard Congress took away my medal, I spent the afternoon drinking bourbon. Then the greatest scout this country has ever seen pissed in his pants.

"YOU STILL OWE me," Tammen says.

"I don't owe you a damned thing." I've worked for him for two years to pay back twenty thousand dollars I borrowed. The way he keeps books, I'll be paying him back when I'm dead. I say, "The debt's paid."

"The hell it is. The interest compounded faster than you made payments."

"Compound this," I say, touching the pearl-handled Colts on the table in front of me. I point the barrels toward Tammen. "I don't want to kill you."

"You son of a bitch," Tammen says. "I think you'd really do it."

"After two years, you're finally getting to know me," I say.

LOUISA LOOKS OUT the huge window from my study, her hands clasped behind her back.

I say, "I've tried to tell myself I did the right thing staying with you all these years, but I can't lie to myself anymore. I've stayed because I've been a coward."

"You've always been a coward, Will, always been weak. You need other people to validate your existence. You're nothing when the cheering stops."

I don't need Louisa to catalogue my weaknesses. "You can have the ranch," I say. "It's all yours. All four thousand acres."

"I've already got the ranch," she says. "I live here."

"For Christ's sake, Louisa—"

"I've asked you not to take the Lord's name in vain. At least you can give me that much."

I stand beside her at the window. To the west the sky's lavender. "I don't believe God joins people together so they'll have to go through life miserable. Do you?"

She doesn't answer.

"Is that your kind of God?"

"Don't talk to me about God," she says, turning toward me. She has the face of an angry principal.

"When a mistake's made, we can change it. There're laws. People get divorces every day now."

"I don't care what 'people' do, Will. Before we're finished, you'll know what it's like to be in hell."

"I already know what hell's like," I say.

I LIE IN bed holding my flaccid penis. It may not be much, but it's all I have to hang on to.

My wife hates me and the other women are gone.

I've made more than a million dollars, but I don't know where it went. I told Katherine that when we were sitting in the bar at the Hoffman House in New York. I remember there was a sign above the bar saying there are three kinds of people: those who make things happen, those who watch things happen and those who ask, "What happened?" I thought it was funny, but now I ask that all the time.

I'd met her when she was on the stage in London, and

I'd financed a show she was doing in New York. She was twenty years younger than me and we'd just finished making love on the black satin sheets in my suite at the Hoffman and my checking account was overdrawn.

I said, "I've given you eighty thousand dollars and we've been to bed ten times."

"I didn't know you were counting, Will."

"It cost me eight thousand dollars every time we did it and I just can't afford that anymore."

DARK CLOUDS GATHER over the mountains as I come down the steps from the courthouse in Cody. I founded the town, but I can't get a divorce in the place that bears my name. It doesn't seem fair. My dream cost me millions.

I button the goose down jacket I'm wearing against the wind that comes down from the Tetons and ignore the reporters standing on the steps. The papers say I'm an American icon, but I don't know what that means.

I'm anachronistic.

Friends told the court how I've suffered over the years, but their testimony didn't help because no one believed a legend can suffer. It's like reading about people starving in other parts of the world; you never quite believe it.

Louisa wore a black dress in court. She spoke so softly the court clerk had to ask her to speak up when she put her hand on the Bible and said she'd tell the whole truth, nothing but the truth, so help her God.

She lied.

"Will is one of the kindest and most generous men I ever knew. When he was sober, he was gentle and considerate. If I had him to myself now, there wouldn't be any trouble. He's gone wrong because of bad companions," she said, looking at my friends, "and drink. His friends caused him to put this upon me."

After the hearing, Louisa said, "I'll never forgive you for this, Will. You humiliated me again."

"I wasn't the liar."

"Your insisting on a divorce broke our daughter's heart. You might as well have killed her."

"For God's sake, Louisa, Arta was a grown woman. She'd have wanted me to be free. You know she died from pneumonia. *Pneumonia.* She just couldn't breathe anymore." She lived in Spokane and all she could talk about was the rainy weather. Now the cold rain falls on her grave.

I walk into the wind, my eyes watering. I can smell the rain in the air. Pretty soon, it will be falling on my grave.

"I DIDN'T THINK you'd try to poison me," I say. "I didn't think you hated me that much."

Louisa says, "It wasn't poison. It was Dragon's Blood, an aphrodisiac I got from a gypsy. He said it would help you to stop drinking and rekindle your love."

"I didn't think you'd want to 'rekindle' my love." I'm lying on the couch in my den but I can see the lights on the Christmas tree in the next room.

"It was good once, Will, in the early days. When you came to the house courting me that first summer in St. Louis. You wore a white suit."

"I remember." We went out onto the veranda after we danced and Louisa asked what I wanted to do with my life and I told her I wanted to conquer the world. She laughed, but that's what I wanted to do. I say, "It's too late for us now. It'll take more than Dragon's Breath to make things right between us."

"I'm sorry about that," Louisa says. She bends over me, straightening the comforter.

"Yeah. So am I."

★

WHEN I AWAKEN, Doctor East is leaning over me, his fingers on my wrist.

"What're my chances?"

He says, "Your condition's being worsened by an eclipse of the moon."

My condition's been made worse by years of pretense and prevarication. I say, "I don't believe in omens." Now that I'm dying it's as if Louisa is finally able to forgive me. She even got me to go to Colorado for a mineral water cure. Doc Holliday died at the sanitarium where I stayed.

East says, "Believe this: you don't have a lot of time left." Louisa stands next to him, her eyes large in the dim light. All she says is "Cody." I can barely hear her.

"How long?"

"The sand is slipping slowly—"

"How long?"

"About twenty-four hours," he says.

I tell Louisa, "The drinking ends today."

THEY WERE LARGE stinking beasts with foul breath. They were always covered with flies.

I can remember when the prairie looked as if it had broken out in cankers there were so many of the filthy beasts. I could never understand why the Indians worshipped them.

I personally shot thousands and thousands and never regretted it. Some days the barrel of my Sharps was hotter than the sun.

Now that they're almost gone the prairies seem as empty as my dreams.

At Freedom's Edge

JUDY MAGNUSON LILLY

As much as I enjoy stories about Bat Masterson and Buffalo Bill, this is what I had in mind when I came up with the idea for *White Hats* and the companion volume, *Black Hats*. This story features an obscure, unknown historical character, a slave named Larry Lapsley, and tells of his actual walk to freedom.

Judy Lilly's fiction has appeared in *Louis L'Amour Magazine* and in the anthology *American West: Twenty Stories from the Western Writers of America*.

★

The black man lay in his neighbor's bed, staring up at the tawny face of his old friend standing beside the Swede doctor. He was used to white faces now, never seeing a black one unless he went into town. He'd heard talk that ex-slaves had settled beyond the bluffs, but he'd never made a visit.

The friend, Luke Parsons, a veteran of the war with the South, laid a hand on the man's bony shoulder. "How you doing, Larry? You got to get yourself well. Remember that trip we're going to take? You hear they call it Oklahoma Territory now? When you're on your feet, we'll see the places that came near doing you in."

With effort, Larry Lapsley nodded. "A long time back, but I 'member those times." He felt Parsons squeeze his arm. Then he closed his eyes, and the sound of voices grew dim, as if he were floating away on a quick-made raft in the dark, silent waters of the Red River. He wanted to tell Parsons that he was already seeing those Oklahoma places: Fort Gibson, North Fork Town, Pine Mountain, Muddy Boggy, Canadian River. They were parading through his mind, real as they were thirty-three years ago. He could see the river, broad and placid, between all that green and yellow and coppery foliage. And he could see himself then too, strong and cocky, dressed in gray homespun, frayed trousers and shirt, toting on his back a lumpy canvas bag stuffed with a castoff split-tail coat and a two-day food supply. He was crouched beside his cousin Wesley, their dark skin tight and shining with youth, on the river's high wooded banks.

He remembered how they'd sweated as they hid in their cage of bushes on the south riverbank, looking over into Indian Territory. The sun was sinking to the horizon. Wesley, broad and beefy, sucked in air through his open mouth and wiped his glistening face. Larry rested on his haunches and listened to the distant sounds of men shouting and dogs barking up and down the river.

"It's the rebel gen'ral and his men, Larry," Wesley said, his voice breathless. "I figure they be down at Colbert's Crossing now. Probably rebel Indians too. I hear talk 'bout getting a hundred dollars a head if they catch us. Maybe we oughta turn around. Go on back."

Lapsley looked at him and then back across the river. "We ain't goin' back." His voice was dry, hoarse. "Price and his men are far enough off. They're heading into Texas. We goin' the other way." Lapsley stood then. "We gotta lash us a raft before the light's gone. Let's get to it." He pushed through the bushes and ducked into a thicket of cedar that led down the river's side hill. Wes scrambled after him.

Lapsley hadn't thought much of running off to the north until two days ago. There was a time when he expected to get his freedom papers, but when his old owners had fled Missouri for Texas a year back, Old Man Stancel bought him. Working in Stancel's distillery was the best he'd known since he was a youngun on the Lapsley plantation in Kentucky. He'd come to think a heap of Stancel. He thought Stancel thought a heap of him too. But day before last, the old man came to him and said how times were tough with the war going bad for the South. "Gotta sell you, Larry. You and Wesley are going to Caleb Cook north from Bonham," he had said. "I hate it, but the corn's all going for food and feed. If it's not the troops eating us poor, it's the refugee Indians camping in the fields, looking for handouts. Nothing else I can do, boy." Stancel had turned away then and gone back to his fine, white house.

So he and Wesley had left that November day after the noon meal, with the clothes on their backs and a gunnysack with food from the kitchen for a couple of meals on the road. In Wesley's pockets rode his good luck stuff, the bone of a cat leg, flint stones and dried rosemary. In Lapsley's pocket, along with a ball of twine and a bone necklace belonging to his old ma, he carried their passing papers that told they were meeting a man in Bonham, Texas. Stancel never even took his goodbyes.

When the two had walked out the back lane, just past the slave cemetery where Wesley's wife and baby lay buried, they turned north, in the direction of the Red River, instead of south toward Bonham. Lapsley had decided he wasn't going to belong to anyone again.

Now down near the river's edge, they gathered logs and yanked vines and roots from the red earth. By sunset they were laying the logs side by side and lashing them together. Once the darkness had grown thick as tar, they car-

ried the finished raft to an area of riverbank hidden by
sumac and brushwood. Piling their bags on the raft, they
stripped off their clothing, threw it over their cargo and
eased themselves into the river. The coldness of the water
shocked them, bit into their legs and torso and then steadied the waves of panic that slogged through their bellies.
Runaway slaves came back mute and slack-eyed. Some
were whipped and hot-iron branded. Stories got worse
every year.

"Ready, Larry?" Wesley's hoarse voice came out of the
darkness.

"Let's go." The heady feel of freedom was pumping
through Lapsley's veins now. They launched from the
bank, kicking as smoothly as otters and using free arms for
paddles. Lapsley thought of how Stancel had told him
what a first-rate job he'd done in the distillery, learned
quicker than most. But it didn't count for nothing in the
end. He should have known better.

A gauzy film covered the moon above them. In the distance gunshots echoed off the night sky. Dogs set up a
now-and-then ruckus. But each time, silence followed the
sounds. When they had reached the north shore, they stole
from the water and dragged the raft into the friendly shadows of the timber. Shaking the river water from his arms
and legs, Larry looked back across the wide expanse. The
dark south side rose like a prison wall, and he was beyond
it. By the time Caleb Cook sent word to the old man, he
and Wesley would be at least a night's walk into Choctaw
country. They were on the edge of freedom now.

IN HIS SICK bed, Lapsley awoke to a rowdy laugh somewhere beyond his sight, down the hall of his neighbor's
house. At first he thought it was Wesley telling his made-up
stories round a Sunday fire, eyes wide, his ginger-colored
cheeks puffed like a bullfrog. But then he remembered. He

had crossed alone, come on to Kansas, the single black
man in Parson's wagon. Only in his memory was his
cousin still a strong, young man, quick with a grin, partial
to talk over actions. Nearly four decades ago it all had happened. But he remembered like it was yesterday.

ONCE THEY HAD crossed the river, they planned to
travel at night and rest during daylight. The first day, before the sun was fully up, they collapsed among hazel
bushes and scrunched up their coats into pillows, hoping to
sleep for hours. But buzzing mosquitoes descended in
clouds and stung their ears and necks. They tried covering
themselves with leaves and branches and then with their
faded coats. Finally, Lapsley gave up sleeping and sat
among the bushes, listening to a rooster crowing somewhere deeper in the woods and the hee-hawing of a contrary mule. He began to lay out their plan in his mind. One
white-haired slave traveling past Stancel's place with Confederate General McCullough had told him the Choctaw
Indians held the southeast corner of Indian Territory.
"They be mostly old men, chil'ens and squaws camping on
the Muddy Boggy and Blue Rivers," he confided at the
meal table. "The young bloods are riding for the South.
You git over the Canadian and you be safer then. The Federals now, they feed the Cherokee, some Creek too, up
there."

As the sun rose higher that first day, they sat among the
prickly bushes, dozing, not daring to move even to eat.
They saw no one pass by, but nearby sounds confirmed a
human presence. Then as the shadows grew long across
the meadow they had just crossed, they crawled from their
hiding place. Ahead they could see tall oaks that began an
upward march. The easy going was over now that they'd
left the river bottomland, the way becoming slanted and
rocky as the timber and undergrowth grew dense. That

night and the next, they were able to travel only two or three hours before clouds blotted the moonlight, and they lost their direction sense. Each night a light rain began, growing finally so heavy that they had to crawl, wet through to their skin, beneath a sandstone shelf or cover themselves with leafy boughs.

At dawn of the third day, they stood exhausted at the edge of a clearing where fog hung in patches. Shivering under their damp coats, they watched light seep from a distant forested ridge. Before either could speak they heard a thrashing sound behind them. They turned and suddenly, out of the shadows, a rabbit beelined for them with a black dog, teeth bared, on its tail. The rabbit shot off to the right, leaving the dog charging forward. Wesley stood frozen in place. Lapsley bent and seized a piece of wood as long as his arm. Hurling it at the animal he cried, "Hey!" His yell caught the dog in its tracks and rolled it up on its hind legs. Wesley began his belly laugh, the sound echoing off the forest floor. The dog dropped to all fours, turned and sailed, snapping and crashing, into the brush. The men lowered themselves to a log lying among the stiff grasses. Without speaking, they sat for a time while the sunlight burned off the fog around them.

Against his good judgment Lapsley had agreed that morning to travel a mile or two farther before finding cover for the day. "Cain't make good time this way," Wesley had whined. They took off around the clearing and followed their own paths through the trees, coming together now and then. Lapsley had just sighted Wesley when again the sound of stirring leaves and cracking wood made them turn. A strapping fellow, his skin darker than either of theirs, stepped into a shaft of light. "Good morning, gentlemen. Heard your merriment. You traveling?" He looked from Lapsley to Wesley, and then he nodded toward the open meadow beyond the trees. Six or seven horsemen waited while the stranger nudged them into the open. The

riders wore faded trousers, dirty wool jackets and slouch
hats over dark hair hanging loose. Not until they came
within a few feet did Lapsley realize they were Indians.

"My name is Moses," the black fellow said, pleasant
enough. "You boys are guests of the Choctaw now. Come
along with us. And don't give nobody trouble."

The Indians shared their poor rations with them that
first day, something Wesley never forgot. The two had
been taken some distance to a rambling house low on the
rocky upgrade they had been climbing the past three
nights. The house had a leaning porch and makeshift addi-
tions to the sides and back. It faced a large open area bound
by a river. Tents and several cabins stood amid tramped-
down grass, cook fires and garden patches. Ponies and
mules grazed beyond the trees, while a few cows and pigs
ambled about. The settlement had the feel of a campsite,
short-lived and forlorn.

After the meal of cornbread, sour milk and beef, their
captors snapped irons on the men's legs and wrists and
kept them in a back room that had only two chairs and
blankets for sleeping. For days, a stream of Indians, mostly
women and children, dressed in ragged shifts or patched
trousers and waists, the clothing of white people, trooped
into the old house to see the "black boys" and jabber at
them in strange huffing sounds. The days passed slowly at
first, as they had nothing to do but walk about the room or
peer out a window. A guard sat outside the door at all
hours. While Wesley seemed almost content to sleep dry
and eat regular, Lapsley bore the long hours like added
weight to his shoulders.

After two weeks and three days, according to the
notches on the bottom side of the jailhouse chair, two
guards, a tall, hawk-nosed Choctaw and one who carried a
rifle on a crippled arm, came to them and removed the
irons from their wrists and feet. While the Indian with the
rifle watched silently, the other men tethered their legs to-

gether at the ankles with short lengths of chain. The prisoners were hauled out and set to work grinding corn with a little steel mill that had been nailed to a tree. The day was unusually warm. Children played in the sunshine and women worked the ground of their gardens. But gaunt-bodied dogs and solemn guards with rifles roamed the camp. Lapsley spoke quietly as he scooped kernels of corn into the grinding mill. "They're getting us out now. That's good. They think we might come around, might want to stay with them like Moses."

Wesley looked at him and then across the camp to a group of children. He went back to shelling corn into a shallow basket. "Ain't half bad here, Larry."

Lapsley stared at him. "Look at us. We're in chains, Wesley. We been owned for all our twenty-two years. We never been in chains b'fo'."

"They gotta know they kin trust us is all. I 'spect soon enough we'll—"

"No, Wes, I ain't gonna do for these Indians like Moses have to. Only thing different than b'fo' is they's skin is closer to us. We still ain't free."

"Shore, Larry. I know. But they looks at me when they tell me somethin'. And they listens to what I say."

Lapsley said no more to Wesley about running. He began to watch how his cousin jawed with the guards and spoke out a few Choctaw words like *kucha* for "go out" and *kawi* for "coffee." One warm day a guard let Wesley remove his chains and play stickball with them. Lapsley stopped his grinding to watch as players kept a small ball in the air with hickory sticks looped at the end and covered with woven strips of leather. The women and children began gathering to watch. Soon everyone was calling Wesley's name, cheering for him, patting him on the back.

The thought struck him that with so much liberty Wesley might try to slip away first, despite what he had said. If that happened, he'd never have a chance. From that moment, he resolved to be like Wesley. He pitched into his act, joking with guards, even asking for *oka,* water, and *paska,* bread. Before this, he had been watched and followed from the moment he stepped from the house into the sunlight. But after a couple of weeks, they let him walk into the woods a hundred yards, following as far as the gate to the path, keeping their weapons ready. Finally the guard got so he didn't even come out of the house, and for solid minutes at a time no one watched him. Vowing to be ever ready, Lapsley kept his pockets full of shelled corn and his knife in his coat pocket.

But slipping away from camp would be one thing, while breaking his ankle chains was another. He had noticed how the Indians carelessly left tools lying around the yard, making no attempt to keep a count of them. One day as they returned with Moses from a rail-cutting jaunt, Lapsley watched the big black man drop his hatchet by the woodpile near the path going to the privy. That night, when he went unescorted on his trip to the woods, he retrieved the hatchet on his way and hid it in floodwater brush beside a hulking oak tree.

A rainy stretch began at what Lapsley calculated was the end of December—four weeks since he and Wesley left Texas. About dusk one evening, as rain came down in sheets, the Choctaw prepared for some kind of celebration to be held inside the house where Lapsley and Wesley were kept. They were hauled out to watch the festivities. Women came bringing pots of stew, while the old men of the camp arrived wearing beaded or yarn bands around their arms and wrists. Some brought sleighbells on a leather strap and rattles made from gourds or turtle shells or steer horns. Younger men wearing gray army coats brought in liquor jugs and took their places around the large main room.

By seven o'clock, both thunder and spirits rocked the foundation of the old house. To a constant drumbeat, men danced in the center of the room, using a kind of stomp step in circles or a go-as-you-please manner. Lapsley sat at a table where men played a game with kernels of corn. He could see Wesley across the room with Moses in a group of Choctaw, his chains clanking around his tapping feet.

The guard that night was a Creek they called Neal Bean, a muscular man with long black hair and a broken nose. His rifle lay at his feet, and he leaned against the back of the chair, clapping calloused hands. Everyone gabbled in Choctaw, even Wesley, who would shout out *"Sa ituk-shila,"* and wait to be passed a jug.

Lapsley pretended to drink when the jug came to him and watched the dancing. Usually only men took to the floor, knees bent, feet moving in short, flat-heeled steps. Their shoulders and heads seemed to bob together to the beat of the drums. Sometimes the women joined in, doing the stomp step and following a leader who had them raising their brown limbs toward the ceiling and then dropping them toward the floor. Through it all Lapsley could feel his blood pumping with the drumbeats.

After a couple of hours, he observed that the liquor was taking good effect. Those who weren't dancing slumped in the corners of the room. Lapsley left his chair and found the guard, having to shake his shoulder to get his attention. *"Kucha! Kucha!"* he said. "Looka here, I'm going to step out. I know it's raining, but I can't wait no more."

Bean waved him away. "Aah, go. Be quick." He turned back to toss kernels of corn, blackened on one side, onto the table. Lapsley moved slowly around the edge of the room. He could hear the rain pounding the roof, and he wished he could go for his old coat. Amid the drum music his leg chains clinked and his heart thumped. Wesley's familiar laughter erupted suddenly behind him, honest and bold. More than anything, he wanted to look at his cousin. But he couldn't risk even one quick last look. Wesley would know. He'd see it all in Lapsley's eyes. Wesley might even turn him in out of some murky need to please his captors and keep Lapsley with him.

Outside the rain was heavy enough to harm his seeing, coming at him sideways. For a moment he felt confused. Then, from a lightning flash, he saw the log pile to his right. The path lay beyond it. He sloshed through water and mud to where a trail entered the woods. Beneath the trees the going was easier and drier. The oak tree stood beyond the privy, and lodged in the winter-dried grass was the hatchet. With the head of the tool, he pried apart the U-rings and slipped the irons from around his ankles. For a moment he felt light enough to rise into the thick branches overhead. Then with one great heave he threw the shackles into the darkness. The rain had suddenly lightened, though the trees dripped heavy enough to splash him. Lapsley began to run, half limping at first, then sure-footed in the direction he had mapped out in his head these past weeks. Despite the shiver that rolled through his body, the words "head north" throbbed in his brain like a drumbeat and pushed him forward.

HE FELT A soft touch on his forehead and, struggling to see through filming eyes, Lapsley recognized the concerned ruddy face of Addie Robinson, the neighbor who cared for him now. Her mouth had a troubled set to it, but her gentle hand moved behind his shoulders and raised him enough to take a spoonful of warm broth. "The doctor says you must eat, Larry," Addie said. "I know you like my chicken soup."

Trying not to cough, he let the liquid slide down his throat. Those weeks in the wilderness had marked him in many ways—frostbitten fingers and toes, loosening teeth—but the memory of hunger scraping at his insides was the worst. Sometimes he'd had nothing to eat but berries or wet kernels of corn that sprouted in his trousers pocket, green shoots three inches long, waving like fine new grass. Once a drove of wild turkeys had flapped down from the trees and strutted near him. By then he had no strength to kill one. When the flock was gone, he wondered if he'd seen them at all.

Oh, the Indians came after him all right the night he escaped—Neal and Moses and others with their dogs. Even the women came along, calling, "Larry, *minti. Minti.*" He had run hard, arms up to shield his face while his muscular legs carried him crashing through the darkness. Mile after mile he ran, over a wide-open prairie, then down the bank of a creek, which he followed until it emptied into a river. By then the clouds had broken, and the moon showed a sliver of itself against a blue-black sky. He lay on his stomach on the riverbank and brought water to his face in his cupped hands. Drinking lightly, he rested for several minutes and then set out again. Some of the bigheaded feeling that drove him at first had seeped away, and now he began to worry that not enough time had passed before they had missed him.

Daybreak caught him several miles down the river where only patches of sumac and hazel provided a place to hide. He went back up the river to where the banks were high and steep and in some places hollowed in and filled with bramble. He hid himself among the brush beneath the overhanging bank. His wet shirt and trousers hugged his shivering body. When the sun was full up, he began stripping off his clothes, thinking to dry them on the bushes. But he heard a stick snap on the bank above him. A horse and rider stood on the high bank opposite him, while two dogs nosed through the scrub oaks and thickets.

He waited, barely breathing, and when he was sure they had gone, he lowered himself into the river and moved upstream some fifty yards to where willow bushes grew out of the water. He climbed among them and within minutes, it seemed, he was surrounded by Indians tramping the high, rocky riverbanks above, raking the grass and thickets with poles and sticks, calling his name as though this were a child's game of hide-and-seek.

All day he watched through the leafy curtain the squaws hunting him and the men driving their dogs up and down the river. His body floated in the water of its own will, numbed by the cold. Throughout the night, he named camp sounds to himself—spitting fires, braying mules, the low beat of a drum.

The second day seemed to bring the hunters out thicker while he sat in the water with his head leaned against the river's muddy brim. Later in the afternoon, the activity grew less and finally ceased, but he stayed in his hiding place until the moon was high, and wolves set to howling.

The country around him was a table of dry grasses and sparse trees beneath a full moon. To the north lay a dark ridge and beyond that, he knew, another. The old slave of the Confederate general had drawn a map in the dirt. "Here's de mountains coming outta Arkansas 'bout a hundred miles," he had said to him and Wesley. "A strong walker can shore make it, but keep off de roads." Lower on the dirt map, he drew what he said was the Red River and two more lines. One angled from the Red River northeast, missing the mountains. The second followed the direction of the mountains and connected with the other. "Dis first one's the Texas Road. 'Bout two hundred miles nawtheast Federals controls it. De other road's the Fort Smith Road, leading to Boggy Depot. Best to stay shy of dat one. Never know who ya'll meet."

Facing north Lapsley figured he had the highest of the uplands ahead of him and probably the road from Fort Smith. He hoped the Texas Road was to his left. The night air was wicked to a body soaked to the skin, but he set out pumping his legs and arms, sticking north over rocky outcroppings. At dawn, hungry and tired, he reached pine-covered mountains and hunted a place to hide. Still he could see signs of settlement: cow paths, a patch of ground cleared for rails, faint curls of smoke. More Choctaw. Maybe some Creek too. The old slave had told him, "Git to where most the Cherokee living before you show yo'-self." So Lapsley lay among the underbrush and tried to sleep.

At dusk he rose and traveled on. That night and the next he walked among the pine, their presence promising some dark menace in wait. Hunger had settled in as a companion. In the light of a coming dawn, he could sometimes find a few hard berries the birds had missed. The corn sprouts in his pockets he ate without satisfaction.

The days and nights that followed became patches of time with no connections to one another. He climbed to a summit and down, only to find another sandstone rise, covered with a blackjack forest, before him. Endlessly he walked and walked and still the trees stood around him.

A little after sundown, while he was still climbing, a large mountain lion leaped from behind a boulder, unaware of Lapsley, and landed on a saucerlike stone that began to slide. The animal and stone tumbled end over end down the steep side of the mountain. Both startled and amused, Lapsley was glad for the sight. It meant he had passed from the concentration of settlements. Taking his chances with the beasts of the wilderness seemed a surer gamble.

He traveled night and day now, resting when he could get no more effort from his exhausted body, or when the sky clouded at night so that he couldn't tell one direction from another. Sometimes the broken shale slid beneath his feet and sent him sprawling, or the bramble raked his clothes and hands. He willed his feet to take each step, aware only of blurs that swayed and swelled around him.

At last he reached a valley of prairie grass as the sun showed midmorning. Traveling the balance of the day and part of the night, he came to a river flowing east. He hunted up a stout walking stick and waded the waist-high water over a rocky bottom. About midway a fish, half his size, it seemed, came tumbling downstream, striking his legs and knocking him underwater, bubbles and waves coming at him, as he worked to right himself. At last, he lay shivering on the north bank, able only to crawl into the relative warmth of cedar boughs growing low to the ground.

FOLKS TOLD HIM later they didn't know how he'd gotten through. Must have traveled two hundred miles on foot. Must have taken the better part of two months to get from the Red River to Fort Gibson. He liked to tell his Swede neighbors in Kansas he was too ignorant or too stubborn to quit.

The day he reached the deserted town, he found wild hogs and dogs had taken over. He was able to manage only a quarter of a mile at a time. His bones seemed to rattle in his skin. Always light-headed now, he struggled to focus on his surroundings. Mostly log houses, smokehouses, empty stores, burnt supply buildings. Once he swore he saw his old ma bending over a cistern. And there standing by a flagpole in his fine red coat was old Marse Lapsley from the Kentucky plantation.

Lapsley picked the first building he came to and hauled himself inside. A good place to die, he thought. Papers covered the floor of the building, and he took to lying on them, pulling some over him, dozing, dreaming. Later he walked around, looking for warm clothes or something to eat. Instead he gathered odds and ends, a dented tin pan, a cracked-handled axe, two ten-pound cannonballs, a dirty army blanket and a nearly empty match tin.

When darkness came that night, Larry heard wolves stealing into town. Their snarling and the squealing of the hogs mixed with his dreams of Wesley and the guard named Neal. In the morning, as he dragged himself to the town pump, he heard a commotion inside one of the vacant buildings. He watched as a fat hog emerged, squinty-eyed, through the doorway of an old supply shed.

He knew what he must do. With a length of rope he found rotting on the flagpole, he fixed the door so that he could fasten it shut once an old hog ventured inside. Morning after morning he checked the shed but found it empty. By now, the ground had begun to swing under his feet. The faces of people he used to know floated before him—Old Man Stancel and Wesley giving him a wave.

One morning, when he dragged himself to the old shed, he heard something scraping and scratching inside. On his hands and knees he crept through the doorway. There rubbing against a post in the middle of the room was a good-sized, bristly hog. Backing out, Lapsley tied the door closed.

He had to study over how to kill it.

With the army blanket he slid the cannonballs and the broken-handled axe over to the shed. The first ball he tossed hit the hog on the snout, and the animal let loose with a wicked squeal. The second ball had the same noisy results. Seeing no other choice, Lapsley picked up the axe and climbed light-footed into the building with the hog.

In the farthest corner of the room, he saw a box bed with splintered crosspieces. The hog had backed into the opposite corner. Lapsley closed the door and approached the hog, holding the axe like a weapon. He struck the hog across the snout. The hog threw up his head and came straight at him, but Lapsley moved behind the center pole in the room. The hog hit the pole dead on, wheeled and ran under the bed. Lapsley hurried to pull a loose board free from the bed and barricaded the animal in his hiding place. Then he sat down to rest. His head ached. What strength he had came from the prospect of eating. He tried not to think of all that needed to be done yet. Lapsley began pulling off more boards from the bottom of the bed. The animal was wedged in so tightly that it couldn't move. With all his strength he struck it with the axe head. The hog squealed.

"It's you or me," he said. "You or me. And it ain't gonna be me." He swung the axe again. Resting briefly, he swung it again and again. Finally, the beast ceased his squealing, blood pooling between his ears. Lapsley sunk to the floor and rested his head on the bed frame.

How many times had he and Wesley butchered a hog? He got his fire going first outside the little shed, gathering loose papers and plenty of wood. The third of four matches from the tin made the paper leap into flame and when it was strong, he stripped off a piece of skin from the hog's ham and then cut a palm-sized slice of meat. Using a long stick, he skewered the ham slice and hung it over the fire. The first bite, fully chewed, doubled him over when the meat hit his gut. He lay on the hard ground beside the fire and waited for the pain to stop.

Three hours passed before he could eat again, this time a smaller bite. But he found himself stronger. He set to work skinning and butchering the hog and lugging its remains out from under the bed and to the fire. Then he smoked the meat, hanging the hams, shoulders and other cuts on the poles over the fire. The rest of the hog he left for the wolves.

THE DECEMBER SUNLIGHT pushing through Abbie Robinson's curtains cheered his sickroom and made him care about living again. The ground was too hard frozen for fieldwork, but there were things he could do. He felt the aches in his old body draining away. He would take that trip into Oklahoma Territory with his friend Parsons. The long-ago trek had been terrible for a fellow to make. He'd suffered more than he'd told about. But he'd have to say now it was worth it. Got him a good life. He'd been his own boss, with the final papers on his claim to prove it.

Lying peaceful in his bed now he could look forward to the coming day. Believing in himself, much like he did the day he set out from North Fork Town over thirty years ago.

HE TOOK A WEEK to build up his strength, going farther each day with a walking stick to keep him steady, feeling his leg muscles hardening and his shoulders growing tight again. The day he left town, he piled the smoked meat in the blanket, knotted it and slung it over his back. He followed the main town road north to where he'd seen a river flowing east, wide but crossable by a natural rock bridge. Beyond the river, the road took up again and bore the scars of heavy wagon travel and the haste of mounted riders.

Two days walking brought him within the tink-tink sound of a cowbell. He saw that the road he had been following continued north, and to his right was a wide river. The sun was low in the west. Men were fishing and walking on both sides of the river. When Lapsley got within two hundred yards, he saw an Indian woman crossing the river toward him in a skiff. She arrived at the bank long before he did and jumped out, preparing to wash clothes on a large rock that erupted from the water. The woman, dressed in a knee-length shift the color of clover, her dark hair plaited down her back, saw him coming toward her. She left her piles of washing and jumped into the skiff.

Larry stopped a few feet from her and put down his sack. "Please, ma'am. I'd like to get across." He gestured to the river and then, thinking to pay her in smoked hog, swung his makeshift sack off his shoulder and started to untie the top. The woman began to speak, loudly, nodding her head and motioning for him to get into the boat. She spoke a different language from that of his Choctaw captors, and something told him that was good. Still, his stomach lurched when he realized that on the far bank Indian men, dressed like settlers with pistols and rifles, stood and watched them.

Lapsley got out of the boat, thinking to let them make the first gesture. But they only looked at him and each other. The only sign he could think to make was to rub his belly. One fellow, his brown face broad and sober, gestured for him to follow and led Lapsley into the woods until they came to a sprawling Indian camp. Makeshift shelters, as well as permanent log cabins, filled every space among the trees. He saw fireplaces built of stone, animal sheds, a crisscross of narrow roads that could send the traveler in any direction. Children carrying wood or playing in the leaves stopped and watched him pass, but no one seemed surprised by the sight of him.

The Indian led Lapsley to a little shanty where an old woman and two girls set about getting him something to eat. They seemed to want to talk, but he could only smile and shrug his shoulders so the woman and girls turned back to their cooking. When the food was ready, the man motioned to Lapsley to sit up to the table. He shook his head, meaning to take his plate outside, but the Indian pulled out one of three straight-back chairs. The old woman sat at the left-hand side of Lapsley and the man at the right. The woman kept his plate full. They had biscuits, coffee and meat. Lapsley's belly began complaining about the food. He stopped and sat back in his chair, stretching to make more room in his insides. Everyone stared at him, even the two young girls. The plateful of food he'd put away too fast was punishing him and he left the table to go outside.

Presently the man came out and motioned Lapsley to go with him. They walked through the town, kicking up leaves and pine needles. He turned and saw that men and young boys were gathering behind him. They began to walk up a grassy incline. Ahead lay brick buildings, grazing animals, cannons and tin canisters, as well as men in blue uniforms. Larry turned at a sound behind him and realized a swarm of Indians followed them. They all seemed eager to talk with him. Now wasn't that strange? Too bad Wesley hadn't come along. He'd have been busting his buttons over this.

From the Salina Republican Journal,
December 17, 1897:

We regret to chronicle the death of Larry Lapsley, the well-known farmer of Liberty Township, who died of heart disease last evening at the home of B.F. and Addie Robinson. Acquainted with Luke Parsons, a veteran of the Third Indian regiment serving during the last war at Fort Gibson, Indian Territory, Mr. Lapsley accompanied him to Kansas after the war. A familiar sight to students at Star School District, he occasionally stopped to visit, admonishing the young people to study hard. "I was 'most thirty years before I learned to read," he used to say, "and I regret terrible those years that I was so ignorant." The Robinsons have erected a monument at their friend's grave which reads, "If the Son shall make you free, you shall be free indeed."

Separating the Wheat from the Tares, Being a True Account of the Death and Life of Orrin Porter Rockwell

ROD MILLER

Rod Miller has the singular distinction of being the only author to send me a *White Hats* and a *Black Hats* story about *the same person.* Orrin Porter Rockwell's was, according to Rod, the most obscure of the larger-than-life legends of the West. Did Rockwell make it into *Black Hats*? I guess you'll have to buy that book, as well, and see.

Rod is a poet and columnist whose work has appeared in such periodicals as *The Denver Post, Elko Daily Free Press, Western Horseman,* and *American Cowboy.* A book of Western humor, *You Ain't No Cowboy If . . . ,* is scheduled to be published in 2002.

★

I am the last man to see Porter Rockwell alive.

In the early hours of the afternoon of 9 June 1878 he passed on to his reward in his office at the Colorado Stables where I am hostler. Since the last words to pass his lips fell upon my ears and mine alone, I feel obliged to set down the events of that day and the night previous, leaving a true and accurate record to refute the rumors and speculations concerning his death.

Having known the man over a number of years it seems my duty, as well, to set straight the facts of his life and rebut the claumny that dogs him even in death. He had not grown cold in his grave when the *Salt Lake Tribune* libeled him in its columns thus:

> *The gallows was cheated of one of the fittest candidates that ever cut a throat or plundered a traveler. Porter Rockwell is another in the long list of Mormon criminals whose deeds of treachery and blood have reddened the soil of Utah, and who has paid no forfeit to the law. He was commissioned by the Prophet Joseph Smith avenger-in-chief for the Lord when the Latter-day Saints were living a troublous life on the border, and arrived in this Territory where the fanatical leaders of the Church suffered no restraint, and the avenging angels were made bloody instruments of these holy men's will. Porter Rockwell was chosen as a fitting agent to lead in these scenes of blood.*

The absurdity of these slanders is plain to all familiar with "Port" but painful to his memory even so. The true facts attest that Porter Rockwell was the finest peace officer, bodyguard, bounty hunter, pioneer, tracker, scout, and guide to ever carry sawed-off .36-caliber Navy Colt pistols in his coat pockets.

Allow me, now, to begin my account at the end.

THE LAST WORDS Porter Rockwell spoke came in reply to a question of mine. We had talked off and on since his arrival at the Colorado Stables at about one o'clock in the morning. He kept a small seldom-used office there.

Most of his time the past few years was spent at his ranch away out on Government Creek, but he occasionally came to town to visit his family and tend to the remnants of his freighting business. He sometimes slept on a cot in that office, as he did that final night.

Port had escorted his daughter Mary to watch Denham Thompson play the lead in *Joshua Whitcomb* at the Salt Lake Theatre. After seeing her home, he spent a quiet hour at a saloon before walking the three blocks to the stable to retire. He arrived here just after one o'clock. He slept a few hours, then awoke complaining of cold and a sick stomach. We talked off and on as he dozed and thrashed uncomfortably through the remainder of the night and morning. Shortly after midday, he was again taken by chills and vomiting. He struggled to sit up and pulled on his boots.

"Port!" I exclaimed. "How are you?"

"Wheat. All wheat," he replied weakly.

He then lapsed into unconsciousness, never to awaken again in this world—to die, as the saying goes, with his boots on.

Perhaps his final words bear explanation. "Wheat" was a favorite expression of Porter Rockwell's, heard often by those who knew him. Some claim it is of uncertain origin, but I know where it comes from and what it means because Port told me. It is from the thirtieth verse of the third chapter of *The Gospel According to St. Matthew:* "Gather ye together first the tares, and bind them in bundles to burn them: but gather the wheat into my barn."

So, all that was good was by Port described as "wheat" variously meaning "all is well" or "that is good" or "everything is fine" and such like. His detractors take it further, using the scripture against him—it is the reason, they say, he killed the forty or eighty or one hundred and more they claim for him; they were but "tares" to be destroyed.

I asked Port one time about the deaths attributed to his

hand. His answer was as simple and direct as the man himself: "I never killed anybody that didn't need killing."

ON THE DAY of his death, Rockwell was, in fact, awaiting trial for the Aiken affair. In the autumn of 1877 he had been indicted, arrested, and jailed for murder. Only fifteen thousand dollars bail posted by friends kept him from languishing in a cell awaiting the term of the district court. Anti-Mormon prosecutors obtained from a grand jury with similar leanings a True Bill accusing Port and Sylvanus Collett of murdering John Aiken *twenty years before!* I heard the story from Port himself, and here is the truth of that matter.

Painted by lawyers for the government as innocent and unsuspecting travelers set upon by Brigham Young's Destroying Angels, the Aiken party was, in reality, a band of opportunistic California gamblers. Decked out in Texas hats and riding silver-studded Mexican saddles on fine horses, the party of six, led by John Aiken and his brother Tom, arrived in the Territory in late fall 1857. Hearing that the United States Army was marching to attack and occupy Utah Territory, they had set out from southern California with a considerable stake and a gambling outfit including playing cards and dice and a faro layout, intending to pick the soldiers clean.

The bunch was arrested before even reaching Great Salt Lake City. Jailed in Ogden and later transferred to the territorial capital, the Aiken party was held for two weeks or so while authorities decided what to do with them. They determined to release the Californians and escort them from the Territory on the southern route to prevent any possible contact with the approaching army. Port was assigned to lead the escort party, duly authorized by law.

"Four of us took four of them south, two of the gamblers being allowed to stay at large in the city until spring,"

Port said. "We was camped on the Sevier River when I was woke up by some commotion, which was our charges attempting an escape. One of them fancy men had the best of Collett and so I shot him, but he run off through the bushes with a bullet of mine in his back. Them two Aikens and the other'n was down and I figured them dead so we dumped the bodies in the river. Come dawn we rode north considering the job a bad one, but a finished one just the same."

The next afternoon, the wounded outlaw stumbled barefoot into the town of Nephi bleeding from his head and the bullet wound in his back. The local sawbones probed for the bullet, and, sure enough, it was the same caliber as Port's Colts. Later in the day, the townfolk were surprised by the arrival of another of the outlaws—this one John Aiken, obviously not as dead as believed—apparently revived by the cold water of the Sevier River. He, too, was barefoot and bleeding from head wounds. Four or five days later, the pair had healed enough to travel and asked to be driven to Great Salt Lake City. Two young men volunteered for the job.

Eight miles north of Nephi, the party had stopped to water the team at Willow Creek when the door of the sheepherder's shack there flew open and blasts from a shotgun cut down the wounded gamblers. The boys lit out of there and Aiken and his traveling companion were never seen again, dead or alive.

Twenty years after the fact, Port and Sylvanus Collett were blamed in the mysterious Aiken affair on the flimsiest of evidence—or a complete lack thereof if you ask me. Port refused even to cooperate in his defense, "Wheat" being his only reply to questions from his lawyers.

Laying the blame on Porter Rockwell is not a recent development. As far back as the thirties, when the Mormons were abused and mobbed by Missouri Pukes, Port was accused of being chief of the "Danite" bands that retaliated against the mobs. Then, when Governor Lilburn Boggs ordered the Mormons evicted from Missouri *or exterminated* and an assassin attempted his life in reply, that, too, was attributed to Rockwell.

There was no credible evidence in either case, and I believe that if Port had set out to kill Boggs he would be dead today. Whether with pistol, rifle, or shotgun, his skills as a marksman were the stuff of legend—as you will see from the facts behind another of his more famous escapades, as related to me by the legend himself.

THE YEAR WAS 1845, and the place was Hancock County in Illinois, not far from the city of Nauvoo and not long after a mob had jailed and murdered the Mormon prophet Joseph Smith and his brother Hyrum.

Port was a favorite of Joseph Smith's, appointed by him in his capacity of mayor of Nauvoo as a deputy marshal and personal bodyguard. In fact, Rockwell's long, flowing locks were the result of his association with Smith, who prophesied, "Orrin Porter Rockwell—so long as ye remain loyal and true to thy faith, ye need fear no enemy. Cut not thy hair and no bullet or blade can harm thee." A true prophecy as it turned out. But I digress.

The other characters in the incident at hand were Frank Worrell, leader of the Carthage Grays, a so-called militia unit that murdered the incarcerated Smiths; and county sheriff Jacob Backenstos, unpopular in the area because the mobocrats accused him of sympathy with the Mormons.

Rockwell tells the tale:

"I was watering my horse alongside the Warsaw Road when I spies Backenstos whipping up his horses and flying down the road towards me in a carriage. Coming over the rise a ways behind was two men a-horseback. Jacob hauled in the lines in a cloud of dust and hollered to me, 'Rock-

well, in the name of the State of Illinois, County of Hancock, I order you to protect me from the mob at my heels!'
I had my pistols and a rifle so I told the sheriff not to
worry. I didn't know so at the time, but five other men was
behind the riders, coming on hard in a rig and a light
wagon.

"One horseman was well ahead of the other. Backenstos
hails him and orders him to halt. Instead, he pulls out a pistol. By now I seen I was facing that sonofabitch Frank
Worrell so I shot him."

The sheriff later said in official reports that the rifle bullet, fired from a distance of 100 to 150 yards, tore through
Worrell's chest and launched him from the saddle. The
other rider, and the men in the two outfits that had by now
arrived on the scene, lost heart at the sight of their leader
bleeding in the dirt. Loading the dying body in the wagon,
they turned tail.

" 'Well, I got him, Jacob. I was afraid my rifle couldn't
reach him, but it did. Only missed a little bit.' 'What do
you mean?' he asks me, and I says, 'I aimed for his belt
buckle.' "

ANOTHER SILENT WITNESS to Port's long-distance
accuracy with his weapons was the unidentified scape-
grace behind the Great Bullion Robbery of 1868. The
Overland Stage, eastbound out of California, was held up
in the Utah desert and relieved of some forty thousand dollars in gold. The driver pushed on to Faust Station, next
along the line, where Port was to board the stage as a Wells
Fargo shotgun guard for the run to Fort Bridger. Instead, he
mounted up and rode off on the stage's back trail in pursuit
of the thief.

"He was a wily one," Port told me one time, "taking
care to cover his tracks and otherwise confuse his movements. But I catched him up on Cherry Creek, two days

after taking up the trail. The gold was in the ground, I figure, so I lay low keeping an eye on him. After a week or so
of skulkin' around out there, he's sure he's not being followed so he sneaks off and digs up the gold. About the
time the last bar comes out of the hole, I draw down on him
and make the arrest without incident.

"Me, that gold, and the outlaw make our way to my
place on Government Creek where I has Hat Shurtliff keep
an eye on him while I gets some sleep, which I had been
missing a lot of, you see. Ol' Hat, though, he fell asleep on
the job and wakes up just as the prisoner clears the corral
gate on one of my horses. I stagger outside whilst trying to
peel back my eyelids and blink out the blur just in time to
see him skyline on a little ridge east of the cabin. Them
stubby Colts of mine ain't much for distance, but I fired all
the same.

"Well, I figures I missed since I didn't see no evidence
to say otherwise. So's I finished up my sleeping and gets
things in shape at the ranch then hauls the gold on into the
Wells Fargo office in Great Salt Lake City, where there's a
report of a dead man found propped up agin a telegraph
pole. Seems his horse had wandered off, leaving the poor
soul to bleed to death from a bullet wound in the back. I
never saw the body. But I suspect I'd of recognized him."

THE INFAMOUS LOT Huntington felt the effect of
Porter Rockwell's marksmanship from a range close
enough to look the fearsome lawman in the pale blue eyes.

The cause of the whole affair was the Honorable John
W. Dawson, vacating Utah in the dead of night following
a glorious three-week term as governor of the Territory,
during which time he had managed to aggravate enough
folks high and low with his debauched behavior that he
feared for his life. Which, by the way, would have been no
great loss.

While waiting at the stage station, the disgraced Dawson was set upon and pistol-whipped by a half dozen drunken cowboys who left him for dead and rode off into the windy winter night. Dawson survived and identified one Lot Huntington, a known petty outlaw and rustler, as leader of the gang. Local police had no success in locating the accused after two weeks of searching, at which time the story takes a curious turn.

A strongbox containing eight hundred dollars cash belonging to the Overland Mail disappeared from the Townsend Stable, along with Brown Sal, one of the finest horses in the Territory. Suspicion again centered on Lot Huntington and his crowd, who were seen leaving the vicinity and heading west. A posse was formed to take up the chase, with Porter Rockwell in the lead. The posse passed through Camp Floyd some several hours behind the bandits and rode hard through the night to Faust Station, where Port spotted Brown Sal under a shed in the corral. He takes up the tale from there, as best I remember his telling it.

"It was coming on morning and we was cold and tired and the wind was hard and bitter. But, wanting to avoid any unnecessary gunplay, I elected to surround the station and wait and see. Along about sunup, Faust himself comes out of the inn to do his chorin' and I beckons him over to where I was hidden. He tells me Huntington is in there with two others eating their breakfast.

"So I sends Faust back inside to explain the situation, figuring they'd see the hopelessness of their plight and come out with hands up as instructed. Well, lo and behold, next thing I know Lot Huntington comes strollin' out pretty as you please with a big ol' .44-caliber cap-and-ball pistol in his fist. I calls out a warning and shoots in the air but he walks on over to them corrals like he ain't got a care in the world. I rushes over to the shed just as he's swingin' onto Brown Sal bareback and I hollers out another warning. Lot aims that pistol at me but before he could fire I unloaded eight balls of buckshot from my Colt into his belly. He gets all tangled up in the fence rails fallin' off that horse and made a strange picture danglin' there and dyin'."

The other two surrendered without further violence, and Port and the posse delivered the corpse, the prisoners, the strongbox, and Brown Sal to the authorities back in the city. While unsaddling his horse minutes later, Port hears gunfire.

"With pistols in hand I ran back to where I left the prisoners with the police. 'What happened?' I asks the constable and he says all matter-of-fact, 'Tried to escape.' But I looked at them bodies close, and both was powder-burnt and one shot in the face. How the hell that happened I couldn't discern, lessen he was runnin' away backwards."

A FINAL INCIDENT, selected from many, must suffice as testimony to Porter Rockwell's skills as horseman and tracker. Known far and wide for his ability to handle horses no other could master and getting more miles from a mount than possible as a practical matter—with no ill effects on the animal—Port was sometimes accused of thinking more like a horse than a horse did. The upshot was a relentlessness on the trail that, combined with seeing sign where there wasn't any, made Port the first one called upon when there were rustlers to be caught.

One story, as I say, will serve. It was told to me not by Rockwell, but by letter from Frank Karrick, a freighter who hauled goods between Sacramento and Great Salt Lake City and was the beneficiary of Port's services in recovering a herd of stolen mules. I quote his missive at some length:

I was 70 miles south of Great Salt Lake City back in '61 when several valuable mules disappeared in the night. Upon discovering my loss in the morning, I left the teamsters to guard the wagons, goods, animals &c while I went off in pursuit but soon lost the trail in a confusion of hoofprints. Knowing no other recourse I reported the crime in Great Salt Lake City where B. Young himself suggested I enlist the support of Orrin Porter Rockwell. Upon retaining his services we repaired to the place I lost the trail, now three days cold. Rockwell examined the ground for a time and pointed out the track we were to follow. Asking how he knew, he answered, "Never mind. They've only taken the shoes off the mules. We'll just stay on this trail."

About dusk the trail again became entangled, having been crossed by a large herd of cattle. Rockwell expressed no dismay and followed up the herd. After dark, we approached the drover's camp, unnoticed until reaching the edge of the firelight where Rockwell reined up. Soon we were looking down the barrels of several firearms in the hands of the startled men in the camp, one of whom hollered, "Stay right where you are or the shooting starts!" Rockwell answered in his squeaky voice, "Wheat, fellers, wheat." Either the voice or the term had meaning in the camp, as the reply came back, "Port! Step down and join us! Supper's soon ready and the coffee's hot."

(Note: Perhaps I neglected to mention that rough and tough though he was, Porter Rockwell's voice did not match; it being rather high pitched and tending to break higher when excited. This fact was not to his liking. Likewise, his hands were small and well formed, almost feminine in appearance and not at all in keeping with what one might expect in a so-called "rough character." Continuing now with Karrick's report.)

After sharing the warmth of the fire through the night and a hot breakfast, both courtesy of the men moving the cattle, we rode out ahead of the cowboys as they were lining out the herd at first light. As if he never doubted their course or destination, Rockwell soon pointed out the tracks of my stolen mules. We pushed hard through the day. Near sunset, we trotted up a rise and saw a faint trace of dust in the far distance. Rockwell rustled about in his saddlebags and produced a telescope. "Two men . . . some horses . . . and mules—come on!" he said. And go on we did, with haste.

For the second time in as many evenings, we rode up on men hunched around a campfire. This time Rockwell did not wait to be noticed but instead rode right into the rustlers' camp (there can be no doubt on this point—my mules were clearly visible in the fading light, grazing on the banks of a nearby stream) with snub-nosed Colt revolver in hand.

I regret my tale lacks the excitement of a shoot-out (although I did not regret it at the time), but the fact is the two were visibly frightened of Rockwell and offered no resistance. They were soon behind bars, my mules back in harness, and Rockwell gone home richer by $500 worth of my gratitude. On reaching my destination in California, I rewarded him further with the shipment of a hand-tooled saddle and demijohn of fine whiskey. I heard later he was vastly more interested in the whiskey than in the saddle.

In all my years of freighting, never once did I have the pleasure of meeting a better man than Porter Rockwell. His ability as a tracker I have never seen equaled. Nor have I seen another who commanded such presence among men, as demonstrated by the gladness and the fear I saw in the faces of the cowboys and the outlaws, respectively, we encountered during our brief expedition. My gifts did not begin to repay Porter Rockwell and I consider myself ever in his debt.

> *Respectfully,*
> *(signed) Frank Karrick*
> *Sacramento, Calif.*

By now it ought to be clear to even the most skeptical that Orrin Porter Rockwell was a credit to his people and a force for law and order. I could tell more. But I fear the lies and venom would yet outweigh any further words I could put to paper.

The reports of his death by poison or by bullets or by a beating administered by various people he is said to have wronged are likewise false. He died, as I have said, in his office at the Colorado Stables in my presence. The coroner's jury, influenced by the testimony of four physicians, determined there was "no evidence of injury, nor any symptoms of poisoning" and the death a result of the "failure of the heart's action, caused by a suspension of the nervous power."

If that description is correct, it is the only time Porter Rockwell ever lost his nerve.

Ribbons and Gee-Strings

CANDY MOULTON

Candy Moulton is invaluable to the Western Writers of America in many ways, not the least of which is in her capacity as editor of its house publication, *Roundup* magazine. She's written nine historical books, including *The Grand Encampment: Settling the High Country* and *Roadside History of Wyoming*. Here Candy proves herself equally adept at fiction with this tale of female freighter Sarah Ferris set, coincidentally enough, in the Grand Encampment.

★

Sarah Ferris cursed her damn dead husband as she slapped the harness over the back of the sixth mule in her hitch. He'd left her to handle the freight runs alone, not even having the decency to die in a tragic accident. Hell no, he'd sat down in the chair by the fire in their cabin, propped his feet up, and let his heart just stop beating. She'd cursed him for that every day since his death.

If he had to up and go and leave her alone to do this job, by the goddamn Sam hell the least he could have done was to die decently, say in an avalanche or a runaway with the team, the way old George Ferris did. George's widow, Julia, had collected the condolences from an entire county, along with all the pity and sympathy any rich window ever reaped. They weren't even as close as apron-string relatives, Sarah Ferris and Julia Ferris, not to even consider shirttails. Sarah never wished they were, she didn't fit in with Julia's cultured ways, her prim and proper attitude.

Dealing with mule teams for years had wiped out any culture Sarah ever thought of having, pitched out the barn door with the manure. But now, as she hooked the last tug on the mule's harness to the singletree, she cursed again. This time she vented against the weather. The wind pushed at her long brown wool skirt. It pulled at her dusty brown hat, pulled low over her eyes and tied down with a scarf so it wouldn't sail to Saratoga.

"Goddammit, mules, let's get on the road," Sarah railed as she hitched her skirt and stepped onto the hub of the tall freight wagon. Settling her bulk onto the rag rug she'd folded over into a pad on the wooden plank seat, Sarah lifted the lines, setting the six leather ribbons between her fingers before kicking the brake. "Kate, Jim, head on out now," Sarah said, twitching the lines ever so slightly.

The lead mules threw up their ears at her command. They leaned into their collars and broke the wagon loose from its ground-tied position.

Sarah hated the hard wooden seat. The rag rug might as well not even have been between her and the board for all the good it did. She wished she could ride her wheel mule, like Gee-String did. It would be much smoother on the back of the mule than on the unforgiving board seat. But, though she drove mule teams and freight wagons, she had yet to abandon her skirts for trousers. The women already looked down their noses at her because she drove the wagon. *Hell, that's probably why they practically ignored me after that damn husband of mine up and let his heart quit beating. If I'da sat around tatting or sewing or gossiping with them like that snippety Julia Ferris, they wouldn'ta treated me like they did.*

In her grief six months earlier, Sarah hadn't realized

where the food came from in the days following the death. She didn't remember making arrangements for his funeral, but she knew that he had a spot in the Grand Encampment Cemetery. She knew the spot well, she'd been there before, once, with him. That's when the hardening began.

But she didn't think of that now. Instead she concentrated on the teams, working the lines, keeping the animals pulling together as they made their way through Grand Encampment's wide streets, past the new red-brick Emerson & Henry building, not seeing the women on the sidewalk, nor the men huddled near the town hall. She had a load of cable she needed to get up the mountain, to deliver to the crews stringing it along the tramway route.

It was a marvel, the tramway being built between the North American Copper Company Smelter down by the river and the Ferris-Haggarty mine sixteen miles away, across the divide at Rudefeha. Not part of her family legacy, the Ferris-Haggarty, but belonging to that rich widow Julia. Damn her for having everything, even a new mansion over in Rawlins City, while Sarah still lived in the one-room log cabin where her damn husband gave it up last winter.

THE TENSION AND anger melted as the mules pulled their load up the rutted road. Driving did that for her, brought peace to a troubled soul. That's why she did it. Not for the money, though the pay was necessary if she and the mules intended to keep eating, but for the chance to be alone, moving at a pace where she could watch for rabbits and coyotes, where she could study the carvings the Basque herders had left on the aspens. Only when she was driving did the turmoil subside.

Sarah rested the team occasionally, letting the mules blow and flexing and relaxing her own fingers that had become cramped from holding and handling the lines. She reached Battle late in the afternoon, stopping the wagon near the livery barn and unhitching with a calm in complete juxtaposition to her morning anger. She fed the mules some grain she'd brought in a burlap bag in the back of the wagon, rubbing their ears after she'd brushed their hides.

If only I could maintain this calmness. But Sarah knew by morning she'd be cursing and angry all over again. The lonely nights did that to her and she faced another one at the hotel just shy of the Continental Divide.

THE SUN BARELY touched the top of the mountain where Sarah harnessed her mules, when Jake kicked her. The blow pitched Sarah against the side of the heavy freight wagon and she groaned in agony as her shoulder popped from its socket, snapping her collarbone in the process. Fighting for balance and control over the pain, she ground her teeth and sucked in high, thin air. No tear escaped from beneath her black lashes. The first wave of pain subsided and Sarah turned to the mules, stripping harness that just minutes before she'd thrown over their backs. Leading them with her uninjured right arm, she put the animals back into the stable yard.

No one else in town stirred as Sarah started walking west. Doc Perdue was in Rambler for the summer. She'd go to him and get her shoulder fixed up. Red waves danced before her eyes as the pain returned, subsided, flooded back. Carefully placing one foot after the other, she stepped from the Atlantic rocks to the Pacific side of the mountain, and descended toward the crystalline blue beacon that was Battle Lake, with the small town of Rambler beside it.

Doc Perdue still had his nightshirt on when Sarah lifted the latchstring on his door.

"Dear heaven, woman, what happened?" Doc asked,

seeing the ashen color of her usually robust face as he guided Sarah through the door.

"Mule knocked me against the wagon. Can you fix up my shoulder?" Sarah sank into the chair he placed behind her knees.

"Let me get some chloroform to ease the pain." Doc turned from his patient.

"Can't. It'll kill me. Bad heart." Sarah said with a grimace. "Heart already got my damn husband, I'm determined it ain't gonna get me too."

"But, Miz Ferris, fixing you up will be mighty painful without something to ease you."

"I can take it, Doc. Just get it fixed up. I got a load to haul up to the mine today."

"Well, then. Bite down on this," Doc said, handing her a piece of fire kindling.

Sarah clenched the wood between strong teeth, squeezed her eyes tightly and grabbed onto the arm of the chair with her good hand. The red haze washed over and over her as Doc pulled her shoulder into position and wrapped bandages to hold her collarbone in place.

When he'd finished, he poured whiskey into two cups. "Here Sarah, to your strength," the doc said, handing her one cup as he slung the other against his own lips.

"I don't drink."

"It's not a libation. It's medicine. Take it."

Sarah downed the whiskey in three swallows, and as it went down the tears fell for the first time since the mule pulled his trick. Sarah coughed and wiped her eyes. "Damn. That burned all the way down. Thanks, Doc." She rose and headed for the door.

"You ought to stay here. I'll hitch the team to my buggy and take you back over to Battle in an hour or so," Doc said to Sarah's back as she cleared the threshold.

"I can walk. Do me good. It'll clear my head."

The birds sang as Sarah made her way around the lake

to the trail leading up the mountain toward its rocky divide.

Sarah struggled with the harness, but managed to get it on the mules and deliver the cable to the mine, handling the ribbons as much as possible in her right hand and only putting three in her left palm when she needed to turn a corner or maneuver across the rocky trail below Rudefeha.

After making the delivery, Sarah turned the team toward home, letting the mules set their own pace and for the most part pick their own route. She made the delivery and then the downhill run in a day, pulled harness from the animals, brushed them only briefly, and then turned them not in to the corral, but instead in to the pasture where the animals rolled, finishing the job of easing their sweaty backs. Sarah closed the gate and went to the cabin, not even taking time to remove her skirt before she climbed into her bed, where she finally gave in to the pain that had started shortly after she threw her first harness of the morning and that had escalated with each twist and turn of the road, each bump and bounce of the hard wagon seat.

THE MULES THREW up their heads in anticipation when Sarah emerged from the cabin days later. "C'mon, get over here. Your holiday is over," Sarah said as she headed toward the pasture. The mules crowded her, each seeking a rub between the ears. It took Sarah longer than usual to harness and hitch; her shoulder ached and she had full use of only her right arm. But she managed, then drove the wagon out of the yard, back along the trail toward the smelter.

"You doing better?" Gee-String called as Sarah stopped her wagon beside his.

"Arm hurts like all bloody hell, but I'll manage," Sarah replied. "Once I get back on the road I'll get the kinks worked out."

"You could take a few more days off," Gee-String said as he climbed onto his left wheel horse, holding the single line, the gee-string, that he used to control his team, eight perfectly matched white horses. He called them his Stack of Whites. Holding the multiple ribbons for her team, Sarah marveled at his skill with the gee-string. The whites leaned into their harness and snaked up and over the hill separating the smelter from the town.

EACH DAY SARAH'S shoulder strengthened so that by the time the chokecherries ripened, she had full dexterity again. Her freight changed with the leaves. The tram cable was now in place so Sarah hauled supplies for the mining operations at the Ferris-Haggarty, returning to town with a load of copper ore in her wagon. Occasionally she took a load to the tie camps on East Fork. She liked going to the tie camps, though understanding the people in them could be a challenge. Most of the cutters were Swedes or Norwegians who spoke their native languages, laced with some English and quite a lot of profanity. At least Sarah understood, and could speak, the latter. They'd built a combination church/schoolhouse at the edge of their camp and the children always ran out to greet Sarah when she drove the mules out front.

Descending the mountain in late October, Sarah hunched her shoulders under the wool coat that had been her husband's. She had nothing of her own that was as warm as his coat and since he had up and goddamn died on her he didn't need it anyway. Snow swirled, making it hard to see the track and harder to see the Stack of Whites coming up the mountain toward her.

"You'll get out of this snow soon," Gee-String called as he rode by on the wheeler. Sarah envied him the warmth of the animal between his legs as she shivered on her hard plank seat. Each day she had layered on more clothes, including her dead husband's old union suit. Once red, it had faded to pink and had holes in the knees. She knew the men at the smelter and those at the mine saw her legs, now covered in the union suit, when she climbed on or off her wagon. When wearing a skirt it was impossible to get aboard without hiking it up. She might be a freighter, but Sarah had no intention of bucking tradition and donning trousers. The union suit was as far as she'd go, and that only because she had to stay warm somehow.

As the snow piled up in the mountain country, Sarah's team took longer to make the run between Grand Encampment and Ferris-Haggarty. What had been a two-day trip became four. Now, returning to town, Sarah thought of her cabin. Even though the stove would be out, she knew it would only take a short time to warm the small space once she got a fire going. Thinking of a cup of tea at the end of the day, she huddled into the collar of her coat, only her eyes showing beneath the wool scarf she'd tied around her head.

The lead team balked when a coyote ran across the track ahead of them, the mules swinging to the left and off of the packed trail. They lunged as their front legs sank in the soft snow, pulling the other teams behind them. Sarah sawed the lines, urging the teams back onto the trail, but the mules panicked in the deep snow, pulling the wagon sideways off the solid snow-packed trail.

Sarah didn't need to stop the team; with all six mules mired to their bellies, they simply couldn't move anymore. Cursing, she climbed from the wagon and went to the lead team, using the shovel she carried with her to clear the snow. "You goddamn stupid mules. Kate, Jim, what the hell were you thinking?" she yelled as she pitched snow so she could unhook the leaders from the other teams. Sarah packed snow ahead of the animals, finally getting them free of their partial burial. Tying them to the wagon, so they stood on the packed trail, Sarah left her coat hanging on the side of the tilted wagon and then shoveled until she had freed the other two teams.

She wanted to remove more clothes, perhaps stripping down to the union suit, because the work was hard and hot and tiring. After moving the teams, Sarah shoveled around the wagon, clearing a path before rehitching the mules. Sweat ran down the animals' sides, just as it did Sarah's, by the time she had the wagon back on the hard-packed track. She'd barely finished the task when Gee-String came up behind her on the trail. Reading the story in the snow, he called with the wind, "Gotta keep 'em on the trail, Sarah."

Sarah threw a withering glance over her shoulder, not bothering to answer, but she saw the twinkle in the old freighter's blue eyes. Some of the other men derided Sarah, constantly telling her she ought to sell her teams and find a job at the boardinghouse. Not Gee-String. He might tease her, but his comments never cut, they never hurt. He'd encouraged her after her husband died. She suspected he recognized her need to drive the teams, to handle the wagon. He made the work of freighting appear as if it wasn't work at all, but rather a lark and a chance to be out in the glorious mountain country day after day.

But as much as the driving soothed her, no question remained—freighting in the Sierra Madre in winter tried spirits. Many of the men put their teams out to pasture, huddling in one of Grand Encampment's thirteen bars when the snow swirled. Sarah made runs on clear days. Or at least she started them on clear days. Often, by the time she went up the mountain to Battle she found herself enveloped in a blizzard.

By February even Sarah and Gee-String, the two most intrepid drivers, kept their teams on pasture.

★

THREE LOAVES OF bread raised on the table and Sarah savored the wood stove's warmth as she knitted a pair of wool socks. Her shoulder ached, throbbing in tune to the wind that pushed against the cabin. At times a gust hit the small log structure, causing it to shudder and creak. Sarah was grateful to be inside, warm, rather than out with a load. It took a minute for her to realize the pounding on the cabin door was human-caused and not wind-created. Setting her knitting beside the yeasty bread, she pulled open the wooden door. Doc Perdue stepped into the warm room; an open door in this weather was invitation enough.

"A skier just came in from East Fork," Doc said, shaking snow from his hat and coat. "Everybody up there is ill. They need medicine and they're short on food."

Sarah poured tea and handed the ceramic mug to the doctor. "It'll have to wait 'til this storm clears. None of the men will venture out in this weather," Sarah said.

"That's what they all said over at the Double O." Doc gulped the hot drink, wishing Sarah had added a dollop of whiskey like he'd gotten there. "Sarah, if they don't get the medicine, a lot of people are going to die."

"Goddammit, Doc, why are you telling me this?" Sarah said, knowing the answer.

"None of the men will make the run."

"And you think I would?" Sarah said, putting her bread in the stove.

"You're the only one, Sarah."

"What about Gee-String? If he won't go, I won't go."

"He would. He can't, fell two days ago and broke his leg."

"I hadn't heard. Haven't been out in this storm." Sarah wiped her hands on her apron. "Doc, it's dangerous out there. I don't think a team can get through the snow. It's too deep."

"Gee-String said he's got something for you; that you need to stop by his place on your way out of town." Doc downed the last of the tea. "Sarah, there are children at East Fork."

Sarah snorted. *Goddamn men, they expect me to make this run.* They'd sent Doc; they knew he could touch her soft spot, as no one else had been able to do in years. Not even her goddamn dead husband had been able to reach it. She finished the socks while the bread cooked.

"I'D MAKE THE run with you if I could." Gee-String grimaced as he shifted his left leg, which lay straight out before him, propped on a small stool. "Use my sled, and in the front stall of my barn you'll find snowshoes for the mules. Take an extra set, in case one of the bindings breaks."

"What the Sam hell are you talking about? Snowshoes for the mules?" Sarah stared at Gee-String, thinking he'd broken his head along with his leg.

The older teamster's blue eyes glinted. "You have snowshoes for yourself, right?"

"You know I do."

"Well, these are for the mules. They work the same way, have webbing on a framework. I got 'em from some of the Norwegians in the camps last time I was up there. I'd spent two days getting from Halfway House to East Fork because my teams were mired constantly."

"Do they work?" Sarah asked incredulously.

"Don't yours?" Gee-String replied.

"I'll return 'em in a few days, then," Sarah said, turning away from her old, and only, friend.

Hitting the well-packed trail, Sarah made good time to Elwood, carrying the medicine Doc had given her in the back of the sled. She had on the old wool coat, and had wrapped a buffalo robe around her legs. Though the wind buffeted her, the snow had stopped falling.

When Sarah turned off the main road above Elwood to

head south toward Halfway House, the pace slowed. Not as tightly packed, the trail slowed the mules, who sank to their forelegs in the snow. By the time she crossed the North Fork, the snow started again. As it piled on the track, Sarah stopped the team and put on the Norwegian snowshoes. The mules stamped their feet, no doubt wondering about the contraptions they now wore. Sarah put on her own webs and led the team up the trail. After a quarter of a mile she figured the animals had their snowshoes figured out, so Sarah took off her own and put them in the back of the sled. Hunched in her wool coat and buffalo robe, snow engulfed Sarah and her team.

The wind rose with the elevation; at times she couldn't see anything and simply trusted Kate and Jim to stay on the trail. She slid into Halfway House long after dark and found it deserted. For the past hour she'd been counting on help there. Sarah unhooked her teams, leading them into the barn where she unharnessed before forking some hay into the manger. From the back of the wagon she retrieved a sack of grain, pouring some into the wooden feed boxes for the mules.

Sarah had never seen Halfway deserted. She wondered where everybody was. At the roadhouse, she found the latchstring out, the stove cold, and a pile of kindling. She started the fire, melted some snow, and found some tea along with a frozen deer haunch. Sarah hacked off a chunk of the meat and fried it in a skillet. She drank a cup of tea, then rolled into her buffalo robe and fell asleep on the bed closest to the stove.

Shortly before dawn, Sarah fed her teams. Then she fried some more deer, drank some tea, washed the dishes, and harnessed. Snow swirled and it got lighter so Sarah figured the sun was up somewhere as she resumed the journey. Even with their snowshoes, the mules had a hard day of it. Sarah rotated the teams so Kate and Jim didn't break trail all of the time. Occasionally she put on her own snowshoes and walked with the animals, lightening the load on the sled. That movement also kept her warmer.

Crossing Soldier Summit, where troops had camped when doing reconnaissance during the Ute uprising in 1879, Sarah lost all sense of direction. Everything was white; the snow covered the ground and it filled the sky. There was no line where the two met. Back on the sled, Sarah, who always took care of her mules before she took care of herself, let them take care of her. Back in the lead Kate and Jim moved slowly, lifting each foot carefully, holding their noses down to the snow-drenched ground. The other teams and Sarah trusted them to stay on the trail; if they veered into the soft snow all of them might die.

I'll be there soon. At least I hope I will be. I hope this isn't my last trip. Her hands were numb, as were her feet encased now in the new wool socks she'd pulled on over the top of her boots. Sarah was so cold she couldn't think. She couldn't even curse. The wind played on the pipe organ of pines; the snow swirled. Kate and Jim plodded on, their snowshoes sinking into the ever-deepening snow with every step.

It had been dark for hours when the mules stopped. Sarah pushed back her buffalo robe, shook the snow from the wool scarf covering her head and realized she could see stars, and, just ahead of Kate and Jim, a light.

"Hello . . ." Her voice came out as a croak. She tried again, "Hello the cabin." Kate heard it, barely, turned toward Sarah and began to bray. The other mules joined in, causing an explosion from the cabin. Men tumbled out, wearing hobnail boots and wool pants held up with wide suspenders over their red union suits.

Voices cried in a babble of languages and Sarah felt someone lifting her from the sled. "My mules," she whispered to the burly man who carried her toward the cabin's light.

"We'll take care, put 'em in the barn with ours," the man told her in broken English.

"The medicine," Sarah began.

"You brought medicine?"

"In the bag beside my snowshoes," Sarah muttered as the man placed her on a rough-hewn bed.

"We'll get it. Bless you, the children are all so ill."

SOMEONE HAD REMOVED Sarah's wool socks and boots, as well as her wool scarf and coat, but she still had on the rest of her clothes. The bed was hard. Built of rough-cut lumber and covered with a mattress stuffed with grass or branches or something equally lumpy, it had no style. But the cabin was warm. It smelled of pine pitch, woodsmoke and sweat. Voices broke over her in a babble of languages. Children lay on beds; men huddled near the stove sitting on rough wooden chairs made by interlocking two wide boards to form an X-shaped seat.

Seeing Sarah sit up, a tiny woman moved from beside one of the children. "Mrs. Ferris, God will reward you richly." Mary Olson placed a knitted shawl around Sarah's shoulders.

"I doubt that, Mrs. Olson, I've cursed too much in my life."

"But the medicine you brought and the food, it will help the children, and the adults who are ill as well." The lines around Mary's eyes had deepened since Sarah last saw her, late in the fall.

"What happened, why is everyone so ill?" Now, three days after Doc asked her to bring the medicine, Sarah realized she didn't even know what it was for.

"We had an influenza outbreak about ten days ago; it spread throughout the camp. Already six adults have died and five children, including my Gertrude. Sven Andersen said he'd ski out and get help, but that was almost a week ago. We didn't think he made it. We didn't think anybody would come in this storm."

"If it weren't for Kate and Jim, and the snowshoes Gee-String gave me for the team, I wouldn't have made it." Sarah shuddered, her bones still cold.

"See, God watches over you, and us. And particularly the children, my others." Mary Olson handed Sarah a cup of tea. "Do you have children?"

The question stunned Sarah. Tears welled, spilling down her cheeks. "I had a daughter, Sally Ann. I lost her when she was only six. Influenza." Sarah brushed the salty streaks on her face, but the tears didn't stop.

"And now you have driven a team through this mountain country, bringing medicine so my children, and the others in our camp, can live. Oh, yes, Mrs. Ferris, you will be blessed."

WILD IRIS TURNED the yard green in front of Peryam's Roadhouse. "Whoa up there, Kate, Jim," Sarah called, setting the brake as the wagon rolled to a stop.

Gee-String saw her through the window, glancing up from his plate of sourdough flapjacks. The rocking chair seemed possessed as it teetered in the back of the wagon.

"So it's true, you're leaving?" he asked as Sarah pulled a chair beside his at the long table.

"Have to. This country is too tough. It got Sally Ann, then it got Jim. It'll take me, too, if I stay."

"Where you headed?"

"Nevada. Heard it's warmer there, not so much snow, fewer blizzards."

"Luck to you, Sarah. You're the toughest freighter in this country. Who'll we depend on next time there's a blizzard and somebody needs to make a run to East Fork or Battle?"

"I guess it'll have to be you, Jack. I put the snowshoes back in your barn."

Historical Note: Sarah Ferris freighted in the Grand Encampment Copper District from 1901 to 1904. In the summer of 1901 she crushed her shoulder between two wagons, walked from Battle to Rambler to get medical attention, and refused the use of chloroform because she, indeed, had a bad heart. In 1903, she was severely depressed and then broke her knee in an accident with her teams. In 1904 she left Grand Encampment for Goldfield, Nevada, where she freighted until December 23, when she moved a shotgun while freighting and the gun accidentally discharged. The shot hit her in the breast; she fell from her wagon and died lying between her teams.

Gee-String Jack Fulkerson also freighted in the Grand Encampment District, handling his teams with one line, known as a gee-string, and riding the left wheel animal in his hitch, which could include up to ten teams. His most well-known hitch was the one he called his "Stack of Whites." He remained in Grand Encampment throughout his life.

The freighters in Grand Encampment's Copper District used Norwegian snowshoes for their teams.

On August 20, 1899, George Ferris died when he was thrown from a wagon pulled by a runaway team. His widow, Julia, did have a mansion in Rawlins. They never made their home in Grand Encampment though they did own interest in the Ferris-Haggarty mine.

Day of Vengeance

JAMES REASONER

Without taking the trouble to go to my shelves and check, I would venture to say that James Reasoner has appeared in more of my anthologies than any other writer. Why? Three reasons. For one thing he's adept at crossing genres, so whether I'm doing a mystery collection or a western collection, he qualifies. Second, he always delivers and never disappoints, as with this gem about the early days of the Texas Rangers.

James is deeply involved right now in writing a series of novels about the Civil War. So far *Manassas, Shiloh, Antietam, Chancellorsville,* and *Vicksburg* have appeared, all from Cumberland House. If I'm not mistaken there are about seventeen more to come. I'm glad James took time out to write this story for us.

Oh yeah, I did say there were three reasons, didn't I? What's the third? That's easy. James never says "No!"

★

Was he on this side of the river, or had he already crossed over? That was the question we asked ourselves all morning as we pursued John Temple.

Of course, being good, upright Texans, and Rangers to boot, we were not going to let a little thing like an international border stop us, even if John Temple was already riding in the land of the *mejicanos.*

Captain Ford called a halt at noontime so that men and animals could rest. He dismounted and came over to me as I swung down from my saddle. In a quiet voice, he asked, "What say you, Doctor? Should Jennings be sent back to Laredo?"

I looked at Dave Jennings. Jennings had not yet dismounted. He sat on his big chestnut gelding, hunched over the saddle, his left arm pressed to his middle. His face was gray.

"If he persists," I said to Captain Ford, "I fear we shall be digging a grave ere long."

The captain nodded, his bearded face solemn. "I think you're right. I'll talk to him."

His tone of voice indicated to me that he would brook no argument. Command came naturally to Captain John Salmon Ford, or "Old Rip" as some of the men called him. The prankster of our company, "Doc" Sullivan, had given him that sobriquet. It seemed somewhat disrespectful to me, but Captain Ford never seemed to mind. I suppose he was confident enough in himself not to mind how people referred to him.

Tall, slender, erect in his carriage, with beard and hair already gone white despite the fact that he was not long past the prime of life, Captain Ford had been given command of this company of Rangers and instructed to bring law and order to the Texas border country. Our area of jurisdiction stretched from the gulf coast in the east to Brownsville in the south and up the Rio Grande far past Laredo. It was a large chunk of Texas, which in those days had either the hide off or the bark on, depending on which colorful descriptive phrase is preferred. The war between the United States and Mexico had been won, and the conflict which tore the states themselves apart was yet to come. The land in which we rode was menaced by Comanches from the west and Mexican bandits from the south, and our small group, which was already becoming known as "the Old Company" despite the relative youth of many of its members, faced daily dangers on its patrols.

Today, however, our quarry was not an Indian or a Mexican but rather a white man, a wanton murderer, which proves, I suppose, that the urge to spill blood is common to all races of men.

Captain Ford put his hand on the flank of Dave Jennings's horse. "Dave," he said, "I've been talking to the doctor, and we think you ought to turn around and go back to Laredo."

Gray-faced, Jennings shook his head and said, "You know I can't do that, Rip. It was my boy that bastard Temple gunned down. I got to see this through. I got to—"

He stopped and bent over even more in the saddle. His face was twisted with pain. His breath came faster. Captain Ford looked over his shoulder at me and said, "Doctor?"

I reached inside my saddlebags and brought out a small bottle of laudanum. It would dull the pain that Dave Jennings felt as his disease gnawed away at his vitals from the inside out. I took the bottle over to Jennings, pressed it in his hand, and said, "Just a little, Dave."

With his hand shaking, he lifted the bottle to his mouth and swigged from it. I reached up and retrieved the medicine before he could gulp down more. Within moments, as the drug's relief spread through his body, he was able to take a deep breath and drag the back of his hand across his mouth. "I'm all right now, Rip," he told Captain Ford. "Let's go get that son of a bitch."

Captain Ford squeezed his arm. "Go back to Laredo, Dave."

"No, sir. And I ain't a Ranger, so you can't order me to."

Captain Ford looked at me and shrugged. Jennings was right about that. He was not under the captain's command, other than to the extent that a civilized society requires any citizen to cooperate with its lawful authorities.

Of course, I am talking about Texas. In those days, and some would say still, the strictures of a civilized society barely applied.

I put the laudanum away. Doc Sullivan came over to me, grinning as usual. He enjoyed the fact that while *I* was a physician and the company's surgeon, *he* was the one called Doc. "Say, Doc," he said to me (he was the only member of the company to call me that), "you reckon Dave's gonna die 'fore we get back to Laredo?"

For all of Sullivan's jocularity, he was not a cruel man, so he couched his question in quiet tones that could not be overheard by Jennings. Speaking likewise, I replied, "I don't know, but I'm afraid he might."

Sullivan shook his head. "He's got a powerful thirst for vengeance. Reckon I would, too, if it was my boy who got kilt over some damned feud. It just don't make sense."

"Murder seldom does."

"But why would John Temple shoot Sam Jennings? Their families been gettin' along better lately."

Captain Ford came up behind Sullivan in time to hear the question. He put his hand on Sullivan's shoulder and said, "It's not our job to say why things happen, Doc. All we do is bring in the lawbreakers."

Sullivan nodded. "Yeah, I reckon. But I know both of them boys, Rip, and somethin' ain't right about this."

Captain Ford frowned and seemed to be thinking about what Sullivan had said, but before the discussion could continue, Roque Maugricio rode in. Half-Comanche, half-Mexican, Roque had been cast out by both and had found a home for himself with the Old Company as Captain Ford's tracker. No one knew the border country better than he.

Roque wore buckskin breeches, a linen shirt, and a broad-brimmed sombrero. He jerked a thumb over his shoulder and said to Captain Ford, "Temple's holed up in a bunch of rocks two miles upriver."

"On the American side?" asked Captain Ford.

Roque nodded. "Yep."

"He may be gone by the time we get there," Sergeant Level said.

"Nope," Roque said. "His horse is dead. He rode it out from under him trying to get away from us. Now he's just sitting there waiting for us."

"Well armed, I suppose," Captain Ford said.

"I wouldn't know. He spotted me, but he didn't take a shot at me."

The horses were rested now and had drunk from the river and cropped some of the sparse grass along its bank. Captain Ford called, "Mount up!"

We rode on, and as the afternoon grew hotter, Dave Jennings looked worse and worse. I kept an eye on him and from time to time saw him swaying in his saddle as if he were about to fall, but somehow he stayed on his horse and kept up with us. The need to avenge the death of his son gave him strength.

It did not take long to cover the two miles to the scattering of boulders where John Temple had taken refuge, but during that time I thought about what had led all of us to this place. The Temples and the Jenningses were two of the families that had come early to Texas, when it was still a colony of Mexico. Men from both families had fought at San Jacinto. Given what they had faced together, they should have been staunch friends.

Instead, a disagreement over a lady had prompted hot words, and guns had been drawn. Shots were exchanged. Neither of the combatants in that initial confrontation were fatally wounded, but blood had been spilled and hatreds forged. A feud was born that day, and since then, a dozen men had died, four on the Jennings side, eight on the Temple. But of late, as Doc Sullivan had said, it appeared that the feud was waning. Those who knew both families, as I did, hoped that it would finally come to an end.

Then, two days previous, John Temple had walked up to Sam Jennings on Laredo's main street, taken out a gun, and shot him in front of a score of witnesses. As he staggered backward, mortally wounded with blood staining his chest, Sam Jennings had cried out, "Why?" and John Temple had answered, "You know why."

Then, as Sam Jennings fell, John Temple had caught up a nearby horse and ridden out of Laredo as fast as the animal would carry him.

A party of Rangers from the Old Company, under the command of Captain Ford, had taken up the pursuit later that day. Dave Jennings, the father of the slain young man, had insisted on accompanying us. I knew that Jennings was in ill health and tried to dissuade him, but he would not listen. When I tried to insist, Captain Ford had said, "Let him come along with us, Doctor. You can't make a man stay behind when his boy's been killed."

The rocks came in sight, large ones scattered along the edge of a gentle bluff that sloped down to the Rio Grande. An ugly heap in front of them was John Temple's dead horse, lying where it had fallen when its heart finally beat its last. As we rode toward the rocks, I saw a puff of smoke from behind one of the boulders. A second later, as a bullet kicked up dirt in front of Captain Ford's horse, a flat crack sounded through the air. Captain Ford reined in and held up a hand, indicating that the company should stop.

In some men, such a reaction might indicate fear, but not on the part of Captain Ford. I knew him to be as very nearly fearless as it is possible for a human being to be. He rested his hands on his saddle and leaned forward to call, "John Temple! This is Captain John S. Ford of the Texas Rangers! Come on out of there!"

"The hell I will!" came the shouted response. "You won't take me back to Laredo to be lynched!"

"There will be no lynching! You will have a fair trial!" the captain promised.

John Temple's only reply was another shot. This one struck the ground near enough to the hooves of Captain Ford's horse that the animal danced nervously aside before the captain's firm hand on the reins calmed it.

Dave Jennings urged his horse forward, alongside Captain Ford's mount. "You see," he said. "He's gone mad. There was no reason for him to murder my boy like that. You have to ride in and take him, Captain."

Despite the nickname that gave the impression of a man who rushed about, Rip Ford was not one to be hurried. He waved the company back and said, "Let's think about this."

"What is there to think about?" Jennings demanded. "There's two dozen of you. If you rush those rocks, Temple won't have a chance!"

"And he'd probably kill two or three of us, at least. I won't waste my men like that, Dave."

"Then what are you going to do?" Jennings's voice was scornful. "Wait him out?"

"Maybe," Captain Ford said.

"He'll get away!"

Captain Ford shook his head. He sent Sergeant Level and two men down to the river south of Temple's position, while Roque Maugricio and two more men circled to the north of the rocks. If Temple attempted to swim across the river and flee into Mexico, the Rangers would be in position to stop him.

That was the plan, at any rate. Roque and his companions had not been gone more than five minutes when they came galloping back. The rest of the company had dismounted by now. I could tell that something was wrong from the way the riders rushed up, so I went over to join Captain Ford as Roque swung down from his saddle to report to the captain.

"Trouble," the tracker said. "A Comanch' war party less'n a mile upstream, coming this way."

"How many men?" asked Captain Ford, always practical.

Roque smiled thinly. "Forty or fifty, I'd say. And I think it's Carne Muerto's bunch."

Carne Muerto. *Dead Meat.* One of the fiercest of the Comanche chieftains, and an old adversary of Captain Ford. He had no great liking for Roque Maugricio, either, regarding the tracker as a traitor to his people.

Captain Ford absorbed the news and gave a curt nod. "Our horses are played out," he said. "We can't outrun them, even if we were of a mind to." He turned toward the rocks where the fugitive John Temple had sought shelter. The captain took up his reins and began to walk, leading his horse.

The rest of us followed him. What else could we do?

"Stay back!" John Temple cried. "I'll shoot, I swear I will!"

"You would be foolish to do so," Captain Ford told him in a loud voice that carried well in the hot, dry air. "There's a Comanche war party bearing down on us, Temple, probably drawn by those shots you fired. We need to fort up in those rocks where you are."

"It's a trick!" Temple shouted back. "You're lying to me! I see Dave Jennings with you!"

Jennings was indeed walking reluctantly toward the rocks with the rest of us. "I say we shoot the son of a bitch and take his guns and ammunition," he muttered.

"We'll need all the fighting men we can get to make it through this alive," Captain Ford said to him. "So you just hush up about that, Dave."

I could tell that Jennings did not like being spoke to that way, but he did not say anything else.

The few moments required to walk over to the boulders were quite nerve-wracking. At any second, one of us might be shot dead by John Temple. But no more shots came from the rocks, and when we strode into their sheltering ring we found Temple sitting with his back against one of the boulders, breathing hard. He looked up at Captain Ford and said, "You're not lying about the Comanches?"

"No, son," the captain said. "It's not a lie. They're coming."

"Oh, Lord." Temple wiped his hand across his mouth.

We were all frightened, of course. Any sane man would be, faced with the fierceness of the foes who were bearing down upon us. I have never made a study of military matters, having been concerned all my life with other things, but I have heard men who should know state that the Comanche warrior is perhaps the finest natural fighting man on the face of the earth. He is certainly one of the most ruthless, and Carne Muerto was a prime example of that. None of us could expect any mercy from him or any of the other Comanches. Defeat meant death. Capture meant a slow, agonizing death.

I looked at my hand. It was steady enough. I had ridden with the Rangers for almost a year and had participated in several skirmishes with the Indians. I had heard the song of lead in the air and smelled the brimstone of burnt powder. I was the ruler of my fear.

But I felt it anyway, and mentally uttered a prayer that I would not die today.

Roque came back from the river, where he had gone to fetch Sergeant Level and the other two men. Our party was back at full strength as they rode in. Two dozen Rangers—and the two feuding civilians, John Temple and Dave Jennings. They regarded each other warily and kept considerable distance between them, as much distance as possible considering that we were all gathered in a relatively small area behind the rocks. The slope leading down to the river was at our backs.

I carried a pistol but no rifle, so I would have to wait

until the Comanches closed in before I could join the battle. In the meantime, I was curious. I went over to John Temple and hunkered on my heels beside him.

"What made you do it, Temple?" I asked. "Why did you kill Sam Jennings?"

From behind me, Captain Ford said quietly, "I'd like an answer to that question, too, John."

Temple looked back and forth between the captain and myself and said defiantly, "He had it coming."

The captain dropped into a crouch beside me, took out his pistol, and began checking the loads in the cylinder. "Why? Because he was a Jennings?"

"Because he raped my wife," Temple said, his voice harsh.

I glanced at Captain Ford. The captain's face, tanned and weathered, seemed tighter than usual. "That's a mighty serious accusation," he said.

"It's true. Last week, I . . . I rode into our place. Sam was riding away. I thought he'd been there looking for me." Temple's eyes cut over toward Dave Jennings. "His pa didn't know anything about it, but Sam and me . . . we'd been trying to patch things up between his family and mine. We figured it was time the killing stopped." Temple swallowed hard. "But he was lyin' to me. It was all a trick. He acted like he wanted to make friends, and then . . . and then . . . "

"You don't have to go on," Captain Ford said. "This will all come out at the trial."

Temple laughed. "There won't be a trial. None of us will get back alive, more than likely. So somebody's got to hear the truth. I found my wife in the house. Sam had . . . had attacked her. Louise said she was all right, she said it didn't matter. I wanted to go after Sam, but she begged me not to. She didn't want me to get hurt. Lord help me, I went along with her. Then, a couple of days ago . . . I'd been out checking on some horses . . . I came in and found her.

She'd thrown a rope over one of the ceiling beams and . . . and put it around her neck . . . "

Again, Temple dragged in a long, ragged breath.

"After I'd cut her down and buried her, I got my horse and rode into town. I figured I'd find Sam Jennings there. I did," he concluded with heavy finality.

For a long moment, none of us said anything, then Captain Ford told Temple, "You shouldn't have run. You should have stayed and told your story to the law."

Temple shook his head. "It wouldn't have done any good. There's not many of us Temples left. Jennings and his bunch are going to win. They've worn us down over the years. Any jury in Laredo would've had more men on it who're friends to their side. I'd've stretched rope, Captain, and you know it."

He was probably right, I thought. Frontier justice is sometimes capricious, despite the efforts of such honest men as Rip Ford. And Temple *had* shot Sam Jennings in cold blood. No matter what the motivation, he would have had to answer for that.

So we had come after a murderer and found an avenger. Dave Jennings, in turn, wanted vengeance on the man who had taken his son from him. And so it went, the wagon wheels of death and hatred ever turning, carrying their cargo of tragedy from the past on into the future.

Ah, but I wax poetic. In truth, I was thinking no such high-flown thoughts at that moment, because it was then that Doc Sullivan called out, "Here come the Comanch', Cap'n, and they've got fire in their eyes!"

"Help hold the horses, Doctor," Captain Ford said to me as he straightened from his crouch. He strode toward the rocks and stood beside one of them with his rifle in his hands, ready for the advance of the Comanches.

Three of us held the reins of the horses. Since I had no rifle, it was logical that I would be one of the three. It was a necessary job, otherwise the animals might bolt when the firing started.

I could look past the boulders and see the Comanches approaching us. They had taken their time getting here, and they still rode their horses leisurely as they came into sight. But then, with a shrill cry, their leader, whom I knew to be Carne Muerto, kicked his mount into a run and galloped toward us.

"Keep a cool head, boys," Captain Ford called to the Rangers. "Make your shots count."

Roque's estimate had been correct. There were at least forty warriors in the band of Comanches, and probably more. Whooping and shouting, they charged the cluster of rocks along the river.

"Hold your fire, hold your fire," Captain Ford said. He had his cheek nestled against the stock of his rifle and was aiming steadily at the onrushing Indians. "Hold on . . . *Now!*"

A volley ripped out from the guns of the Old Company. But already the Comanches were splitting into two parties and veering aside. They wheeled away, each group circling back out of range. None of the Indians had fallen, and none of their horses had stumbled. Our shots had gone for naught.

With narrowed eyes, Captain Ford stared at the distant foe. "He's a canny rascal, that Carne Muerto is," he said. "He made us waste some bullets and established the range of our guns."

Sergeant Level said, "His rifles won't shoot any farther than ours."

"No, and he probably has fewer of them. But he has more men. He'll circle us so that we can't escape, then wait until dark and move in to finish us off."

Captain Ford's prediction soon gave evidence of being correct. The large war party split up, and smaller groups were sent out on our flanks. The Indians crossed the river to sit on horseback on the bluffs of the opposite bank, watching us. We were surrounded.

The prospect of waiting here for several more hours for night to fall and bring with it another attack was unpleasant. Doc Sullivan suggested, "They're thinned out now, Rip. Maybe we could bust through 'em and light a shuck outta here."

"We could do that," Captain Ford agreed, "if we could rest our horses overnight. They can outrun those Indian ponies, but not when they're as tired as they are now." He shook his head. "No, we're not going anywhere. We have to make the best of it right here."

Hunched over from the pain inside him, Dave Jennings walked up to John Temple and said, "This is all your fault, Temple. We wouldn't be here if it wasn't for you, goddamn it!"

Temple swung around to face him, tightly gripping the rifle in his hands. "Get away from me, Dave," he said, his voice shaking.

"Don't you tell me what to do, you murderer! You killed my boy!"

"Because Sam raped my wife."

Jennings stepped back violently, as if Temple had just struck him in the face. In a way, I suppose he had. "That's a damned lie! Sam wouldn't . . . he would never do such a thing!"

"He did, and Louise killed herself because of it." Temple's face was hard as stone. "I reckon you don't like to hear it, Jennings, but it's the truth."

Captain Ford moved to get between them. "We don't need to be fighting amongst ourselves right now," he said. "We've got our hands full with the Comanches."

Jennings pointed a shaking finger at Temple. "He's lying about my boy! I'll see you in hell for this, Temple!" The barrel of his rifle started to come up.

Captain Ford clamped a hand on the rifle barrel and

forced it down. "Stop it!" he said, his voice ringing with command now. "Dave, get back over there behind that rock where you were. And John, you hush up."

"I'm just telling the truth," Temple muttered.

Captain Ford waited until Jennings had reluctantly returned to his position, then said quietly to Temple, "I don't know the truth of what happened at your place, John, and I reckon the only two people who really knew are both dead."

"Louise wouldn't have lied to me! She had no reason."

"What you say makes sense, but what I'm saying is that nobody really knows now what happened. You wanted vengeance for your wife, so you shot Sam Jennings. Dave wants vengeance for his boy, so we came out hunting you after you ran." Captain Ford nodded his head toward the Comanches, who were sitting on their horses, far out on the desert, waiting. "They want vengeance for the things they think we've done to them. When do you reckon it all ends, John? When we're all dead?"

The captain was expressing in words the things I had thought earlier. But John Temple had no more answers than I did.

Roque came up to Captain Ford and said, "If we wait until it's dark, we won't have a chance, Cap'n. We need to draw them in now."

Captain Ford nodded. "I agree. You were thinking maybe a feint?"

"Me and a couple of the boys can make it look like we're trying to make a break for it over the river," Roque said. "The shooting might bring in Carne Muerto from the front."

"It'll be dangerous."

Roque grinned. "I don't mind taking the chance."

Doc Sullivan spoke up, saying, "Neither do I."

John Temple stepped forward. "I'll go," he said.

Instantly, Dave Jennings protested. "Don't let him go, Ford. He's just trying to get away."

Temple laughed coldly. "If you're so worried about me getting away, Dave, why don't you come with me?"

Jennings stared at him for a moment, then jerked his head in a nod. "All right," he said. "I'll just do that."

"Dave," Captain Ford said, "you're in no shape to—"

"I'm fine," Jennings cut in. "Just lemme get my horse."

But he wasn't fine. Pain was etched on his face, and it was all he could do not to double over from it. Even if we got out of this trap somehow, I thought, it was unlikely that Jennings would survive the ride back to Laredo.

So he had nothing to lose by daring the Comanches to kill him, I realized as I watched him clamber into the saddle. And neither did John Temple, who faced only a hang rope if he returned to a trial. One way or another, the long-standing hatred between their families had already claimed them both.

Roque and Sullivan mounted up, joining the two feudists. Temple, whose own mount had perished in his flight, borrowed a horse from one of the other men. "Good luck, boys," Captain Ford said to them.

"Don't worry, Cap'n," Sullivan said. "We'll be back in time for the real fun."

With that, he took off his hat, waved it over his head, and let out a whoop as he and the others spurred their horses down the slope toward the Rio Grande.

The Comanches waiting on the other side of the river saw them coming and closed in. Guns began to bang heavily. As they waited on the other side of the rocks, Carne Muerto and the rest of the war party wouldn't be able to see what was going on, but they could hear the firing. Would Carne Muerto be able to resist the temptation, or would he have to rush in to see what was happening? On that question rode the lives of many men.

The Comanches met Roque, Sullivan, Temple, and Jennings in the middle of the shallow, sluggish river. I watched as powdersmoke spurted into the air and saw flickers of motion as arrows whipped around the party of Rangers. The Indians outnumbered them two to one. Bent over in his saddle, Jennings fired his rifle until an arrow pierced his side. Still he stayed on his horse and fired again, this time blowing one of the attackers off his mount. Beside Jennings, Doc Sullivan emptied his revolver into the swarm of Comanches, then swung the empty weapon as a club. Next to him, Roque Maugricio had revolver in one hand, Bowie knife in the other and was fighting fiercely with each. At the end of the line, John Temple flailed at the onrushing Indians with his own empty rifle until one of the Comanches buried a knife blade in his back. Temple sagged forward but managed to turn and sweep his rifle around so that its stock shattered the Indian's skull.

The rest of us watched the battle from the top of the bluff, unable to fire into the cluster of struggling figures for fear of hitting our men. Then we had our own challenges to meet. Captain Ford called, "Here they come!"

It was true. Carne Muerto and the rest of the war party swept toward our makeshift stronghold. The riflemen began to fire, and several of the Comanches tumbled off their mounts. But there were too many of them for us to stop all of them. In what seemed like a matter of only heartbeats, they were among us, leaping their horses through the gaps between the boulders.

In later days, what followed next would be described as a fine fight. There was nothing fine about it while it was going on. I hung on with one hand to the reins of the terror-stricken horses while drawing my pistol with the other. I was acting mostly on instinct as I looped my thumb over the hammer of the Colt, pulled it back, and found a target. The gun bucked heavily in my hand as I fired. Stinging smoke drifted into my eyes, partially blinding me.

I cocked the gun and fired again, not knowing if my first shot had had any effect. I was surrounded by screaming and yelling and shooting. I may have even shouted myself; I am not sure about that. But I know that what must have been no more than a handful of minutes seemed more like hours or even days, and just when it seemed that the tumult would go on for an eternity, it all ended suddenly. The rattle of hoofbeats indicated that the Comanches, those of them who had survived the battle, were fleeing.

Nothing is more exhausting than fighting for one's life. My grip on the reins was all that held me up as I wanted to fall to my knees. My gun was empty, though I did not remember firing all of its shots. I replaced it in its holster and looked around.

Captain Ford walked among the company, checking on those men who were wounded. As the company surgeon, it was my job to tend to their injuries, and the duty I felt to my calling forced what was left of my fear into the back of my mind. I went to the nearest fallen man, who had been shot through the leg, and used his bandanna to bind up the wound. Then I moved on to the next case.

Within a half hour, I had seen to all the wounded. Three men were dead, two more seriously injured, but the others would all be all right, I thought. I reported this to Captain Ford, who said, "Good job, Doctor. But your three casualties don't include Temple and Jennings, do they?"

I shook my head. I had forgotten about them. When I looked around, I saw their bodies draped over the saddles on their horses, which had been brought back in by Roque and Sullivan. Both the tracker and Sullivan had minor injuries, but otherwise had come through the fracas in the river unscathed.

"We wiped out more than half of Carne Muerto's war party," Captain Ford went on. "He'll be licking his wounds long enough for us to make it back to Laredo if we hurry."

I gestured toward the bodies of Temple and Jennings.

"They had their vengeance, I suppose. And it got them nothing but two more graves to add to all the others."

"You know what it says in the Good Book, Doctor: 'The rage of a man will not spare in the day of vengeance.'" Captain Ford turned toward his horse. "If we're lucky, maybe some of us will still be around when that day is done."

The Diamond Ring Fling

LORI VAN PELT

Lori is a Wyoming rancher and author. She recently published *Dreams and Schemers: Profiles from Carbon County, Wyoming's Past* (High Plains Press, 1999), a nonfiction collection, the title of which is fairly self-explanatory. Oddly enough, one of the chapters is about "Gee-String" Jack Fulkerson (see Candy Moulton's story in this collection).

Here she chose as her White Hat lawyer Willis Van Devanter, who eventually became the first United States Supreme Court Justice from Wyoming. She chose, however, to tell the story from the point of view of a fictional prostitute. It makes for interesting reading.

★

I first met Willis at an execution. I recall the event clearly, for this murder occurred not on the gallows as one might expect of such a grisly deed but inside the raucous environs of the Cottonwood Saloon in Cheyenne, Wyoming. Providence decreed that the murder was not my own nor was it my doing. But the blood remains on my hands. I played a part whether I like to admit it was so or not. Willis saved my life.

Cheyenne had earned a reputation as the "Magic City of the Plains." The nickname attached itself because the town had sprung up with great alacrity on the barren plains penetrated by the steel rods of the railroad. I found this city to be anything but magical through my own folly entirely.

On that particular October evening in 1895, four men surrounded a table in the center of the smoky room, intent on winning money through the luck of the draw. Among them, confident and assured, sat Marcus Dalton. I sat at Marcus's side, gaily watching the proceedings. Other girls seduced younger men slick with liquor up the back stairs to Miss Ruthie's special rooms.

Marcus and I had no need of such diversions on this night. He gambled with funds he'd saved from his work on the railroad, planning to increase his holdings and then purchase land. Land! Every man's savior. Any man who ventured west and found himself on this humble open space filled with winter winds and harsh lessons desired to own property. As if he could take it over and make the lonely acres entirely his own. But land—and the passion for its ownership—is a demanding mistress. Land led astray many more men than it ever gave sterling living and well-bred respect to, or so I believed.

I pulled my frills tighter around my neck. Marcus did not appreciate my wiles displayed even modestly when other men were present. The other *nymphs du prairie* had noticed my special feelings for Marcus. They had helped me with Miss Ruthie by taking care of the slack when Marcus came to visit me. And he paid extra, most of which I presented to Miss Ruthie, thus satisfying her greed and assuaging any anger she might have felt at my near-exclusive status.

I took pains to please Marcus Dalton most especially. Marcus was tall and slender but muscular, with a dark, thick mustache and dark hair. He had the bluest eyes. They were a bit pale, like the sky on the coldest of winter's mornings. Marcus was unfailingly kind to me. He alone knew of my past indiscretions and he had pledged to help me find a better life. His large, rough, working-man's hands dwarfed the money he left on the dresser after our dalliances. In my own delicate hands, the bills appeared larger and more numerous.

"I'm going to buy land, Charlotte," he announced early one morning as we cuddled beneath the covers. "I want to own my own piece of land, to have the pleasure of being my own man, my own. The landowner. And then I will build a cabin and purchase beef cattle and become a rancher. And marry and have children."

"Grand dreams," I said, snuggling closer, and luxuriating in the warmth of his skin next to my own. "But do you not have pleasure here?"

He smiled at me. He stroked my hair. "Ah, Charlotte. Yes, my darling. I am pleasured here for certain. But land. Now that's something that lasts forever. All wealth comes from land."

I kissed the vee of his collarbone, placed my hands on his hairy chest and rolled on top of him. "I don't feel like talking any longer, Marcus," I said.

"You have insatiable appetites, for a woman," he answered, swallowing with his lips any reply I might have made.

Before the earliest morning light warmed the windows, Marcus dressed and left down the back stairs. He must not be late to his work on the railroad crew. Enough men had come through Cheyenne in recent years that the slightest infraction could throw them out of a job. And Marcus needed a bit more before he could afford to buy his land. I stood at the door and blew him a kiss, a gesture not missed by one of my coworkers, Lily. Lily did not like me. I knew from the look in her eyes she would find a way to use Marcus's overnight stay against me. I shuddered to consider how. Lily's door had opened at nearly the same time as my own. I supposed she was contemplating a chilly journey to the outhouse. A smile found her lips, the sideways grin that meant she thought of something titillating to do. She was the only one of the girls who did not help me in my quest for Marcus. Jealousy beamed from her like the heat in a kerosene lamp piped toward the ceiling. She would do something. What, I did not know.

THE NEXT EVENING as Marcus enjoyed his card game, a smoky haze from the burning of cigars filled the room. The piano player delighted the sparse crowd with a variety of tunes. I recognized old favorites like "I'll Take You Home Again, Kathleen," "Oh My Darling Clementine," and "Oh, Dem Golden Slippers" and sang the words I could remember. Marcus placed his elbow on the arm of his wooden chair, moving nearer to me as I sang. I laid my hand on his starched sleeve.

Cold air rushed in, swirling the heavy cloud of smoke, when the saloon doors swung open to reveal Hank Terwilliger. Tall, blond, more lithe than I remembered.

I stood, grateful that I had covered myself somewhat demurely.

"Hank," I said. "Hank Terwilliger."

His eyes searched the barroom. When they at last rested on me, he shook his head.

"Oh, Charlotte." His voice broke, as if he'd returned to adolescence again and could not speak a sentence without an unplanned and somewhat musical lilting. He took steps forward but I remained at Marcus's side. "They told me you'd been here. Oh, Charlotte. How did you ever go so wrong?"

The "they" he mentioned most certainly included darling Lily. My hand touched the ruffles covering my throat. "You're not Hank. Hank is dead."

"Oh, but I am Hank, dear Charlotte. I've returned for you, my dear."

Marcus tensed beside me. I kept my eyes on Hank.

I shook my head. "No. Hank died in a railroad accident two years ago. Had he not, he would have found me before now."

The man smiled. "Charlotte, it was a terrible mistake. Another man died in my stead. Did you not receive my telegraph letter?"

"You know I did not," I said sharply. "For if I had I would have returned to my fiancé and my home with him."

"You have defiled yourself, woman, under the eyes of God." His hazel eyes narrowed, judging me.

"The frontier has not been as I thought it would be," I replied more calmly than I believed possible as I felt the heat of anger course through my blood. I had not meant to use my body as a tool to make money. I possessed few skills that would have allowed me to eat. I could not cook. I had not learned to sew, for my mother had been ill for most of my childhood. "I arrived in this godforsaken city to discover the fiancé who sent for me was dead. I never would have come here but for you, Hank," I retorted. With both my parents dead, I found no reason to return East and could not have managed the train fare on my own when the brief opportunity existed. "I accepted my fate and have done the best I could with my circumstances."

Lily laughed out loud, then covered her mouth with her hand to muffle her hiccuping giggles.

"You did not have the courtesy to let me know you were alive," I continued, ignoring her outburst. "When I arrived here, your employer told me you'd been killed in an accident. Why did you not come for me yourself?"

Hank dropped his eyes and his chin fell to his neck. He did not answer me immediately. Instead, he took a deep breath. When he raised his face again, I saw more shame. This time, though, I sensed his shame was for his own misdeeds rather than my own. "I was a fool, Charlotte. The thought of caring for a wife and a family in this rugged country—" He stopped, swallowing hard. "I could not see myself doing that. I did not feel that I could live up to such an obligation. When the other man was killed, I let them believe it was me. I only wanted to get my feet under me again. I needed time to get used to the idea."

"And why did you return now?"

"I found out you were here. I could not believe it. And now that I've seen you . . ." He shook his head. "Charlotte, I must ask for the return of my grandmother's diamond ring."

Marcus looked startled. "This is true?"

"Of course," I replied. Walking as proudly as I could, I mounted the stairs to my room. The barroom had become strangely silent during the conversation, except for Lily's snorting. She had found Hank and brought him here, hoping no doubt to discredit me in some manner. Biting back tears, I retrieved the ring from its hiding place within my dresser. I felt the cold gold band between my fingers. Though I had not confided in Marcus, I too had hoped to purchase a new life through saving what funds I could. The diamond had been the bulk of my savings. Miss Ruthie took more than she allowed the girls to retain, thus ensuring her work force remained on the premises.

Hank's return had never occurred to me. Had I been of more sterling character, I suppose I could have returned the ring to his family when I had thought him dead. However, he'd given it to me. I had kept it at first as a remembrance. I did not want such an ugly reminder now. I returned to the saloon.

The card players had not returned to their game. Activity ceased for those brief moments. No one talked. The piano player sat with his hands in his lap. Men at the bar had turned away from the bar to face the card game at the table in the center of the room.

I returned to my place near Marcus. I held the ring between my thumb and index finger and raised it to eye level.

The diamond caught the light and sparkled like a star fallen from the sky.

"Do not give it back, Charlotte," Marcus said in a low tone. "He does not deserve to have it returned. Any man who would treat a woman in this disrespectful manner should be grateful that she would deign to speak to him."

Hank pressed his lips together in a line. He raked his eyes over Marcus, who remained seated at the card table. Hank's right hand lingered near his belt. His gun holster was near. He reached for the ring with his left hand. "I'll thank you not to enter into business which does not concern you, mister," he said in a menacing tone.

"Perhaps it does, Hank," I said. "I'll say here and now that I'll not remain betrothed to a coward."

I flung the ring toward him. It landed on the wood floor and made a tinkling sound like a dainty bell. It rolled to a stop near his feet. He kept his gaze riveted on me. His eyes narrowed.

"Shut pan, woman, I'll show you who's cowardly," he said, his face red with rage. His right hand lowered.

I closed my eyes and fell to my knees. A shot rang out. When I opened my eyes again, Hank lay dead on the floor.

Marcus's chair made a scraping noise as he stood. He unbuckled his holster and laid it on the table, gun still in place. I hadn't seen him produce it before. He must have pulled the trigger from beneath the table. But surely not my Marcus! An underhanded shot branded him as much a coward as Hank. I looked up at Marcus and he lifted his chin. A man I did not know had come to stand beside him.

"I'll go with you to the sheriff," he said, and Marcus nodded.

I crawled on the floor toward Hank's body. I reached for my ring. A slender man's hand covered my own.

"No, ma'am. That ring will be used as evidence in the trial."

I looked squarely into the kindly visage of Willis Van

Devanter, probably the most prominent lawyer in Cheyenne. He introduced himself as I relinquished the ring to his control. I couldn't fathom the reason he was inside the Cottonwood and I hadn't even noticed him until now. But I knew, as did most folks, that he had defended the cattlemen in the Johnson County War just a few years back and had done so right here in Cheyenne. He defended their right to murder rustlers Nate Champion and Nick Ray. Mr. Van Devanter was also known and well respected in highfalutin political circles. I did not much like that about him.

He gave my hand a squeeze. "Come to my office in a half hour," he said.

I gazed in amazement as he left the saloon. He followed Marcus, who was being led away by the unknown man.

"Things will work out all right, Charlotte," Marcus assured me. He kissed my hand—a most gallant gesture and one not often offered to one of my kind. I was not convinced.

I believed that his unfortunate shot cost me all hopes of happiness. And I puzzled about what Mr. Van Devanter had in mind.

Lily sat smug at the end of the bar. She said, "About time you got what's comin' to ya, Miss High-and-Mighty. I've always wondered. What makes *you* so special?" She sneered.

There was no reason to answer her question so I did not. Instead, I held her gaze until she looked away.

MR. VAN DEVANTER was much nicer than I expected, given his penchant for politics.

"I saw the whole thing, Charlotte," he said, tapping his hands on his shiny oak desk. His fine wood chair creaked slightly as he shifted his weight and leaned back. "I've discussed this case with Marcus. We will plead self-defense. I will, however, need your testimony."

His office—in the interior of the building used by the increasingly famous law firm of Lacey and Van Devanter—smelled musty, the result of papers stacked from floor to ceiling near bookshelves filled to capacity, both gilded with a fine layer of dust.

"I didn't see anything until the whole thing was over," I responded.

"You are the reason for the argument that ensued between the two men, are you not?"

I nodded. Then I took a deep breath and said, "If you don't mind my asking, sir, why would an attorney of your stature consider taking on a case of such low magnitude?"

He peered at me. An unbidden image of butterflies stabbed to a collector's board filled my mind. "Why," he said and stopped, holding me in suspension for an uncomfortable moment. "For the principle of the matter, Miss—"

"Oliver. Charlotte Oliver."

A small smile lifted his lips. "You see, Miss Oliver, Mr. Dalton shot to defend himself from a startling and unexpected attack. The fact that he fired through his holster and that the other man had not yet"—he paused and cleared his throat, then continued—"supposedly, had not yet drawn his weapon is immaterial."

"If that is so, why do you need my word, then?" I folded my shaking hands demurely in my lap, held them tightly together, and stared at them. "Most people won't believe a woman such as myself."

"Miss Oliver, do not sell yourself short. Your occupation is not on trial in this case. Some people will believe you. Some will not." He stood up and walked around his chair. "A jury will be called first. This could take some weeks. Mr. Dalton will, of course, remain in jail until this trial is decided."

"He'll lose his job," I said.

He turned to me. "That is unfortunate but true. However, I am confident that he will find other employment after this blows over."

"I will do what is in my power to help Marcus go free," I said. "But I do not have the proper funds at my disposal for a person of your abilities."

Willis Van Devànter bit his lip. "I see. Perhaps we can manage something." He didn't offer any further comments. Instead, he remained standing. He lifted his right eyebrow slightly. His conversation with me was completed.

I stood and stepped toward the door. "Mr. Van Devanter," I said, stopping and turning to face him again. "What is so important about this principle that you would argue the case of a common gambler accused of murder without proper payment?" I could not understand how a man could murder another in front of witnesses and then not be punished for the crime, but this thought I did not speak aloud.

He shook his head, waved an index finger in the air. "I must, Miss Oliver. I must defend those principles I believe in with all my human ability to protect them. For if I don't, then I lower myself and all of us by virtue of cowardice."

"But Marcus—"

Mr. Van Devanter walked to the front of his desk, nearer to me. "Marcus made a decision he will live with every remaining day of his life." He walked past me. A breeze scented with bay rum cologne tickled my nose. "I have done the same." Mr. Van Devanter placed his hand on the doorknob. "No, I cannot say that murder is ever justified. That is not for me to say. But I am a man of principles. And principles, Miss Oliver, deserve a strong defense."

He opened the door and ushered me into the narrow corridor. "I will let you know when you are to appear at the trial, ma'am."

★

I SIT, FIDGETING with the sturdy midnight blue brocade of the dress I made myself for this day of judgment. The fabric is smooth and comforting beneath my calloused fingers. My thumb feels numb after days of pushing the needle through fabric and my index and third fingers have roughened with numerous needle and pin pricks.

After I visited with Mr. Van Devanter in his office, I returned to Miss Ruthie's. Not long after that, Elise the dressmaker came to ask for my assistance in her shop.

"The governor is hosting a ball at Christmas," she explained. Elise, a short, stout woman, never failed to look neat and freshly groomed. A virtue of her trade, perhaps? "You have learned the basics of hems through your frequent visits to me, Charlotte. I would appreciate your coming to the shop these next few weeks and helping us with the increased orders." She watched me for a moment, sizing me up in some way. Then she added, "I will, of course, pay you for your work. We can start you at fifty cents per day. As you progress in skill, perhaps we can increase that amount."

I stared, bewildered, at the tiny woman who'd taken precious moments of her time when I begged her to teach me to wield a needle during my own stolen hours. "Elise." I surprised myself by being able to speak. "I would love to work with you at your shop."

"Good." She nodded. "And I will speak to Miss Ruthie. Surely she can provide you room and board for the next few weeks until we find something more"—she cleared her throat and touched the stiff collar around her neck— "suitable."

Somehow Elise had done as she promised. I was now employed properly at a dressmaking shop. I had even progressed to sewing straight seams upon the sewing machine. With Elise's help, I had made this dress I wore now in the lonely foyer of the courthouse. Elise was kind and encouraging. That provided me some comfort as I pon dered the tumultuous events of the previous weeks of my life. A decision came to me as I sat waiting on a chilly polished wooden bench to testify on behalf of Marcus who had murdered my fiancé.

The large wooden doors to my right creaked open. Lily stepped out and saw me. Her eyes narrowed. She undoubtedly felt jealous of my new dress, my new life unfolding before her eyes. In my mind, I saw my new life as a wondrous and pleasant blessing. Lily probably did as well. The fact of my improvement in social standing in the midst of such devastating circumstances caused her consternation, I feel sure.

She said, "He'll be in jail forever. I saw the whole thing and told them all I knew."

The guard touched her elbow and reminded her she was free to go now. She threw a final haughty look in my direction and strode away. "Ma'am?" the guard said, nodding at me.

I stood, took a deep breath, and smoothed my skirt yet again. I refused to let Lily's venomous attitude shake me.

Inside the courtroom, I saw Marcus and then the firm countenance of Mr. Van Devanter. The attorney representing Hank Terwilliger's family reminded me of a weasel. His eyes were much too large for his face, and his neck too long for his body. I had seen such an animal once near a barn. I felt an involuntary shiver shake me. I took another deep breath and resolved to remain strong until the questions were finished. I did not look at the jury, nor at the people gathered in the room to listen to the proceedings.

The event passed in a blur. Hank's attorney made much of my previous profession, explaining that I had done my fiancé wrong by not waiting for him, and by that decision had perhaps instigated the entire incident.

Mr. Van Devanter argued in my behalf by asking me about Hank and learning that I had thought him dead and had done what I must to survive. "I'll remind you also, sir, that Miss Oliver is not on trial in this matter," he said, voice resounding throughout the room like a chord played on a church organ.

We finished more quickly than I had thought, and I waited outside on the same bench for the news of the decision. The jury deliberated for less than two hours. Marcus was set free. They ruled that he had pulled the trigger in self-defense. Mr. Van Devanter looked pleased with himself. Marcus rushed from the courtroom and hugged me tightly and kissed me on the cheek.

I endured his attentions for a moment and then gently pushed him away.

"We'll marry, Charlotte. I can buy land now, we'll marry and . . ."

My lack of enthusiasm stopped him. He frowned. "Charlotte?"

I shook my head. "No, Marcus. I'm sorry. I cannot marry you."

"Why not, Charlotte?"

"I cannot marry a murderer."

"But I wasn't convicted."

I allowed him a small smile. "That makes little difference to me, Marcus. You murdered someone almost before my eyes. I cannot reconcile myself to that fact."

"Charlotte," he said quietly. "Now's a fine time for you, of all people, to seek the high ground."

Mr. Van Devanter cleared his throat and excused himself to the courtroom.

"I cannot help it, Marcus. I would never fully trust you. I will not marry a man I cannot trust."

He blinked. "I see." He took a deep breath. "I believe you are making a tragic mistake."

I held my hand toward him. "Good luck, Marcus."

He took my hand in his own and then lifted it to his lips and kissed it. He held my eyes with his own for a long moment, and then turned on his heel and left the courthouse. I watched him go.

Mr. Van Devanter returned. "This belongs to you, I believe."

He handed me a small package, which contained the diamond ring I'd flung onto the barroom floor that fateful October day.

"I thought Hank's family would want it," I said.

"No. They want to be finished with the whole sad thing. His mother wants no reminders of her son's premature death." He squeezed my hands. "She said Hank gave it to you and it is yours to keep."

"Thank you, Mr. Van Devanter," I said. "I was hoping to purchase a sewing machine. I think I might be able to use this ring as a portion of the payment."

He motioned toward the doors, and escorted me into the deceitful November sunshine, which promised warmth but delivered only light.

"I must say I was hoping you might," he responded, smiling. "And please, call me Willis, Miss Oliver." He left me standing on the steps as he trotted down them and strode purposefully toward his office. I felt no need to explain that the next dress Elise assigned to me, at the special request of the customer, was the elegant gown Dellice Van Devanter would wear to the governor's Christmas ball.

The Cotton Road

L. J. WASHBURN

Livia is an award-winning author with a foot in many genres—mystery, Western, historical, romance, fantasy—which must make it real difficult for her to buy shoes. I have had many dealings with her in the past, as her work has appeared in *many* of my anthologies, and I have spoken to her on the phone, but we have never met. I'm dying to see what she looks like with all those feet.

Of Sally Skull she e-mailed me that she didn't exactly know if Sally would be a White Hat or a Black Hat, but "the way I'll handle the story would be White Hat about the Cotton Road." Sally Skull was, apparently, an Old West version of the bogeyman.

★

"Durn you, Thomas Jefferson McKelvey, you better be good, or Sally Skull will get you!"

I don't know how many times my mama told me that when I was growing up, but I heard it a lot. I reckon that was because I was the rambunctious sort who was always getting into some kind of mischief. Mama couldn't stand mischief. She was a proper lady back in St. Louie before Pa dragged her down here to the wilds of Texas and they had a passel of kids, of which I was the youngest. Pa wouldn't hardly take a switch to me, since I was the baby in the family, and that annoyed Mama to no end.

I didn't know who Sally Skull was, but the name was scary enough by itself to make me toe the line, at least part of the time. The way Mama said it, she made ol' Sally Skull sound like just about the fearsomest creature on heaven or earth.

Then come a day when I was twelve years old and met Sally Skull, and I found out that Mama didn't know the half of it.

WE WERE HOMESTEADING then on some land about halfway between Corpus Christi and Victoria, not far from the old road that had once been called the Camino Real, back in the days when the Spaniards ruled all of Texas except that what belonged to the Comanch' and the rattlesnake. Which was a fair bit. I was churning butter in the shade of the dogtrot when I heard the squeal of wagon wheels turning. I looked up, shaded my eyes against the bright sunshine, and saw a wagon rolling toward the log cabin we called home.

It wasn't just a wagon, though. Three riders came along behind it on big, fine-looking horses. The riders wore tall, broad-brimmed hats—sombreros, they was called—and I knew from that the riders were Mexicans.

The face of the woman on the seat of the wagon was as dark as that of a Mexican, but she was white, I reckon. She wore a black sunbonnet, but except for that she was dressed like a man, in a buckskin shirt, rawhide trousers, and high-topped boots.

And the two cap-and-ball pistols she wore in holsters on her hips, they were like a man's, too.

She brought the wagon to a halt by pulling back hard on the reins hitched to a team of six mules. Big ugly brutes, those mules were, but I got the feeling their strength was no match for that of this unlikely woman. She looked down at me with dark, snapping eyes over a nose that was like the beak of a hawk.

"You alone here, boy?"

I was a mite scared, don't you think for a minute I wasn't. She wasn't like any woman I'd ever seen. She was old, real old, probably forty at least, but she handled those mules like a man half that age.

"My mama's gone to town," I told her, afraid to lie, "and my pa and my brothers and sisters are workin' out in the fields."

"You look like a right strong boy. How come you ain't out in the fields, too?"

"Mama said this butter had to be churned today. She told me to do it."

"You like churnin' butter?"

"Hell, no," I answered without thinking. That was the first time I ever said a cuss word in front of a grown-up. My brothers used 'em all the time in front of Pa, but never when Mama was around.

For a second the woman looked like she was going to smile, then she said, "I got a wheel about to come off. Reckon it'd be all right for me an' my vaqueros to work on it here?"

"I don't know. . . ." I didn't much want her or the Mexicans around the place when Mama got back.

She looked at me, then shrugged a little. "That's all right, son. I wouldn't want to get you in trouble with your folks. We'll move on."

If she'd said it a-purpose, she couldn't have come up with anything more likely to make me give in. I was a tad rebellious back then, ready to do most anything that'd bother Pa or Mama, especially Mama.

"No, ma'am," I told her, "you just stay right here and work on that wagon wheel. It'll be fine."

"You're sure?" she asked me.

"I'm sure." And I was.

"All right, then." She tied the reins around the brake lever, then started to swing down off the seat. "By the way, folks call me Sally Skull."

Well, sir, that might near floored me. After being threatened with her so many times when I was acting up, I'd about half-decided that Sally Skull didn't really exist. I just stared at her.

"That ain't my real name, o' course," she continued as she reached the ground. "That's Sarah Horsdorff. I'll answer to either one, though."

I swallowed hard. "I . . . I didn't know you was real, ma'am."

"I'm real, all right." Again I thought she was going to smile, but she didn't. "Lemme guess. When your mama don't like what you're doin', she tells you to behave or ol' Sally Skull will get you and take you away. Is that right?"

I nodded.

"I ain't stole any little boys for a long time. Been too busy." She jerked a thumb over her shoulder at the wagon. The back of it was piled full of bales of cotton. "I'm takin' this here cotton to Matamoros."

I nodded again and said, "Yes, ma'am."

"You know why?"

I shook my head.

"Your folks ever talk about the war?"

"No, ma'am, not much, 'cept to say they don't hold with slavery. That's why Pa ain't off fightin' for the Confederates."

"Well, now, I ain't argyin' either way when it comes to havin' slaves. Never owned any myself. But that there cotton, it's worth a small fortune if folks in the South can get it over to England. So I take it down the Cotton Road to Matamoros, and the Mexes ship it out."

"I never heard of no Cotton Road."

"Same thing as the old Camino Real. You must'a heard of that, livin' so close to it."

I nodded again. "Yes, ma'm."

I reckon she figured she'd educated me enough. She turned to the Mexicans who were riding with her and jabbered at 'em for a while in their lingo. They got down off their horses and started working on the wagon. They had to jack it up to get the wheel off. It was a warm day so they took off their short jackets. Under the jackets they wore white shirts with fancy, colorful embroidery on them. I really admired those shirts and told myself that one day I was going to get one just like 'em.

Sally ramrodded the work. When she noticed me watching, she pointed at the butter churn and said, "You'd better get back to your own rat-killin', boy. I don't want your mama mad at me when she comes home."

I sighed and started churning again.

"What's your name, anyway?"

"Thomas Jefferson McKelvey, ma'am."

"Don't ma'am me, Tom. Just call me Sally."

I couldn't help but grin. "Yes, ma'am—I mean, Sally."

The hub on that wheel was plumb worn out, and it took the Mexicans a while to repair it and get it back on the wagon. While Sally was waiting, I told her she was welcome to get a drink from our well, and she said thank you kindly and hauled up the bucket. I was getting a mite more brave, so as she was sipping from the dipper, I asked, "How come folks tell their kids you'll get 'em if they don't behave?"

"Oh, I guess I'm known in these parts to be a rough, tough sort. Been around South Texas since the Mexes run the place, ranchin' and farmin' with my husbands."

"Husbands? You got more'n one? I never heard of a lady havin' more'n one husband."

This time she really did smile. "I didn't have 'em all at the same time. I ain't had the best luck with husbands. One of 'em got washed away in a river when we were tryin' to cross with a herd, and I had to divorce myself from a couple more. You know what divorce is?"

I shook my head.

"It's man puttin' asunder what God hadn't ought to put together in the first place." I didn't really understand that, but she went on, "Anyway, I got married up again to a fella name of George Horsdorff. Horselaugh, some folks call him. He's younger'n me, so he's good for a few things that you wouldn't know about yet, but he ain't much for ridin' the trails. Don't really need him, though. These Mex boys what ride with me are good hands."

"Is that all you do, take cotton to Matamoros?"

"I take supplies from England and other countries back north to Alleyton. There's a railroad there, so the stuff can be shipped from there all over the Confederacy by train." Sally tossed the dipper back in the bucket. "And I do a mite of horse tradin' and such-like." She got a faraway look in her eyes, like she was remembering something. "One time at a fandango, a fella said the bellies of my horses were all wet from the water of the Rio Grande. Like I'd stole 'em and brought 'em across the border, you know? So I told him he was a snake-crawlin', skunk-smellin' son of a bitch. He got so mad he hauled out his pistol like he was fixin' to shoot me."

My eyes were wide with wonder by this time. "What'd you do?"

She looked at me and patted the butts of the holstered cap-and-ball pistols. "I hauled iron, too. And I'm still here, so I reckon you can figure out for yourself what happened. You look like a smart boy."

I could feel my eyes bugging out even more. "You *shot* him?"

"Seemed like the thing to do at the time," Sally Skull said.

I'd never met anybody who had killed someone. I had

stopped churning again while I was listening to her. She told me to get back to it.

When the Mexicans were finished working on the wagon, they started taking it down off the jack, and as they did, it slipped and almost fell. Sally lit into them for being careless, spouting cuss words like a river. Some of them words were English and some of them were Mexican, but I could tell from the way she was saying 'em that they were cuss words. Even some of the English ones I'd never heard before, not even from Pa, and he could cuss a blue streak when he hit his thumb with a hammer or something like that. Some of what Sally told those Mexicans to do made me dizzy it was so far-fetched. But they just took it and grinned among themselves, so I reckon they were used to it and didn't take no real offense from it.

Finally, the wagon was ready to go. As Sally went to climb up on the seat, I called out to her, "Wait!"

She stopped and looked back at me. "What is it, Tom?"

I had this idea in the back of my head. Mama wasn't back from town yet and she probably should have been, so I took that delay as a sign that I should go ahead and say what was on my mind. I looked at Sally Skull and said, "Take me with you."

She frowned at me. "What?"

"Take me with you," I repeated. "I want to ride the Cotton Road and see Matamoros. I ain't never been off this farm 'cept to go into the settlement, and it ain't nothin'."

"Boy, you're loco. I can't just take you away from your home. Your folks'd have the law on me."

"They wouldn't care," I said. "They don't like me much anyway." I reckon that was a lie. For all her fussing, I knew Mama loved me, and Pa always acted like he was glad to have me around. But my head was full of the grand adventure she'd told me about, and I wanted to see it for myself, to be a part of it.

Sally shook her head. "I been known to take kids with

me on my trips to help out, but only when their folks said it was all right. I can't take you without your folks givin' their permission, Tom."

"Well . . ." I cast around desperately in my thoughts. "They'll be back anytime now. You could wait and ask 'em." I knew they wouldn't let me go, though.

"I'm sorry," Sally said, and she sounded like she meant it. "But this damned wheel's already held me up too long. I won't make the camp I wanted to tonight. I got to get goin'."

"But, Sally . . ."

"Tell you what. This farm ain't too far off my reg'lar route. I'll stop back by here sometime and say howdy to you. How's that?"

I could tell I wasn't going to get anywhere arguing with her. She was a woman who was used to getting her own way. I nodded and said, "All right, I guess."

"Well, then, there you go." She stepped up onto the wagon box, sat down, and took the reins of the mule team. "So long, Thomas Jefferson McKelvey."

She slapped the reins against the backs of the mules, hollered at them, and drove away from the cabin, followed on horseback by the vaqueros.

I wondered if I would ever see Sally Skull again.

I WAS ABOUT fit to bust by the time Mama got home a little later. She said she was sorry it had taken so long, that she had started talking to Mrs. Scrimshaw at the general store and lost track of the time. I didn't care. I just wanted to tell her what had happened.

"We had a visitor today," I said.

Mama looked at me. "Who?" Her voice was sharp and suspicious-like.

"Sally Skull."

"What?"

"Sally Skull stopped by here. She had to fix her wagon."

Mama's eyes got narrow. "I'll fix your wagon, young man, if you start lying to me and spinning wild stories like that."

"It's not a wild story!" I said. "She was really here. Look, you can see the wagon tracks and the hoofprints of the horses her vaqueros were riding." I pointed out the marks in the dust.

Mama couldn't dispute that *somebody* had been there, but seeing the evidence with her own eyes just seemed to make her more mad. "Who was here? You'd better tell me the truth, or you're going to be in a lot of trouble, Thomas Jefferson McKelvey. I'm already annoyed with you because you didn't finish the churning while I was gone."

"It was Sally Skull. She was really here, Mama."

"Oh, Sally Skull doesn't even exist! She's just made up, something that parents use to frighten their children."

"She's real, Mama. Just because you never seen her doesn't mean she don't exist."

"Doesn't exist," she corrected me. "And you should say, just because you never saw her, not seen her."

Mama was like that, always trying to get me to talk right. Some of it stuck and some of it didn't.

I was getting just about as mad as she was by now. "I ain't lyin'," I said. "Sally Skull was here."

"All right," Mama said, and for a second I thought she believed me. Then she went on, "When your father gets home, I'm going to have him cut a switch and see if he can get the truth out of you."

I just stared at her, and then I turned and ran out of the yard in front of the cabin. She hollered at me to come back and threatened me some more, but I didn't go back. I was too mad, so mad I thought I might slip and use some of those new cuss words. I knew if I cussed at Mama, Pa really would take a switch to me.

So I went up on a hill not far from our place and sat there for a while, thinking mean thoughts about Mama and trying not to cry since I was too old for that. While I was sitting under a tree, I looked off to the northwest, and there I could see the Camino Real. The Cotton Road. I found myself looking at it for a long time, and I forgot about wanting to cry.

A while later, Pa came looking for me, hollering my name, and I went down to meet him.

"Am I goin' to get a whippin'?" I asked him. I noticed right off that he didn't have a switch with him.

"You deserve one for sassin' your mama that way, Tom," he said.

"But she wouldn't believe me!"

"About Sally Skull, you mean?" So she'd told him what I had said.

"Yeah."

"I've heard tall tales about Sally Skull ever since we moved to this part of Texas," Pa said. "Maybe she's real, maybe she's not. I don't know."

"I know," I said. "I talked to her."

"Well, if you did, you're lucky she didn't shoot you or carry you off. She's supposed to be a ring-tailed roarer."

I didn't tell him that I'd asked Sally to take me with her. Pa was the tolerant sort, but I didn't figure he'd much like that.

He said if I'd come back with him and tell Mama I was sorry, there wouldn't be a whipping. I knew that was the best deal I was going to get, so I took it.

Mama wasn't through, though. After I'd dug my toe in the dirt of the dogtrot and hung my head and told her I was sorry, she said, "I accept your apology, Thomas, but you must be punished anyway. There'll be no supper for you tonight."

No supper? My stomach was already starting to think my throat'd been cut. But Mama wouldn't budge, and all

Pa and my brothers or sisters could do was give me sympathetic looks.

I went into the side of the cabin where us kids slept and climbed up the ladder into the loft. If I wasn't going to eat, I might as well sleep, I told myself. There wasn't any point in staying up.

But I couldn't go to sleep. I lay there and thought about Sally Skull and how she was going down the Cotton Road all the way to Matamoros, which I knew was somewhere in Mexico without being sure exactly about it. Sally had said something about making camp, and it had been fairly late in the day when the Mexicans got the wagon fixed and they started out again, so I figured they couldn't have gone too far.

My next oldest brother, Herbert, slept in the loft with me. After supper he climbed up there and stretched out on the corn shuck mattress. "Sorry you didn't get no supper," he said to me. "Pa's mad at Mama for not lettin' you eat, but she don't care. She says liars got to be punished." He dropped his voice to a whisper. "Did you really see Sally Skull?"

"I saw her," I said.

"Did she have snakes for hair, and fire comin' out her ears?"

"Hell, no. She just looked like an old woman . . . 'cept for she dressed like a man and carried two six-shooters."

"*Two* guns?"

"Yep."

Herbert gave a low whistle, he was so impressed by what I'd told him. "Wish I'd been here."

"I do, too. If we'd both seen her, Mama would have to believe us."

Herbert was tired from working all day, so he rolled over on his side, and it wasn't long before he was snoring to beat the band. I still couldn't sleep. A powerful yearning was growing inside me, the likes of which I'd never felt before. I wanted to see the open road stretching out in front of me, the hills and the plains and maybe even mountains, but always something new, something fresh, something I hadn't ever seen before.

No two ways about it, I had me a serious case of fiddlefoot coming on.

I heard more snoring coming from down below in the cabin. It was good and dark by this time. My family, like everybody else, pretty much went to sleep with the chickens. Pa and Mama might have a lamp burning in their side of the cabin, but all my brothers and sisters were asleep by now.

I sat up and gathered my shirt and trousers and shoes. I bundled them up in my arms and climbed down the ladder in my long johns.

Our old dog, Skeeter, was sleeping in the dogtrot when I stepped out into it. He woke up and growled a little but didn't bark. When he saw it was me he crawled on his belly and wagged his stub of a tail.

I waited until I was outside to get dressed. My hat hung on a nail inside the dogtrot. I took it down and settled it on my head.

I tried hard not to think too much about what I was doing. If somebody had asked me right then, I would have told them I wasn't running away from home. I really wasn't. I intended to come back. But not until I'd been down the Cotton Road.

I headed for the barn, Skeeter trailing along behind me with his tongue hanging out and a doggish grin on his face, like he knew that whatever I was up to, it was bound to be something foolish. In a whisper, I turned and told him to go back to the cabin. I didn't want him following me when I left.

The single window on Pa and Mama's side of the cabin was dark. I was grateful for that. I was extra quiet as I slipped into the barn and went to the stall where Pa's saddle horse, a roan mare, was kept.

Now I was just about to become a horse thief, I told myself. But I wasn't really stealing the mare. When I caught up to Sally Skull and she agreed to take me with her and the Mexicans, I'd slap that old mare on the rump and send her home. I knew she could find her way.

That's all I was trying to do, to find my way. I knew I couldn't do it around here.

I got a hackamore on the roan and led her out of the stall. I didn't need a saddle, having been riding bareback since almost before I could walk. I used a milking stool to climb up onto her back, then took tight hold of the reins and heeled her into a walk. I rode out of the barn, keeping the pace slow and quiet, and headed for the Cotton Road.

A big moon floated in the sky, so I had plenty of light to see by. I headed in the right direction, knowing I'd hit the road sooner or later. When I did, I turned to the southwest and followed it. I was far enough away from home now that I could put the mare into a trot.

I should have been scared, a youngster out by myself like that in the middle of the night. But I wasn't. I was too full of excitement to even think about being scared. Nothing bad was going to happen to me. I was sure of that.

It was likely that Sally and the Mexicans would have a fire going. That was how I planned to find them. Time was, showing a light at night was a good way for a pilgrim to get his hair lifted, but the Comanch' hadn't raided this far south in years and years, not since the Rangers whipped 'em at Plum Creek.

After a while I spotted the glow of a fire off to the left. I pulled the mare back to a walk, then slid off her and went ahead on foot, leading her by the hackamore. The trees and brush grew pretty thick along here, but there was a path I could follow and I was pretty sure it would lead to the clearing where Sally was camped.

A minute later I caught sight of the wagon through the trees and recognized the bales of cotton piled high inside it. Right then, the mare lifted her head, pulling on the reins, and let out a loud whinny. To my left, somebody cussed, and to the right, somebody else said, "Who the hell? Grab that kid!"

The voices belonged to men, and they weren't the Mexicans who rode with Sally. They were white men, I could tell that much, and they sounded rough. I could think of only one reason some fellas would be skulking around in the brush just outside of Sally's camp.

That cotton's worth a small fortune . . .

"Sally Skull!" I sang out as loud as I could. "Look out! Robbers!"

A big, dark shadow lunged at me out of the brush. I let go of the mare's reins and ducked under the shape as it came at me. At the same time, a noise like a thunderstorm filled the night, but I knew it wasn't thunder. It was guns going off.

I turned around and tried to run, but I tripped over a root and went sprawling on my belly. That was probably the best place for me, because I heard rustling noises above my head that I figured out must be bullets tearing through the brush. Somewhere close by a man grunted and then fell with a crash. I wiggled around until I was turned toward Sally's camp and started crawling in that direction.

Funny thing about it, I was scared now—who wouldn't be, with all them bullets flying around—but my head was still clear. I wanted to see what was going on. When I came to the edge of the brush I raised up just enough to watch through a gap in the branches.

I saw Sally Skull standing with her back against the sideboard of the wagon, still dressed in her man's clothes, with her long gray hair loose now around her head. She had a cap-and-ball pistol in each hand, and every time a shot came from the woods, Sally jerked one of those pistols toward the muzzle flash and fired. She had both guns going at the same time, her thumbs blurring as she eared back the hammers, flame and smoke spouting from the barrels, the glow of the campfire casting a red glow over her face.

I had never seen anything like it in my life.

The three vaqueros were getting in on the fight, too, one of them kneeling next to Sally, the other two flanking the wagon. They had those new-fangled Henry rifles, the kind you load on Sunday and shoot all week.

After a minute or so that seemed a whole lot longer, Sally stopped shooting and slowly lowered her pistols. "Hold on," she said to the Mexicans. "I think we got 'em all."

I thought she was right. No more shots came from the woods. Somebody was moaning a ways off to my right.

Sally said something in Mex to the vaqueros, and two of them set their rifles aside and drew knives from sheaths on their belts. They slid off into the trees, and after a minute, whoever was moaning stopped. Several more minutes went by. I figured the Mexicans were checking the bushwhackers. When they finally stepped back into the clearing, they both nodded to Sally.

She holstered her left-hand gun and started reloading the right-hand one with caps and balls from a pouch at her belt. She said, "Somebody hollered just before the ball started. Who was it?"

I took a deep breath and called, "It was me, Sally."

Her head jerked around toward where I was hiding in the brush. "Tom?" she said. "Tom McKelvey? That you, boy?"

I got to my feet and came out into the open. "Howdy, Sally," I said.

"Boy, what in Hades are you doin' out here in the middle of the night?"

"I come to go with you down the Cotton Road to Mexico." I swept my arm toward the trees where the dead bushwhackers lay. "Good thing I did, too, or those fellas would've killed you and stole your cotton."

"The hell they would have," Sally said. "We knowed they was out there. We was just waitin' for 'em to get close enough so we could blow their lights out."

"You . . . knew?"

Sally snorted. "Shoot, I been dealin' with thieves and highwaymen ever since I took to the road, Tom. Nobody, not even a Injun, can sneak up on ol' Sally Skull."

That like to crushed me. Here I'd thought I saved her life and she'd have to take me with her out of gratitude, and all I'd done was nearly messed things up.

She finished reloading the pistol and slid it back into its holster. "Tom, I told you I can't take you with me."

I sighed. "Reckon I'd better go see if I can catch that mare, then. Pa'll skin me alive if I lose her."

Sally said something to one of the vaqueros, who nodded and started saddling one of their horses. "Juan'll get your hoss and bring it back here. I reckon you can stay the night. I don't want you traipsin' around in the dark. You can go home come mornin'."

"I don't want to go home," I mumbled. "They don't even believe you're real."

Sally didn't say anything to that for a minute. Then she said, "Huh." She turned toward the wagon. "I got an extra bedroll. You can sleep under the wagon."

I DIDN'T SLEEP much, so I was tired the next morning. Not too tired to keep from being surprised when Sally turned the wagon back toward my folks' farm, though. "I want to make sure you get home safe," she said.

I felt my excitement growing as I rode the mare alongside the wagon. Pa and Mama and my brothers and sisters were going to see Sally Skull for themselves.

There was a bit of commotion around the place when we came in sight of it. Folks were hurrying around. As we came closer, I saw my pa trying to put his saddle on one of the mules. They had realized I was gone, I figured out, and Pa was going to look for me.

Everything stopped, though, when Skeeter started barking at us and everybody looked around to see us coming. Pa stepped into the cabin to get his shotgun, then came out to meet us. He must've told Mama to stay back, but she wouldn't do it. She ran past him and rushed up to hug me as I reined in and then slid down off the mare.

Sally brought the mules to a stop and nodded at Pa. "Howdy," she said. "You'd be Mr. McKelvey, this boy's pa?"

"That's right," he said, and he sounded like he had something in his throat. "We're much obliged to you for findin' him and bringin' him back, Mrs. . . . ?"

"Horsdorff. But you can call me Sally Skull."

Mama was still hugging me and running her hand over my hair, but I was watching Pa and I saw his eyes go wide. "Sally Skull?" he said.

"That's right. I'm takin' this here cotton down to Mexico, and your boy there saved us from gettin' jumped by a bunch of no-good thieves last night. Reckon we owe you our thanks for what he done."

"You . . . you're much obliged."

I hardly ever saw my pa at a loss for words, but that morning was one of those times.

Sally turned and grinned down at me. "Boy, how old are you?"

"Twelve," I told her. I was getting tired of Mama fussing over me, so I sort of pulled away from her.

"When's your birthday?"

"August twelfth."

"Tell you what. First trip I make by here after you turn

thirteen, I'll stop by and see if your folks'll let you go down to Mexico with me. How 'bout that?"

Mama took hold of my shoulders. "I should say not. That's much too dangerous a trip for a boy."

Sally just looked at her and said, "Once a boy's heard the call of the trail, he ain't much of a boy no more."

I glanced at Pa and saw by the look in his eyes that he knew what she meant. After all, he'd come all the way down here to Texas from Missouri. When the time came, he'd do his best to see that Mama let me go. Suddenly, I had me a feeling that Pa was going to win that argument for a change.

Sally picked up the reins. "Well, I got to be goin'. This cotton won't take itself to Mexico. Adios."

"Good-bye," Pa said. "And thank you."

I pulled free from Mama and ran over to the wagon. "Sally," I said.

"So long, Tom," she said as she looked down at me. "I'll see you again. 'Tween now and then, you better be good."

I grinned. "Or Sally Skull will get me?"

"Be good . . . or I won't get you."

Pa put a hand on my shoulder and I stepped back so Sally could turn the wagon around and leave. I watched her and the Mexicans until they were clean out of sight. Mama came up beside me and rested her hand on my other shoulder.

"He's too much like you," she said to Pa. "But maybe that's not completely a bad thing."

He just grinned.

Me, I waved to Sally Skull even though she couldn't see me anymore, and thought about the Cotton Road.

A Commercial Proposition

RICHARD S. WHEELER

Dick Wheeler is much honored and much revered in the Western genre. He won the Best Novel Spur Award from WWA for his novel *Masterson* (Forge, 2000) and recently edited the WWA Spur winners anthology *Tales of the American West* (Penguin, 2001). His most recent novel is *Restitution* (NAL, 2001). He's a busy man, but when I asked him for a favor—"please write me a *great* White Hats story"—he dropped everything and did it.

I mean, he did it!

Here is a wonderful tale about Eleanore Dumont, also known as Madame Mustache.

*

The pox was steaming up the river. I heard it while dealing, which is how I get my news. Some passengers aboard the *W. B. Dance* had it, and the captain intended to unload them at Fort Benton, along with his cargo. That's all anyone knew. And we would not have known that but for the horseman who arrived ahead of the stern-wheeler.

At first I welcomed the proposition. A good round of smallpox would clear Fort Benton of all those vermin-ridden Blackfeet skulking around, and the whole town would be better for it. The redskins were peculiarly vulnerable to the pox, and died in a magnificent hurry. White men died of the pox a little less, and a little slower.

It was a matter of indifference to me whether the paddle wheeler delivered its cargo of pox or not. I had been scratched with Jenner's vaccine years ago, and was immune. But most of the gentlemen in my establishment would undoubtedly expire, and I would lose trade.

I am Eleanore Dumont, and I run a house of notorious repute on Front Street, facing the Missouri River, in Fort Benton, Montana Territory. I am amazed at what comes up the river from distant Independence or even St. Louis. Barrels and crates of all sorts, dandies, preachers, and the pox. Men of all sorts, rarely women, which is why I prosper. Most of the men are gold-fevered.

I am known by another name, Madame Mustache, and I do not discourage it. I am a fat slattern, and I do not discourage them from thinking that, either. I have a coarse dark mustache above my lips. I could easily shave it off, but I don't, because it draws customers, who sit at my table and glance furtively at my hairy lip, a great oddity in a woman, even a slattern, and so they gamble and think about my facial hair, and lose, and I am the better off for it.

Once, an infinity ago, I was beautiful. But that was back in the days of the California Gold Rush, when my gambler husband and I, newly arrived from France, opened an elegant casino. I dealt. The woman-starved miners flocked to my game. I wore decorous clothing, nothing provocative, and I required them to mind their manners. A coarse word earned my rebuke, and ungentlemanly conduct resulted in banishment from my table. They learned swiftly, and those who lost in genteel fashion were allowed to stay until their dust was gone.

I had a little hair above my lip even then, but it was downy and blond and no one noticed, or if they did they did not consider it bizarre. Age and hard living coarsened it, and me. But that is a long story, not important here. *Mon Dieu!* Suffice it to say that I lost my first husband by perforation, and the second tried to squeeze me out of my own business before he died also of a lead pill, and then I refrained from welcoming men to my bed, and made my living entirely by my own devices.

Now I am simply Madame Mustache, the notorious female entrepreneur of a dozen frontier boomtowns where the pickings are easy. Fort Benton fit the bill especially well, because those who arrive here after an easy trip up the Missouri River are ripe for plucking. St. Louis is a long ways away, but they travel in ease. It is my intent always to make sure they are properly motivated by poverty when they leave Fort Benton for the gold fields in Bannack and Virginia City and Last Chance Gulch.

Cards are my vocation. Spirits and the nymphs du prairie are my sidelines. My board and batten business house, facing the turbid river across Front Street in what is considered the rowdiest block in the West, consists of a gambling hall and saloon on the first floor, and a brothel on the second. I will make money by whatever species of sin I can offer, and if there is one sou left in the pockets of my customers, I would regard myself a failure.

I recently saw an account of myself published by someone who had wandered through those double doors on Front Street. I was rather taken by it. "She was fat," he wrote, "showing unmistakably the signs of age. Rouge and powder, apparently applied only half-heartedly, failed to hide the sagging lines of her face, the pouches under her eyes, the general marks of dissipation. Her one badge of respectability was a black silk dress, worn high around her neck."

I keep the clipping on my dresser. Only the last sentence disappoints me. If the journalist thinks I possess any badge of respectability, he has not looked closely.

Respectable men ignore me. The merchants pretend I

don't exist. I rarely see any of them in my establishment, except one or two who sneak up the dark stair. I like it that way.

I was dealing vingt-et-un one early June evening, and losing for a change, the chips sliding from my fingers to the growing heaps of the players semicircled around me. That's when the news arrived: an anguished whisper that whirled like a dust devil at the bar, and roared like a tornado through my house of pleasure.

"Pox!"

My customers looked nervously about. One pushed outside, leaving the double doors swinging, to examine the river for the sight of that fateful boat. He would look, of course, for the smoke rising over the distant trees that hid the river bend, beyond the island that parted the channels just east of town. But he saw nothing.

I heard the whispers:

"Pox on the *Dance*. Half a dozen passengers at death's door, more feeling poorly, three buried at a riverbank somewhere. Captain's gonna unload 'em right into town here, fixing to start a contagion. Pox, pox, pox . . ."

"You gonna let 'em in here?" a miner asked me. Actually, he had not mined an ounce of dust in his life. He was off one of the two other packets out of Independence and St. Joseph that were hawsered tightly to the levee. His hands were smooth clerk's hands, and his flannels were stiff out of the box.

"Monsieur, play ze game," I said. "Or donate your seat to someone who wants to win riches from me."

He laid out two grimy greenbacks, and I exchanged them for my battered blue chips, and he wagered them. *Bien.* They would soon be mine.

"The pox, it makes bad for business," I said. I showed a jack and six. He motioned for a card and busted. I collected his chips without a smile. I don't waste smiles.

"We have to stop that boat," said Zach, one of my regulars, whom I regard fondly as a sort of annuity. "I don't relish fetching the pox, and I never been vaccinated neither. I'd just croak, slow and miserable."

"Shoot the first sonofabitch off that boat that sets foot on the levee," said another. "That's what I say."

"Turn her around and get her outa here. I don't want the sickness," proclaimed a wall-eyed drummer at my table.

I frowned. They weren't focusing on the game, and I was losing money. Speed is what earns profits, as any croupier knows.

"Messieurs, bets down or give up your seat."

They played, but I could sense that their minds weren't on the game. An odd quiet had stolen through the saloon, and I did not miss the nervous glances.

A bag-eyed, consumptive bartender who lost his tips at my table each night folded. "I just think I'll load up a mule and go visit the camps," he said. It was empty talk. He couldn't afford one hoof of a mule.

Men nodded.

"My friend, finish up what you started. You still have three dollars to play," I said.

He started to pick up his chips.

"Double or nothing, turn the card," I said, wanting those dollars.

He shrugged, cut a seven of diamonds, and I cut a jack. I wiped his coin off the table. He looked angry.

The place was stirring. Men slipped through the double doors into the late afternoon sunlight. I was losing trade.

"When is she due?" someone asked.

"Two hours. She's eight or nine miles out."

The gents quit playing. I glared at them, but no one was betting. They were thinking about larger things.

"Maybe I'm gettin' out of here," said one.

"Got no place to go," said another. "I can't even buy a stage ticket."

"We got to stop that damned boat. If I had a cannon I'd blow it to hell."

"Those packets are well armed," said another.

The other games died too. The chuck-a-luck stopped rattling. The roulette wheel stood idle. Blue haze rose from the poker tables, where men sat with their cards glued to their bellies, thinking about death. The bar was quiet. Men stared through the grimy window at the river front, which was heaped with barrels and crates. And would soon receive a cargo of death.

No disease was more contagious or brutal: high fever, vomiting, headache, delirium, convulsions, diarrhea, and then the eruptions—pink or red spots on the face and hands, and then everywhere, turning into suppurating sores—and if one survived all that, one faced wild itching during the healing. But most died of hemorrhages long before that. The disease lived in clothing, in the very air, and pounced on its victims.

Sacré bleu! I listened. There wasn't much else to do. I couldn't keep the game going, not with these peckerheads wetting their pants. I couldn't even get one to give up a seat. My house had shut down without my permission, except maybe the girls upstairs. Clap, syphilis, pox, what difference did it make to them?

My customers were nervous:

"I'll find the federal marshal, Wilbert, he's on duty," said one. "All he has to do is tell 'em they can't land, public health, quarantine, all that."

"The marshal? Don't count on him. He's a political paper pusher."

"We could all just line up along that levee with our pieces and tell that captain to shove off."

"Yeah, you think he's gonna bother with that? He's just gonna start unloading."

"You want to stop a sick man getting off?"

"I'd stop him. Shoot him in his tracks."

"Big talk."

"What if they're sick women?"

"Don't let 'em off."

It was all jabber and huff and puff. Outside, I saw a crowd gathering along the levee. They seemed quiet enough, but I knew when that boat hove into view, they'd scatter like field mice. They'd rather face a thousand wild Indians than the pox. They were thinking about the sickness, no doctors in the camp, no hospitals, no medicine, everyone fevered up, lying in some alley with fouled pants, the bodies dumped in the river every day, feeding fish, floating down to St. Louis, half the place sick or dying, pustules on their bodies, puke, thirst, terror.

I was thinking my business was going to hell. I might have to shutter it. Maybe move to Kansas, which is like moving to hell.

"It's just a rumor," I said.

"The hell it's a rumor. Jake Gibbon himself told me; he come busting into town from Cow Island. The *Dance* stopped there to unload some milling stuff for teamsters, and he got wind of it and come racing over here, breaking down two horses."

"Find him," I said. "I want to hear it myself."

"He's spreading the word. Over in the Exchange, and the Elite Saloon, last I knew. Like he's Paul Revere, the redcoats are coming."

I had never heard of Paul Revere. "Drinks on the house," I said. That was my ace in the hole.

Usually that started a stampede for the bar rail, but no one moved. I couldn't believe it. *No one moved.* I folded my cards.

"This game's over. Clear off ze table or I'll keep what's on it," I said.

I watched the cash vanish into purses and pockets.

"The hand of God. He is sending us the plague for our iniquities," said the preacher, looking opium-eyed.

I never learned his name. He really was a preacher, but the drinkingest one I ever saw. Each afternoon for that past month he had showed up, downed a half dozen popskull whiskeys, wiped the sweat off his florid face, eyed the heavenly host, dusted his black suit, and teetered out to save the world. Some said he couldn't keep a congregation back East. He sure lacked one in Fort Benton.

Now he was spreading the fear of perdition around my house of ill repute.

"Get you out!" I snarled. I am usually more civil.

"The hand of God will strike Fort Benton and scythe down its wicked denizens. Just as Sodom and Gomorrah fell, so will Fort Benton."

They were all listening.

"It's just a rumor," I said. But they were all staring into their opened graves and I might as well have been talking to the dead.

That's how it went. No one had a plan. The mob collected along the muddy levee, waiting for its own doom in the dying sun, which gilded the yellow bluffs across the river. My sporting house was all but deserted.

Then, faintly, something changed.

"Here she comes!" someone yelled.

I couldn't see anything, but then, I can hardly see the pasteboards these days with my cataracts. Sure enough, first there was a disturbance of the air downriver, a flight of crows, faint smoke, and then the rattle of the escapement, the staccato thunder that announced the imminent arrival of a packet from below, from what they called the States out here, because Fort Benton just wasn't in the States.

The death ship rounded the bend, its smoke disturbing the sky, white plumes of steam ricocheting against the cobalt eastern horizon. The horizontal sun gilded its white enamel and made it glow like a grinning skull. It slowed; the river is tricky here. It whistled its arrival, shattering the silence. A stir ran through the mob, and the entire crowd backed up ten or twenty steps, smitten by an unseen and murderous hand.

I peered through my window. Business was lousy and going to get worse. I stared at the emptied-out saloon, with my consumptive dealers slouched over their tables and filling the spittoons, and the bar men standing like aproned statues.

Only the preacher remained, grinning wolfishly, as if he had personally called down the plague.

"I haven't made a dollar in fifteen minutes," I snapped.

My nymphs du prairie emerged from the stairwell in their wrappers, weeping copiously. Lulu was a little tetched, which is how I acquired her, but even Maybelle was whining.

"You are not permitted down here," I snapped.

"Are we going to die?" Maybelle asked.

"Any time," I replied. "From clap or consumption or opium or cyanide. It will be no loss."

They shrank back.

I peered out the window. The glistening white riverboat was drifting into the levee now. Passengers and crew lined the rail waiting to debark.

"Isn't there a man in town?" I snarled.

No one replied.

"Well, then, it's up to a woman," I said.

Hanging from pegs along one wall were assorted weapons on their belts. I required that they be placed there upon entering. Gambling, drinking and whoring stirred up the heat in men, and I didn't want any more blood on my plank floors than necessary. It was bad for business.

I eyed the row of revolvers, and selected a slick black gunbelt with a pair of clean, newly blued Navy revolvers poking from their nests.

I plucked it and wrapped it around my bulging middle,

black belt over black silk, and hitched the belt tight, feeling the weight of those six-guns.

Then I plunged through the double doors into the twilit gloom of Front Street, and shouldered my way through a pack of gutless sopranos until I stood on the levee, scarcely twenty feet from the closing packet.

The captain, dressed in natty blue, with a visored cap over his bewhiskered face, peered down at me from the hurricane deck, in front of the pilot house. Good. His river men were readying the gangway. Passengers with baggage in hand stood ready.

The boat slid silently to shore, but no one reached for the hawsers that the boatmen threw.

I pulled those twin engines of death from their sheaths and pointed both of them directly at the captain.

"No one gets off this boat," I yelled hoarsely.

That caught the attention of the crowd.

"Madam," the captain replied through a megaphone, "put down those revolvers and you won't get hurt."

"You got pox on board?"

He nodded, reluctantly.

"Then put on the steam and get out. No one with the pox lands here."

"Madam, I have not come two thousand miles just to turn around with my cargo. I have one hundred ninety-eight tons to unload."

"You heard me. If that gangway touches land, you'll be the first to die. Anyone steps on that gangway, he's dead."

I saw now that several of the passengers were armed, some with rifles and some with their own revolvers, but the captain wasn't, and I kept my revolvers pointing straight at him.

"You risk your life, madam."

"No, I'm risking yours. You heard me. You turn this bateau around and go away."

"And what am I to do with this cargo?"

"Take it somewhere else. And take the pox with you."

By now the crowd behind me was stirring. Those closest to me were sliding out of danger from flying lead. It wasn't but a moment and I was entirely alone, a fat woman on the levee, with all those bravados and knights of Fort Benton skulking in shadow out of harm's way.

The captain stirred.

The boat bumped land, and began sliding along the levee, drawn by the current. It would collide with the *Waverly* just downstream.

The captain turned to the helmsman and tugged on bells. A great chuff of steam erupted from the escapement, and the *Walter B. Dance* shuddered to life. Its wheels turned over thunderously, and with a mighty splash halted the drafting vessel just twenty yards from the *Waverly*, and soon the pox boat gained against the current and pulled away. There was precious little turning room in that channel, but the skilled helmsman swung the boat around, and the packet slowly thrashed eastward and vanished into the twilight, leaving a strange hush in its wake.

Only then did I lower my revolvers.

"You did it!" someone cried. "Madame Mustache did it!"

"You spared us the pox!"

"You chased him off!"

"Madam, you have spared the entire city of Fort Benton."

"Lot of help I got from you brave gents," I said, stuffing my borrowed revolvers back in their sheaths. My arms were tired.

"Hurrah for Madame Mustache!"

They were clapping me on the back, a rude American indignity I never would have permitted earlier in my life. They were cheering, tossing hats, whistling, discharging their pieces with ear-splitting volleys, laughing, bawling like cattle, strutting as if they had faced down the Devil, grinning, and building up a grand thirst.

I survived the cosseting, entered my notorious house, and unbuckled the borrowed gunbelt. I never did find out whose it was. But his revolvers had rescued the city.

"Drinks on the house," I said, hoping it would not be too costly a gesture. But one drink would lead to another, and I stood to make a tidy profit this day.

They crowded in, all these smelly, rank, unshaven men, and filled my bawdyhouse with their good humor.

"We should erect a statue to you, madam." That from one of the town's leading citizens, a merchant who had never deigned to speak to me before.

"You pay for any erection here," I said, trying to get to my table. But they would not let me. My barkeeps were pouring redeye and popskull by the gallon. I never gave away good whiskey, and the mob was downing the stuff with single gulps.

"Madam, you have saved the day," said the preacher. "You are the horn of our salvation. You have driven away the plague. Out of the tenderness of your womanly heart, you have poured compassion upon the vulnerable and the frightened."

I laughed. I haven't laughed in years.

"Compassion," I said, and wheezed cheerfully at that preposterous idea. "Compassion you call it? Ha! You are an idiot. Tonight I will claw more gold out of everyone than I do in a month. Here now, let me get to my table so you can donate your greenbacks to me. It was a purely commercial proposition."

The Bull's Head

SANDY WHITING

Sandy Whiting chose to write about the Bull's Head Saloon in Abilene, Kansas, which was owned by gambler Phil Coe in partnership with gambler—and gunman—Ben Thompson. This story, however, has very little to do with a bull's head, and much more to do with another part of the animal's anatomy.

Sandy is a computer programmer by day and a writer by night. She has worked with the Wichita, Kansas, Area Girl Scouts at Cowtown, a reproduction frontier city circa 1876, where both girls and adults dress as though they actually live in that time period. Cooking over an open fire in a floor-length dress during a Kansas summer makes her appreciate "just visiting" the frontier with words. She is a member of the Western Writers of America and has been published in various Western-themed magazines.

★

A saloon at the terminus of the Chisholm Trail could have been called anything from the Turkey Trot to the Spider's Legs to the Snake's Tail. This one, however, had been dubbed the Bull's Head, deriving its name from the majestic bull painted on the second-floor facade. A body wouldn't think a lone bull—a painted one at that—would cause a ruckus, but it had stirred up the women like bees about to swarm.

Now a decent man doesn't go around exposing certain bodily attributes the way animals do, it'd be downright improper. But to protest the God-given features of a bull, well, it appeared the fairer sex had again sat on a hive of those stinging insects. And here they came again. Must have been worried someone was going to steal their honey.

G. W. "Wes" Westmorland propped himself beside the door neighboring the Bull's Head, these thoughts meandering through his mind. Dust enough for a whole herd of critters boiled in the air, brewing a trail that led straight toward the saloon. It hadn't rained in days, and the dust lay thicker than wool on winter sheep.

Wes shaded his eyes and scanned the sky. Not a puff of white anywhere. Perhaps some rain would settle things, and not just the earth. He pulled a fresh cigar from his pocket and turned his gaze back to the approaching herd of women.

"Mr. Thompson, what are you going to do about that, that—!" Mary Crowell stuck a finger in the direction of the offending portrait. Two toddlers clung to her faded yellow dress that brushed the tops of her shoes. The small crowd of women, sprinkled with a few men every now and again, voiced support of her one-sided view.

Ben Thompson, one of the two owners of the saloon, strolled from the boardwalk, scratched his head and gazed long and hard at the painting that towered at least eight feet tall on the false second-story front. "Well, Mrs. Crowell, I might get a body to touch up the paint a bit." He shinnied up a roof pillar. From an unseen pocket, he plucked a handkerchief and proceeded to remove the growing layer of grime that clung to the portrait, paying particular attention to the offending feature hanging from the posterior of said bull.

Mary slapped a hand over her children's eyes. "Mr.

Thompson, there are children here! Have you no decency?"

Ben shrugged his shoulders, surprise arching his brows. "Ma'am, I'm just clearing away the dirt." He leaned over the roof's edge. "You do dust things at home, don't you?" His voice was courteous yet patronizing.

A vein pulsed wildly in Mary's neck, her left eye twitched. "I keep a respectable home! I do not cater to the dregs of society as you most certainly do!"

Ben jumped down from the rooftop and rolled his sleeves. "Hey, Wes, are you a dreg?"

Wes studied his reflection in the glass storefront. "Could be. What's a dreg?" Keeping a straight face, he sauntered toward the saloon, his stride chewing up the distance in mere seconds.

Mary gave Wes a glare that screeched for him to buzz around his own hive, then resumed her tirade with Ben. "You have not answered my question!"

Ben stuffed the handkerchief into a pocket and nodded to Wes. "Mrs. Crowell thinks this 'ere paintin' I got is ruining the eyes of her youngsters. Whatcha think? Do ya reckon them kids'll go blind?"

Wes blew smoke rings and winked at the children. "Nah, might give 'em a little edge-u-kay-shun."

"I'll thank you to stay out of this, *Mr.* Westmorland!" Mary spit the words.

Ben leaned toward her. "Answer me this, *Mrs.* Crowell. Your husband owns some breedin' stock and I'll bet you've seen them, what's the biblical term, *know* each other? T'aint nothing wrong with that so why is it wrong for a picture of one to have all the proper God-grown parts?"

The twitch in Mary's eye quickened. "It's . . . it's immoral, degrading and disgusting!" The crowd behind her nodded in a sea of mass approval.

Ben spread his hands in resignation. "It's a bull, that's

all. Now what in tarnation is wrong with that? You Kansans got a problem with a bull, you take it up with God when you see Him. In the meantime, good day." He tipped his hat and disappeared into the saloon, Wes on his heels.

"Whiskey, straight," Ben snapped then rested his elbows on the bar. "Have you ever seen such a bunch of high and mighty females? All of 'em upset over a little thing like that." He gulped his drink. "And I was thinkin' about givin' them the right to vote. Musta been outta my mind. We give them the vote and they'd have us throwed in jail for spittin' in the dirt. And ain't Mrs. Crowell your wife's sister?"

"Yep, sure is. Kinda makes you feel sorry for me, being relations with her and all." Wes pursed his lips. "But it's more'n the women. There's a few menfolk out there upset too."

Ben raised his eyebrows. "How 'bout Reverend Harker? What's he say?"

Wes pushed his hat back with a finger. "I ain't been over t'ask him."

Ben slid the empty shot glass back and forth on the counter between his hands. "Well, next time you're feeling religious, ask him."

Wes blew more rings. "I get religious every Sunday whether I care to or not, makes the missus happy." He lost himself in thought. "Funny thing about religion, I believe in God and most of what the Good Book says, but seems like folks around here use religion as a big bully. Right or wrong, if a body gets the church behind it a man has about as much chance winnin' 'gainst it as a chunk of ice in August 'round here." He tapped his ashes and took a step toward the door. "See ya for round two."

Ben snatched Wes's arm and spun him around. "Don't ya reckon those women'll let it go? I mean it's just a paintin'. It's not like we're dangling the hindside of a breeding bull out there."

"Not likely. Kansans love causes and you're it! Better get your pardner in here and decide what you're gonna do, 'cause, mind you, push will come to shove and it won't be these folks that'll be kissin' up. See ya." He headed out the door, wondering if Ben understood. After all, Ben hailed from Texas, a place where folks wouldn't find a picture of a mature bull the least bit offensive.

Things stayed quiet for two days on Texas Street but Wes knew it wouldn't last. A small herd of cattle had been driven through town just after sunup, and with no rain to speak of, the dust hung like a winter fog. The dryness reminded him of the parched condition of his throat. He headed to the Bull's Head to quench the gnawing thirst that threatened to choke him.

"Hey Phil, give me something wet!"

"Comin' right up!" Phil Coe, the other half of the two owners, set a hefty mug on the counter and filled it to the brim. "Heard you had some fun here the other day. Sorry I missed it."

Wes took a long draw. "Well, I think it's gonna be your turn in about ten minutes."

Phil raised his eyebrows. "Them women comin' back? Ben told me about 'em."

"Yep."

"How ya know?" Phil leaned over the counter. "Ya inta mind readin'?"

"I got my connections, and you can tell that pardner of yours that Reverend Harker is being a mugwump on this." Wes took another soothing draw.

"How's that?"

"A mugwump, you know, has his mug on one side of the fence and his 'wump' on the other. He doesn't want to lose his flock by tellin' them they're full of it but he won't back them either."

Phil drummed his fingers on the counter. "What about them other two gospel pushers? What'd they say?"

"I knew ya'd ask." Wes wet his whistle. "One of 'em was laughin' so hard when I asked him he like to busted a gut. T'other one wouldn't let me wedge a foot in the door without me agreein' to get dunked. I'd say he'd be more than happy to burn this place."

"That bad, huh?"

"Yep, and looks like they're comin' for you." Wes gestured with his head in the direction of the door. "Better say yer prayers."

After sneaking a quick drink from under the counter, Phil ambled toward the door. Wes followed along, taking up his self-appointed spot in front of the saloon.

Phil tipped his hat toward the gathering, which, of course, included Mrs. Crowell and her children. "Afternoon, folks. Is there something I can do for you?"

One of the men stomped to the walk. "It's about that picture you got there. Now these ladies have asked you very nicely to cover it up and you ain't so much as lifted a finger to honor them."

"Well, I ain't got no reason to cover it up. I figured that's the way God made the critter and it'd be an injustice to make it without all its parts."

"We'll give you three days to remove the picture or else!" yelled a deep-voiced member of the throng.

"Or else what? This is a free country, and I'll do as I damned well please!"

"Mr. Coe! Watch your mouth!" Mary cried as she slapped her hands over her children's ears.

"I'll watch my mouth when you tend to your own beeswax!" Phil retorted, his words slurred from the effects of dipping under the bar a few too many times.

"The welfare and decency of this town are my business!"

Hands on his hips, Phil stepped off the boardwalk, dogging Mary. "What? You the mayor? I don't remember no election. No man in his right mind would vote for you anyway! You ain't got 'nut' parts."

A sober Phil would never consider insulting a woman but a drunk Phil, well, a drunk Phil tended to turn loose of the reins on his tongue.

Wes put himself between the warring parties. " 'Nuf said. Everybody go home! Have yourselves some lemonade and cool off," Wes shouted to the warlike crowd. "And Mary, next time you're in a protesting mood, leave the young'uns with your sister."

"I'll do as I see fit," Mary snapped.

Slowly the crowd dispersed. Wes aimed Phil to an inside table.

"How'd I do?" Phil asked, stumbling into a chair.

"Okay, seeing how you had a slight case of bottle fever. A word of advice? Stay off the red-eye till this is over."

On the brink of the fourth day, the three-day time limit expired, the crowd reappeared, more boisterous than a thousand churchgoers at a tent revival. This time they carried protest signs.

"Down with the Bull's Head!" the crowd chanted, marching in circles in front of the saloon.

Wes sat on the edge of the boardwalk in front of the adjacent store. Mary's two older children, Ruth, five, and Joshua Joseph, seven, quickly joined him. Both children had determined in less than a minute that parading around and around on a scorching bone-dry day held little joy.

Joshua Joseph tugged at Wes's sleeve. "Unca Wes, why is Mama so mad? I wanted t'go swimmin' today but Mama said we had ta iron wrinkles outta some bad Texicans. Is she really gonna put a iron on 'em?"

Wes chuckled as he reached for a cigar then remembered he had promised his wife that he wouldn't use tobacco around children. As much as he wanted it, but being a man of his word, he tucked it in his pocket.

"No, JJ, your mama ain't gonna put a hot iron to them.

What she means is she wants Mr. Coe and Mr. Thompson to mend their bad ways."

Joshua shuffled his feet, stirring up miniature dust tornadoes. "What's she wanna change? Are they bank robbers?"

Wes pointed to the picture of the bull that could be seen from their perch. "See that part that hangs down toward the back of the bull? Your mama and all these other folks want that part gone."

Joshua scrunched his face up and studied the picture. "What is it?"

"They're called testicles. All males, that is, boys of all God's animals have them."

The boy screwed his face into a question. "What's it for?"

Wes tugged at his collar, it choking him all of a sudden. The thought that answering one simple question would turn into a discussion of the creation of babies hadn't crossed his mind.

He cleared his throat, wishing for a cool respite, or any respite at the moment. "Uh . . . they're used to make babies, or with a bull, baby cows with mama cows. Without 'em, you wouldn't have Fourfoot, that little calf that likes to lick your face."

"Oh." Joshua kicked his feet against the ground, turning his tiny dust tornadoes into a full-fledged dirt storm. "Do you have 'em?"

Wes cleared his throat, desperately needing that drink. "Yes, and you do too. How about I take you swimmin' later? Maybe make it a weekly event?" A hand tugged on his other arm.

"Unca, do I have ted-di-culs?"

"No, Ruth." At last, an easy answer. His satisfaction lasted about two seconds, long enough for Ruth's face to turn into a rain cloud but not the hoped-for and critically needed variety.

"But I want dem too! Jos'a gets ever-fing!" Ruth set to letting out a squall that could be heard clear to Topeka.

Mary, the baby on her hip, stalked over to investigate. "Ruth Crowell, why are you screaming?"

"I want ted-di-culs!"

"What?" Mary looked to Wes for a translation to the wailing.

Wes bit down hard on his lip and squinted as he stood. Okay, out of the frying pan, into the fire, down to the coals and cellar, and on to China. He swallowed hard. "She wants—"

"Testicles!" Joshua shouted, which served to bring the crowd's protest to a grinding halt and Phil and Ben, the latter having joined the festivities, over to flanking Wes.

Mary's falling jaw like to put a crater in the ground clear to Texas—or at the very least, Wichita.

"I want ted-di-culs too!" Ruth again screeched at the top of her five-year-old lungs. Mary slapped her hand over the child's mouth.

"Where did you hear that word, Joshua Joseph?" Mary asked, the anger barely bridled in her voice.

Feeling like he'd caused the scene, Wes stepped in. "It ain't nothin' to get upset about, Mary. I was just answerin' a question and—"

"*Mr.* Westmorland, I was not speaking to you!" The words were as cold as the day was hot. "Answer my question, Joshua Joseph."

"Unca Wes—" the boy began.

Mary cut him off. "Enough!" If eyes could kill, Wes would have been dead a thousand times over. "Well, I never!"

"Looks to me like you did, more'n a few times too," Phil piped up. "An' if my guess is right, you got 'nother-'un in there."

"Must be testicle fever," Ben whispered to Phil just loud enough for Mary and Wes to overhear.

Tongue-tied, Mary merely stared at the three of them. Slowly she raised her fist at the saloon owners. "You two are the most disgusting, irreverent, despicable drunkards that have ever walked the face of this earth. And you!" Mary's eyes spit fire at her brother-in-law. "I don't know why of all the men she could have had, my sister married you!"

Wes sighed. "Mary, aren't you carryin' this a bit far? It's just a bull, for land o'goshen sakes."

"Being decent may be too far for you, *Mr. Westmorland,* but I'll not have my children subjected to such despicable displays of vulgarity!" She pushed Ruth and Joshua behind her. "And Mr. Thompson, I'll thank you to keep your comments to yourself."

Ben elbowed his partner and snickered. "If I were her, I'd keep more than my comments to m'self."

"Yeah," Phil whispered, "and I'd avoid getting close to testicles, painted or otherwise. They been known to cause swellin'!"

"Mr. Coe! Please!"

"Please what? Don't call 'em what they are? Testicles?" Phil found perverse pleasure in heckling Mary. "Would your gentle ears prefer we say the 'male' part of the bull?"

"Actually, I prefer mountain oysters," Ben boasted. "Just think how tasty oysters that size there would be." The oysters in the painting being the size of fresh melons.

Not to be outdone, Phil added his two bits. "How 'bout balls? That's what they look like."

"Yeah, bull's balls. You like that, Mrs. Crowell?" Ben stared at Mary, barely able to restrain his amusement at the embarrassment he and his partner were obviously causing her.

"Then . . . then," Phil choked through his snickering, "we could dry 'em out and use 'em in that new game they're playin' back East called baseball and call it bulls-balls."

Wes bit at his lip, but bullsballs pushed him over the barrel. He broke into a contagious belly laugh that poor young Joshua couldn't help but to join.

"Joshua Joseph!" Mary reprimanded. The boy paid no attention to his mother and promptly received a slap across the face.

Wes grabbed her hand before she could deliver a second blow. "Mary! The boy ain't done nothin'. If you feel like hitting, then hit me." His eyes bored into hers. Before he could step away, she backhanded him hard enough to send his face into early next week.

Wes shook his head and inhaled deeply to clear his mind. His eyes watered from the sting. Scarcely able to control the urge to put her across his knee, he faced her. "Go home, Mary," he commanded. "I'll be by later to take the children swimming."

Having exacted her revenge, Mary put her nose in the air, spun on her heel and left, leaving Wes with the outline of her hand on his cheek.

Wes watched as the crowd parted faster than he suspected the Red Sea had done for Moses.

"Gotcha good, didn't she?" asked Phil.

Wes rubbed the side of his face. "Gee willikers, for a little bit of a thing, she sure packs a wallop."

"Come on. I'll get ya a drink before ya head off," Ben said as he steered Wes inside.

A day later as dusk set, Wes meandered down Texas Street toward home. True, he could have gone one of at least ten other ways but the company along Texas Street never bothered him. A half dozen or so ladies waved to him as he strolled through this less civilized part of town. Offhandedly he decided the girls must be new otherwise they'd know trying to sell their wares to him was a lesson in futility. Not that he begrudged what they did, he simply found one woman to be all he wanted.

Coming to the Bull's Head, he stopped and stared at the

portrait on the upper story and whistled under his breath. "That's one fine specimen. Dozen like that critter building the local herds and them longhorns going East would be a thing of the past."

A shadow where none should be caught his eye. "What the—?" The phantom slunk around to the back of the saloon. Wes followed, staying well into the shadows himself. Through the walls, he heard the low murmuring of patrons and soft tinkling of glass on glass. Maybe the shadow had simply sneaked behind the saloon for a little relief. Couldn't blame a man for that—what with the stench of a summertime privy.

A flash of light broke the darkness. The shadow became flesh and blood but Wes couldn't see a face. "Hey, what are you doing?"

The tiny light erupted into flames, temporarily blinding him. The specter stole into the night.

"Fire!" Wes shouted, stomping the flames with his feet.

Like whiskey from a broken bottle, patrons poured out the doors and windows. By the time the owners had scrambled to the rear of their establishment, the flames had transformed to dying embers. The two of them stared at the blackened wall that someone had tried to make into a funeral pyre. "Thanks, Wes. We owe you one. It was set, wasn't it? Did you see who?"

Wes shook his head. "Nope. Just somebody small dressed for the occasion—all in black."

Coe's eyes held questions in the lamp-lit dimness. "Could it have been a woman? Your sister-in-law wasn't none too happy when she left here."

Wes raised his eyebrows. "Mary? Nah. Not with all those young'uns to tend to and her condition. Probably just another of your many admirers." He tipped his hat. "Glad I was here to help. Now if you'll excuse me, the missus is expecting me home."

★

WES SNUGGLED NEXT to his wife, who had already fallen asleep. The day's heat had spilled into the night so he opted for only a sheet over his hips and left his chest and arms to hang out. He closed his eyes but couldn't remove from his head the image the brief burst of flame had left there. Could it have been Mary? The size was right. Would she have been foolish enough to set a fire? Maybe she didn't approve of the picture of the bull but that didn't give her or anyone else the right to burn another's property.

Two days later Wes again walked smack-dab into the rally in front of the Bull's Head. A rock grazed the side of his face. He snatched the hand that threw it. Pulling, he discovered it attached to one Mary Crowell, Joshua by her side. "I thought I told you to leave the young'uns home if you were in a protesting mood."

Mary yanked her hand free. "Joshua Joseph needs to see the law in action."

"Law? You're nothing but a bunch of bullies throwing a tantrum. Someone's gonna get hurt." He glanced at her belly. "You might even lose that baby you're carrying if one of those rocks hits you."

Mary clamped her jaw. "My condition is none of your concern, and I'll thank you not to mention it. There are children present."

Wes shook his head. "Mary, havin' a baby's not a sin but throwing a rock at someone is. You'd be better off spending more time studying that Good Book you're standing behind than throwing it at people. By the way, your husband said I could borrow JJ for the day."

"Yippee!" Joshua shouted as he latched onto his uncle's hand.

Mary's eyes narrowed. If it'd been up to her, her son would never be allowed within ten acres of Wes. But she couldn't keep the boy away and still see her sister. "I want him home before supper."

Wes tipped his hat. "He'll be home when the work's

done, not a moment before." He knew that as far as Joshua was concerned, if the work took less than a week, it'd be too soon.

Much later than he'd anticipated, Wes, astride his horse, headed to the Crowell home with one fast asleep Joshua draped over his arm. He took the direct route, straight down Texas Street. Monday nights were always calm along this venue but tonight it seemed downright lonesome. Not a soul stirred on either boardwalk.

He paused in front of the Bull's Head. "Someone's gonna get hurt over that paintin'." The image of Mary lying in the street floated through his head. As much as he disliked her, he'd never wish her harm. Guns roared in his head. In his mind's eye three more bodies joined Mary on the street. He shook his head trying to quiet the thoughts. They refused to be silent. "This is stupid. Somebody's gotta do something about this."

Joshua stirred in his arms. "Huh? Unca Wes, are we done?"

Wes smiled. Joshua's part of the work had ended when he'd fallen asleep in his supper. "Yes, we're—" Wes glanced at the portrait. "No, wait. Are you up to one more chore? It'll be lots of fun."

Leaning back into his uncle's arms, Joshua's eyes drooped then closed. "Sure, Unca Wes."

Wes spurred his horse home. Being mouse silent, he pulled a brush and can of brown paint out of the barn.

Joshua, having been asleep all evening, slowly awakened. "Whatcha gonna do with the paint, Unca Wes?"

They rode back into town. "Not me, you. I'd sound like a herd of buffalo on that roof but you're small."

Wes stopped beside the walk in front of the Bull's Head. "Remember we talked about that part that hangs down on the bull? Well, I'm gonna boost you onto the roof and I want you to paint it out. But you gotta be quiet and you can't tell anybody—especially not your mother."

"Sure. Will Mama stop protesting? I hate protesting."

Wes boosted his nephew to the roof. "At least about this she will." Wes watched from the shadows.

The deed done, Joshua began to giggle as they stole away. "Won't folks be surprised come morning?"

"They sure will but you can't tell them and if you don't stop giggling, your mama's gonna know we're up to something." Wes reined to a stop then turned the horse around. "Maybe you'd better spend the night with us. I might as well wait to face your mother in the morning as bring you home tonight. She ain't gonna be any happier now than she'll be tomorrow."

Late the next morning Wes set off with Joshua toward the boy's home. Unnoticed, they walked behind the crowd gathered around the Bull's Head.

"It's gone!" shouted a member of the crowd. "We won!"

A man, whom Wes recognized from the nights the local had spent in the jail for one thing or another, strutted to the front. "Yep. It's gone and I did it. It's about time someone took responsibility 'round here. Abilene's gonna be a civilized town if we gotsta do it one place at a time. We got to pass laws, make this a respectable community."

Joshua gazed up at his uncle. "He's lying."

Wes winked. "Sure is. I saw the sheriff throw him in jail yesterday. Sheriff says his 'guests' always spend the night so we *know* it wasn't him."

Joshua giggled. "Are we gonna tell? Maybe his mama'll send him to bed without supper. That's what my mama does to me."

Wes squinted at the boy. "You've been telling fibs? You wanna be like that fool? Look at him. Thinks he's all high and mighty, puffed up on himself like he done saved the world. One poke with a pin and he'd go flatter than a flapjack. You want to be a flapjack? Flapping your mouth, acting like a jackass—I mean fool?" Oops. Knowing to rein in his tongue was easy. Doing it an entirely different rope.

Joshua's chin dropped. "Uh-uh. But do I gotta tell the truth all the time?"

"Let's put it this way. If you always tell the truth then you won't ever have to remember which lie you told to who."

Wes studied the painting. "I think we should've used darker paint."

Joshua followed his uncle's gaze. Underneath the brown paint showed the object of controversy, muted from pale pink to dirty brown. "You can still see 'em, Unca Wes. You think Mama will still be mad?"

Absentmindedly, Wes rubbed where Mary had slapped him. "I hope not. Don't think my face could stand up to another one of your mama's 'corrections.'"

Joshua gazed at the uncle he so admired. "Mama sure hits hard, don't she?"

"Ow! She does at that. Speaking of which, let's get you home before I'm in trouble again."

Later, back at home, Wes checked the can of paint. He dipped the brush into the murky contents then spread it on the barn. Water! The can held nothing but muddy water. It left a dirty streak but nothing the color of what he'd seen on the bull. It hadn't been them after all. But who? Who would've done the deed? Coe? Thompson? Mary? An act of God? Then again, what did it matter anyway? Folks would just find something else to fuss about. He dumped the water out and chuckled. "I guess we'll never know."

COPYRIGHT AND PERMISSION CREDITS